THE WRESTLER WHO LOST HIS HEAD

By

H. Churchill Mallison

Copyright © 1992, 2001 by H. Churchill Mallison
All rights reserved.
No part of this book may be reproduced, stored in a retrieval system, or transmitted by any means, electronic, mechanical, photocopying, recording, or otherwise, without written permission from the author.

ISBN: 0-75963-725-3

This book is printed on acid free paper.

1stBooks – rev. 7/17/01

SPECIAL THANKS

to the following who provided me with expert information and advice, and answered all my questions cheerfully, regardless of how frequently I bugged them.

Jerry Brisco, promoter and former wrestler, who also did an editorial read-through for me to help me maintain an air of realism.
Rick D. Look, FDLE Special Agent Supervisor, who also did an editorial read-through for me to help me maintain an air of realism.
Paul Spiegel, former wrestler, promotes local fights and let me use his name as a local promoter, though his character and all the character's events are strictly based on fiction.

I'd also like to thank my husband Norm D. for his moral support and willingness to eat lots of hotdogs for dinner.

DISCLAIMER:

All the characters and events in this story are purely fictional. Any resemblance to persons living or dead are coincidental, and the crimes herein committed are products of the writer's imagination and do not represent any real life events. Names of any persons known to me and used herein bear no relation to such persons' actual character or to any events pertaining to those persons' lives.

I have taken liberties with the geography of the area.

Read and enjoy.

Churchill Mallison

CHAPTER I

Jack Robinson pulled into the vacant parking lot of Waterway Seafood, a restaurant that bellied-up three months after it opened in a restaurant that had filed Chapter 7 six months before that. Fourth restaurant to die on this spot. The restaurants might not survive on this part of the beach, but its boardwalk was one of Jack's favorite fishing holes—he knew he'd never catch a damned thing edible.

So why fish here? Well, he could play at casting, let his mind go blank, and if he did snag a catfish or a blowfish, he'd just chuck it back in—last thing he wanted to do was gut and scale a fish—and Ali sure as hell wouldn't.

He parked his Toyota truck in the shade of a small cluster of palmetto palms. From the truck bed he retrieved a fishing rod with a small silver spoon already attached to a short leader wire—no tackle box— and pocketed a hunting knife just in case he accidentally caught some hapless fish. Jack loped around the faded shell-pink cement-block building with a Cape Cod shingled facade roof, choosing to go to the right of the building to avoid the stinking dumpster in the back parking lot. The sun, high in the summer sky, raised the smell of its deserted garbage to new heights. Even thrashing through overgrown weeds along the south end of the building, Jack wrinkled his nose and silently cursed the Sanitation Department. He definitely had to call them when he got home. He emerged from the weeds, stepping onto the dry-rotted boardwalk which followed the seawall. Irritated, he turned to stare at the offending putrefaction. *Damn, no way I can stand that all afternoon.*

Then something clicked in his brain making him stare harder. He noticed the back bumper of a car parked behind the dumpster. Nobody would leave a car next to something as foul as that. He leaned forward, squinting, slowly walking towards it. *That somebody sitting there?* He crept forward a bit more. The car door was open, and there appeared to be a large person in the driver's seat. It looked like he was searching for something on the car floor. Curious, Jack watched for a minute, but the hulking figure never moved.

Then something else familiar clicked in his mind—something he wished he hadn't recognized—that odor. Taking out a handkerchief to cover his nose and mouth, he approached the car. The front end of the car faced north, away from him, but the angle was such that he could not see what was going on beyond the fact that there appeared to be someone bending forward on the front seat. He came close enough to the right side of the car to get a good look at its interior. Inside sat a corpse so bloated that the steering wheel was half buried in its belly. An arm hung over the car seat almost touching the floor. Flies swarmed all over: inside, outside, far more around the corpse than the garbage in the dumpster.

Now he saw why it appeared the man was looking for something on the floor—this guy had no head. No fucking head at all! A bright cerulean blue, glittering sequined cloth was draped ceremoniously over a bloody stump of a neck. That was it for clothing—he was starkers! Naked as a jaybird, and no head in sight.

Making as wide a circle as possible, Jack walked carefully around the vehicle as best he could, cautious not to disturb the crime scene. The guy had been safety conscious—the seat belt was still bucked, cutting deeply into its swollen ward. The shoulder strap had kept the body from falling over. The condition of the body distorted all its limbs, but he had apparently put up some struggle judging from wounds on its hands—assuming an animal hadn't gotten to it and decided not to finish him off. Jack, backing away to a reasonable distance, scanned the scene for any obvious evidence.

He retraced his steps to the boardwalk, returning to his truck the same way he'd come. Feeling more sickened than disgusted now, he tossed the rod and reel in the bed of the truck, and reached in through his driver's side door to grab his radio mike. Activating it, he said, "Sally, ten-five double-oh-one, we have a

The Wrestler Who Lost His Head

code five at the Waterway Fishing Place on Gulf Boulevard in Madeira Beach stinking up my fishing hole. Then ten-five MBPD. MBPD can call for the Sheriff's Mobile Crime Lab and get the M.E. out here. Ten forty-eight?"

Sally answered in a tone of voice that asked why the hell agents couldn't just speak English instead of using all those stupid code numbers that everyone on God's green earth knew anyway—except her. Well, she knew most of them, but she was still green at being a dispatcher. "Ten-four. You gotta stiff at the Waterway Fishing Place, tell the boss and call Madeira Police. Let Madeira call the medical examiner, and get the Sheriff's lab crew. I'm assuming the boss says that's okay? What's the..." she quickly ran over the list of numbers, "yeah, ten-twenty?"

"Hell, I don't know the street number. It used to be the Boardwalk Oyster Bar, on the Inland Waterway and Gulf Boulevard. No bigger than Madeira Beach is, I'm sure MBPD will know how to find it. Wait a minute," he scanned the deserted restaurant for a street number, but it didn't have one on it, as least not from his point of view. Then he looked across the street at several miscellaneous commercial buildings, but none of them had any street numbers visible either from where he stood. "I don't see any numbers anywhere around here. Look in the phone book."

When she asked if he was going to hang around until the police arrived, Jack stared at the mike like it was crazy. "Are you okay today, Sally? Of course. Then I'm going to find some place quiet and go fishing!"

Madeira Beach, a small west coast Florida beach community in the Tampa Bay area, had a police force that encompassed about fifteen men divided among three ten-hour shifts. Five minutes every man on duty in the Madeira Police force except the dispatcher, with sirens screaming, came screeching into the parking lot, each in its own white, blue-trimmed squad car. All but the chief, that is, who arrived with his cop-chauffeur driving him two minutes later. Jack suppressed a smile, after all, what's the rush? This guy wasn't going anywhere but the morgue. Next came three ambulances, also sirens wailing, lights flashing—the first one skidding a little on sand when the driver almost missed the place.

Men piled out of vehicles. A sergeant approached Jack, his gold badge glittering against a light blue shirt with sweat stains circling the arm pits. Despite the heat, his dark blue trousers still held a sharp crease. Madeira Beach had a new Chief, had lost some of its former staff, and Jack didn't know anyone on this crew. The sergeant stopped a few feet from Jack, giving him the once-over. He slowly turned towards the dumpster and the victim's car, then with deliberate slow motion, back to Jack again.

"Yew call this in?" The sergeant, Jack's height and half his weight, stared at Jack through black shades. A beak-like nose held the glasses securely in place. Thin lips worked around his teeth like he was chewing grass. Then he winced, pulling out his handkerchief, complaining, "Whew, that guy sure does stink, don't he?"

"Yes, I called it in to my supervisor and he notified MBPD. Jack observed several officers rubber-necking the scene.

"Somebody said you're FDLE?" It was an accusatory question.

"That's right, but I don't think we need go get involved. You boys can handle this." Jack kept an eye on the rubber-necks, making sure they didn't foul the scene. They looked straight out of school. This was probably their first murder. Hopefully the Chief would be more experienced.

Chief Charlie Daniels arrived in the third squad car to careen into the parking lot. He hefted himself out of the passenger's side like he held the weight of the world on his shoulders. Immediately his face folded into a mass of bulldog wrinkles. Voice pitched in high falsetto, he exclaimed , "Holy God, what a stink! Jesus. Where's the special investigator who called this in?" He pronounced it "in-vests-ti-gator" with a smile stating that he didn't need any fucking FDLE agent interfering. The sergeant flipped a thumb in Jack's direction.

The Wrestler Who Lost His Head

Jack, noting the chief's sarcasm, knew he was hard to spot since he was the only person on the scene who wasn't in either MBPD blues or medic-green pajamas. Used to this reaction, he simply put his friendliest face forward. He remembered feeling somewhat the same when he was a cop on the beat. The FDLE, the state of Florida's equivalent of the Fed's "FBI," suffered the same resentment from the lower departments of law enforcement as did its U.S. counterparts.

Chief Charlie, as he preferred to be called by his men, barked, "Rope off the area." Then the chief literally screamed at one of his rookies, "Joe! Get the fuck away from that car! Don't touch a fucking thing! Jesus, didn't I teach you nothin'" To Jack he explained, "New man. Greenhorn."

Joe, a patrolman who looked to be all of 18 with beach boy blond hair that hung past his matching eyebrows, freckles scattered across cheeks and pert nose, backed away fast after a quick look. Turned pea-soup green. A minute later he was barfing over the seawall.

The sergeant and another patrolman began setting up weighted aluminum poles and stretching the crime scene tape to block off the area.

"You touch or disturb anything?" Chief Charlie directed at Jack, slinging arrows.

"No. Walked around the perimeter–went behind the dumpster so as not to disturb anything between the opened door and the dumpster. Any luck, you've got a clean scene. I can't imagine that any kids or anybody else would have seen this and not called it in."

"I called for the Sheriff's mobile lab unit and notified the M.E.," Chief Charlie replied. "Should be here by now. Don't believe I've met you before," he continued, sticking out a hand at long last, "Charles Daniels, Charlie. You?"

"Jack Robinson, Special Agent, FDLE. I used to be with the Clearwater PD...up to about a year ago." He accepted the extended hand and they shook. "You come up from Dade County fairly recently, didn't you?" Jack added, trying to establish rapport. "MBPD's lucky to have a man of your experience."

Now that the scene was being secured, they backed off as far as the seawall and up-wind to get away from the heated smell as best they could, and still keep an eye on the men. Two of the ambulance crews left. One stayed behind waiting for the Medical Examiner.

Chief Charlie looked Jack up and down. Jack wore a faded red and yellow plaid short-sleeved shirt and jeans that had been around a while. Worn-out loafers, no socks. Twenty dollar shades. Jack stood a little over six lean feet; his arms were sinuous muscle and bone with large veins puffed from the 93 degree heat and 90 percent humidity—probably even hotter on the steaming asphalt, maybe a hundred. Had a deep tan, but who didn't in Florida?

"You got some I.D. on you?"

Jack's head jerked back at an angle as if he'd slapped his forehead, "Meant to show it." He pulled it from his hip pocket; flipped open the leather casing. Chief gave it a quick look and a nod, and Jack pocketed it.

"So what brings you out here to this desolate place?"

"Like fishing off the boardwalk sometimes."

Chief Charlie shoved both hands deep into his back pants pockets, elbows splayed, shifting his weight from one foot to the other. While he spoke to Jack, he kept watch on the activities of his officers to make damned sure they didn't screw things up right in front of a Special Agent and make him look bad.

The Chief's thick sandy hair stirred with a rising breeze out of the east. He'd left his hat in the car—too hot to wear it unless he had to impress somebody, and he wasn't about to make a special effort to impress the agent. His name tag read "Charles Daniels, Chief, Madeira Beach Police Department"; the gold badge announced his status in relief. Aside from his sergeant, the rest of his rank and file wore silver tone badges. He stood at five feet ten, heavy boned and stocky, a six-month pregnant belly shoving his belt downward in a supportive arch. His eyes were

The Wrestler Who Lost His Head

the color of dawn's first shades of blue, pale with a lingering anticipation of brilliance. Like most stocky men, his features were heavy, lips full, but his nose bobbed slightly making it almost feminine. Women probably found him pleasantly attractive—he looked like a nice enough guy. Jack figured he could get along with the man.

"That your Toyota out front?"

"Yep."

"Ever catch anything off here?"

"Nope."

"Then why the hell do you fish here?"

Jack gave him a lopsided grin, "It's just a place to piddle away some time and clear my head. I want to do any real fishing I go out with a guy down in Boca Grande. All you catch out here is catfish, blowfish, a croaker or two. Crabs. Sometimes I surf cast a little, too."

The sheriff's mobile unit pulled into the parking lot.

"Welp," Jack sighed, "Chief Daniels, I reckon if you're through with me, I'll leave this to you boys and go find somewhere less stinky to fish."

"Oh, no you ain't," Chief Charlie shot him a joker's smile. "You and me're going to my office and we're going to have us a conversation and do this thing up nice and proper-like. I'll try real hard not to keep you too long. Not much I can do here 'til the lab crew and the M.E.'s finished anyway, so why don't you follow me to the station and let's get this over with."

"Yes, sir," Jack sagged with disappointment as the two of them started across the parking lot towards the front. "Of course, Chief, as you know, you want any assist, we're always willing to lend a hand."

"Well, now," Chief Charlie drawled, "I reckon we can handle this. We're little, but we're mighty. I guess I've worked a murder or two myself, coming from Miami and all, and I've got a sergeant with pretty impressive credentials who can handle this just fine. Besides, it's so quiet around here, this'll give the boys some experience. 'Preciate the offer, though. See you in a few minutes at the station house." Chief Charlie whistled at his driver, jerking his head towards the police car. The driver sprinted over from his safe observation position where he'd been watching the action.

Jack climbed into his Toyota, pulling onto Gulf Boulevard behind the Chief, grumbling under his breath, wondering if he was going to get any fishing time in before Ali got off work.

Chapter II

Jack lived with his fiancé, Alexandra—she liked to be called Ali, in her beach-front apartment, a renovated upstairs of one of a few remaining private homes on this stretch of beach. Ali had insisted they live together a while before making any permanent commitments. Jack had met Ali before he'd left his ex and, although his marriage had been long dead, until he met Ali, he'd put off the inevitable. He and Susan had become downright hostile to each other, and thank God, there were no children involved. Ali had just gotten out of prison when he'd met her, a little more than a year ago.

Ali had been a divorced woman supporting a teenage son, Graham, when an abusive relationship exploded and tore her family and her life apart. She'd gotten involved with a man who'd turned violent and she'd stabbed him when he'd attacked her while she worked in the kitchen preparing dinner. That had been in the 1970's when women were sent to prison for defending themselves from abusive men. She'd explained that she simply had never been physically attacked before and her first reaction had been self defense. The judge, however, firmly believed that women who tolerated abuse deserved to be abused. She did hard time for three years on manslaughter, a short parole, and then was released..

Needless to say, neither Jack nor Ali had been ready to tie the knot until they'd been together a while.

Jack met her on her first job working at a Half-Way House as a para-counselor in Clearwater. Their meeting had strange coincidences: first time he was tracking the dealer, and later a case involving suspicions that a serial killer was working the Gulf States who preyed on female ex-cons. It had been his observations that had triggered nationwide information-sharing. Over a period of several years, while on hunting trips with friends in Texas and Louisiana, he'd come across news stories from time to time with crimes so strikingly similar that he'd

H. Churchill Mallison

finally put two and two together. Unknown to either Jack or Ali, Ali was the next intended victim and Jack had figured it out almost too late.

This Sunday morning they sat round the dining table sharing the sunrise and *The St. Petersburg Times*. He ate a bowl of some kind of oat stuff Ali had insisted upon—she'd been a nut about his health ever since he'd been shot rescuing her from her psycho and he'd almost died. Ali sipped coffee. She was already healthy.

He lowered the front page section to look at her. Short, mussed umber curls framed the prettiest woman he'd ever seen, from the coiled locks to her pretty little feet. She possessed gorgeous feet: small and narrow, high arches, all the toes faced in the right direction and the toenails were neat and square. Jack adored her feet.

"Where's my funnies?" Ali grumbled.

"I gave 'em to you."

"Did not."

"Did too."

"Give me my funnies or suffer, buddy. You always give me the sports pages and you know I don't read the sports." She glanced over the largest headlines on the first page of the sports section while he searched through the stack of papers to find the Florida section with the funnies. He sailed them over so they'd land atop the Sports page in her hands.

"Good God!" Ali gasped. "Did you see that about the wrestler?" *LONG KONG KILLER'S MURDER ROCKS THE SPORTS WORLD* screamed across the page in large bold letters. A large color print of the wrestler in his costume topped the article. In it he stood with legs spread, neck and arm muscles bulging, hands clinched at navel level, with a scowl on his face. Long Kong, a Korean immigrant almost the size of a Sumo wrestler, had catapulted to stardom from the first time he'd entered the ring. He wore a bright blue sequined loin cloth and tight matching boots that accentuated massively bulging calf muscles. The first couple of paragraphs summarized what the

The Wrestler Who Lost His Head

front section explicitly detailed, but the rest of the article consisted of quotes from other athletes expressing their shock and sorrow.

"Yeah, it's on the front page, too," Jack mumbled. He, too, was reading about it.

"That the body you found at that deserted restaurant?"

"Yes, it is." Jack finished reading the piece, flipping quickly through the rest of the front section, then folded it and placed it on Ali's pile. Silently, Jack finished off his oats, then took his coffee onto the deck to stare at the calm waters of the Gulf of Mexico. Sea gulls gathered above. Ali fed them scraps of bread sometimes, so whenever either of them walked out onto the deck, they'd fly over to inspect. As a result, sometimes they dumped enough *fertilizer* to start a farm. He checked the deck chairs before sitting down.

Ali Harrel finished the funnies, laughed at Garfield's antics, then joined Jack on the deck. "Oh, I forgot..." she returned to the apartment, reappearing with a couple slices of bread. The birds began screaming, appearing in numbers seemingly from nowhere as if produced by a magician. She tossed crumbs skyward and watched them dive. Jack took a slice from her and began tossing, too.

"If we stop this, we could have poopless chairs."

"Yeah, but it wouldn't be as much fun," she replied. She put her arm around his waist, giving him a long hug. He kissed her upturned mouth.

"Thank God there's my little Ali," Jack's wide, thin lips puckered a little and turned up at the corners in a sweet smile. "Weren't for you...for nice people like you..."

"Yeah," she agreed, meaning him, too. It wasn't necessary to say that when you were a cop, or, as Ali was now, a counselor for abused women, sometimes it seemed that all the world had gone insane and there weren't any good people left. Ali avoided reading about killings because not only had she killed a man, and another had tried to murder her, it seemed that nowadays that's all there was to read in the papers. Jack lived with murder every day and seemed hardened sometimes, but felt deep down where the soul lives, that somebody had to try to do something about it. Some evenings they would quietly talk in the dark about how sorry life could be at times. After a few hours of cool night air and deep conversation, the sea would begin murmuring to them as if to say, hey, life really does go on and most folks really are okay, so cheer up.

* * * * *

"Time?" Jack asked. They were once again enjoying the deck at sunrise.

Ali glanced over her shoulder to peer through the opened French doors and serve-through bar that separated the kitchen from the great room. She frowned at the wall clock above the range.

"What's up?" she asked.

"Work. Why couldn't you be rich or something instead of having such cute little hands and feet?" Jack turned to go inside, dragging a reluctant woman with him, "Gotta get going."

"Can we dress first?"

Jack dressed in a white-on-white short-sleeved shirt, a red, white, and black geometric print tie, and a navy pin-stripe suit. He looked good in a suit— especially since he'd let his hair grow out a little— not a minor victory for Ali. Of course, when he'd worked for the Clearwater police he'd been a plain-clothes man, but since he'd begun working for The Florida Department of Law Enforcement, he dressed more like a business professional. Part of it was better money, but Ali claimed most of the credit. She'd never known a man who shopped worth a damn. Rule one: don't let 'em see the price tag.

Ali wore summery, sleeveless outfits to work, making it a point not to dress like a fashion model. Most of her clients were up against hard financial and emotional times. Sometimes they were physically wrecked. A client could hardly relate to somebody who looked like they'd never wanted for anything in their lives.

Today she wore a cotton hibiscus print dress in shades of orange, purple and apple green on white. The only jewelry she wore was a small ring on her left hand: a ruby flower with a diamond center. Jack gave it to her as their pre-engagement ring the day he'd moved in with her.

"Call you if I'm going to be late," they said simultaneously, kissing goodby in the parking lot between the two storied house and Gulf Boulevard, the only street that ran through this narrow stretch of Indian Rocks Beach. He drove north and she drove south. Jack only had to drive a few miles down Highway 688 to his office. Ali worked in Hyde Park on Tampa's south side. Usually it took her forty-five minutes to get there, even using the less-traveled Gandy Bridge.

* * * * *

A little checking around and Jack found out Chief Charlie Daniels ate breakfast with diehard regularity at Moe's Beach Shack, which was one of the few places on the beach that survived year round because the year-rounders claimed it as theirs. Tourists accidentally stumbled across it from time to time, but not enough to run off the regulars. It sat in the middle of a strip shopping center that had about as much pizzaz as an industrial park in Ybor City.

Moe's Beach Shack, a hole in the wall in the architectural style known as *gun shot*, ran narrow and long with no wall variation. As he walked inside, to the left stood a long, old white enamel and plate glass refrigerated case stocked with all manner of foods, from almond cheesecake to Zeuxis— a meat pie Moe created and named for the ancient Greek artist because he claimed it to be such a grand creation. Beyond the tempting case an old brass cash register, a genuine antique, occupied most of the small counter. There a dingy wall right-angled, it's kitchen door, ever open, showed a well used but reasonably clean

H. Churchill Mallison

kitchen with all its equipment along the outside wall. Jack could see a couple of sweaty men in freshly smeared chef's aprons turning sideways to let each other pass. One of them came in his direction and gave Jack a big white grin.

"Mornin', what can I get for you?" Moe looked like he ate his own cooking and that attested to his success. A grayed white envelope cap perched on a desert-barren balloon head. Watery eyes peered through bifocals.

"Coffee and..." Jack studied an ancient plastic menu on the wall behind Moe, "How about a scrambled eggs and jalapeño hoagie?" Yeah, he'd already had breakfast, but he decided he'd seem a bit more legit if he ate something. Besides, an egg and peppers sandwich sounded delicious. He'd skip lunch.

"Be three twenty-five," Moe punched in the amount on the old register and little white cards popped up displaying the figure in bold black letters.

Jack turned and looked down the alley of darkly stained oak booths, the kind with no padding, just old pharmacy booths from the 1920s or '30s. Maybe a quarter were occupied, and those mostly with one or two people. Jack saw Chief Charlie about halfway back.

"Mind if I sit?" Jack asked the chief.

"Nah, help yourself. Pretty crowded in here; I don't mind sharing." He rolled his eyes up at the tall— skinny by Chief's estimation— agent. "Lemme see if I can guess why you tracked me down."

Jack started to lie and say, No, no, I just happened to come in here and what do you know... Instead he said, "I'm just unofficially interested, that's all. After all, he did ruin my day off. Mind?"

The Chief rolled an exaggerating finger towards the bench opposite and gave Jack a hound dog look. Jack sat and gave the man a big grin.

"Actually, I've heard about this place for years but never had an excuse to come in here. How's the food?"

The Wrestler Who Lost His Head

Chief Charlie cocked his eyebrows and pulled the corners of his mouth down, nodding his head affirmatively, in an expression that implied enthusiastic approval. He said, "It's all in the papers."

"It's never all in the papers," Jack replied. "You're too smart for that. You're fast, I might add." The body had been found just the day before.

"Well, shit," Chief Charlie drawled, "piece of cake. Ran the auto tag through and had him in five fuckin' minutes. Registered to Johnny Kon, a.k.a. Long Kong Killer, who just happens to be— or was— a rising star. He wrestled in Tampa the night before. So when I find out he's a wrestler, I check the week's back issues for an ad. First paper I picked up. Match at a club in north Tampa called Outlandish. Barkeep there says call Paul Spiegel. I call this Paul Spiegel and he IDs Kon for me. Says Kon's wife telephoned the him late that night, complaining that Johnny hadn't come home. This guy, Paul Spiegel, sets up these local matches.

"Prints we get off the corpse match those all over his car— that was his Honda he was found in. Plus some we lifted in the trailer out back they use for a makeup room. Never did find the head. Maybe the killer threw it in the inland waterway and it'll show up one of these days."

The Chief finished off his coffee and Moe arrived with Jack's order. Chief pointed at his cup and Moe left to get the pot for a refill.

"Anyway, got the names of a lot of people near the— get this, *heel's entrance* for the bad guys— the good guys— they call 'em *baby faces* use a different way in. Apparently a lot of the same crowd goes to these things and Spiegel or the barkeep knew some of them by name. You ever been to one of those things?"

"Wrestling match? No, can't say I have. Seen a few on television."

"Anyway, I meet this Spiegel at the *Outlandish.* Of course, the ring's down. Place is a sort of country-type bar, but they

15

occasionally have wrestling matches. Getting set up now for mud wrestling, too. Now, if it's women, that might be interesting. Rest of the time they have a country band and dancing.

"So I ask Spiegel if he saw Kong leave with anybody. Says no, but there were some...I forget what he called 'em...anyway, groupies hanging around that night. Workin' them now. I figure maybe a jealous boyfriend, or maybe some wrestler's pissed because this guy's making it up the ladder pretty fast.

"I understand that's a tough business to get ahead in— get a-head. Shit, poor sucker lost his. Left a wife and two little chinks. Wife? Hardly speaks English. How's she gonna support two kids? Well, I reckon she can get a job in one of them Oriental markets they got all over hell and back now. They live in one of those run down trailer parks on the outskirts of Ruskin. God Almighty."

CHAPTER III

Jack put fresh Folger's Mountain-grown in the filter-lined plastic drainer and shoved it into the slots, then started pouring a pot of cold water in the container of the automatic coffee maker. "What the— " Water began pouring through the strainer all over the coffee maker and counter top. Jack shoved the full pot of water under the running mess that now not only dripped through the strainer, but also poured over its top washing grounds over the sides. Frantically, he checked the switch— it was off— grabbed a dish towel and tried to stop the flow which threatened to cascade to the kitchenette floor. By this time, the coffee pot, filled beyond the brim, began spilling— he hadn't enough hands to dump it before trying to collect the waterfall. Two other agents entered the room for a cup of coffee and cruelly burst into guffaws, standing aside, watching Jack trying to dam the Nile with only two hands.

"What'd you do?" Ralph Landers joined the audience.

Wouldn't you know the supervisor would want coffee right at this moment? Jack couldn't even look over his shoulder at the gleeful congregation.

"Goddamned if I know! I've made ten thousands pots of coffee in this thing and this certainly never happened! Maybe somebody filled the water container when it was off and left the filter empty?" At last the flow came under control.

His boss, Landers, huffed, "Call *The Coffeepot* and tell 'em to check it out. Their number's on the back of the coffee maker somewhere. Wouldn't you know the thing would go on the blink right when we've got a big conference. Hank or Allen, why don't one of you take a run across the lot and see if Kentucky Fried can provide us with several pots of coffee? I want all of you in the conference room at ten thirty."

"Sure," Jack said, shooting a quick glance over his shoulder. He rung the soggy towel into the small sink and then tried to rinse the coffee grounds off the cloth under the spigot before re-attacking the incredibly mess. "Jesus," Jack muttered, "there's more fucking coffee grounds on the counter than there was in the whole goddamned filter to begin with."

The smirking agents left him to his housekeeping. Allen went for the coffee leaving Hank stuck taking a phone call from a habitual nut *witness* who saw crimes committed every time she peeked out of her apartment windows. Some pissed off cop told her to notify the FDLE instead of his police department a couple of months ago and they'd been stuck with her ever since. They nicknamed her *Sally's Aunt* and usually passed the calls off on Sally if she wasn't too busy.

Jack located the telephone number on the coffee pot and buzzed Sally, instructing her to get the coffee service over here pronto— it was a matter of life or death. She bitched that Hank had just stuck her with *Auntie* again and to do it himself, thank you. So he washed his hands, placed the call, then joined Landers, who was setting up the conference room for a pow wow.

Landers popped what he thought was a funny. "Folks get married every day, Jack. You shouldn't let it upset you. Don't worry, we'll relieve you of coffee duty 'til after the wedding."

Jack tilted his head a little and shot Landers a look that said he wouldn't crack a smile if it killed him. Landers' body jiggled with a laugh that never made it to the vocal chords.

"How long is it 'til dooms day now?" Landers kept it up.

"October first. Two weeks."

"Two weeks."

"Yep."

"Hey, joking aside. You're a lucky guy. Ali's not only gorgeous, she's a sweet lady. You mark your calendar, September 30th, that's the Friday before; me and the guys're throwing you a bachelor party."

"Oh, no— "

"Nah, not like we did when we were kids. Just a boys night out, you know. The girls are throwing a little shower thing for Alexandria that night, too. Don't tell her though, I think it's

The Wrestler Who Lost His Head

supposed to be some kind of surprise. You know how women are."

Allen returned with the coffee and Hank followed him inside. Another agent joined them, Jesse Hood, who'd just gotten back in town from an investigation that had taken him all the way to Williston, California, about two hundred miles north of San Francisco. The men collected around the end of the conference table. After they were seated and passed out the styrofoams, Landers buzzed Sally and told her to hold the calls if possible until notified, and to please call around and find someone to cater sandwiches and coffee for lunch for everyone in the office and four or five visitors.

"Okay, now let's get down to business." Landers had taken down the latest crime chart and placed two new ones on the wall.

One chart consisted of two maps: a smaller one of the United States in the upper left corner, and an enlargement of the state of Florida. There were four red dots on the U.S. map and three on the Florida map, two of which were in the Tampa Bay area, the third in Miami. The fourth dot obliterated Los Angeles on the smaller map. The second chart was a blow-up street map of the Tampa Bay area which included not only Hillsborough and Pinellas counties, but also southern Pasco and northern Manatee.

Landers continued, "I'm expecting the Sheriffs of Pinellas and Hillsborough counties to send a couple of CIDs, and Chief Daniels of Madeira Beach to join us, as well as Detective Joe O'Leary representing TPD." He looked at his watch.

As if on cue, the intercom buzzed on the phone. Sally announced the simultaneous arrival of Charlie Daniels and the detective from Tampa. Landers went up front to escort them back to the conference room himself. The reception area of the FDLE was a secured room and folks couldn't just open the door and go inside. No point in making it too easy for somebody seeking revenge.

The three men entered the conference room. All the agents rose. Landers made the introductions and then everybody settled down around the table while Landers resumed preparing the display board writing information on a dry-erase board with a black marker. While they awaited the sheriffs' men, Jack Robinson and Joe O'Leary shook hands and swapped a little gossip. Jack and Joe had gone through the Police Academy together, worked at TPD together for a while, and had both been involved in the Norman killings. They'd been hunting buddies ever since they'd met. The sheriffs' CIDs arrived shortly thereafter and Landers went through the introduction routine again without a flaw.

"Let me introduce the gentlemen from Pinellas and Hillsborough County Sheriffs' Departments. Respectively, CID Hatcher and CID Marco. Chief Daniels, Madeira Beach, and Detective O'Leary from TPD. Thank you for your attendance at this briefing. What we have gathered here in this room is the Bay area's most experienced men when it comes to unusual or old, unsolved crimes. Each and every one of us has worked on several serial killing cases in this area. I don't think the FBI could come up with a more experienced gathering of minds. Well, maybe I'm exaggerating a little, but I'm not off base by much.

"Ordinarily when crimes of a similar nature occur around the state or the country, it's years before somebody accidentally stumbles across a connection and we find out we have a serial killer on the loose. However, in this particular case, the victims are all famous people belonging to one of two country-wide organizations. Actually, they're known world-wide: Universal Championship Wrestling and Federated Championship International. Uh, UCW and FCI. So when these two organizations start losing wrestlers with exactly the same M.O., they start screaming loud and clear. It's like somebody suddenly starts murdering Hollywood's most famous movie stars— it gets noticed in a hurry.

"Now, one of my Special Agents, Jack Robinson here, stumbled across a decapitated wrestler in Chief Daniel's territory and the Chief took over that case. That was June 18, 1982. Two days ago an officer found a decapitated corpse in a wooded area

The Wrestler Who Lost His Head

near MacDill Air Force Base in south Tampa— again, a wrestler. That's when it hit the fan and the UCW and FCI started screaming at the FBI and told them about a crime back in 1979, February 15th, to be exact, in Los Angeles with the same M.O. A wrestler called Bulldog, real name Horace Muncy. I've been in contact with the LAPD and they sent what they had, but it and these other cases remain unsolved." Landers looked up at his chart. "The red dots represent the general location of the murders. Chief Daniels, what can you tell us about your investigation into the Johnny Kon murder."

Charlie Daniels cleared his throat and began to speak. Landers interrupted him, "Excuse me, Chief, but could you stand up so everybody can hear you better?"

Chief Charlie rose. "Uh, as previously mentioned, Special Agent Robinson found the body in a Honda Accord behind a dumpster at the back of Waterway Seafood, a restaurant that now, and was then, too, out of business. Robinson then notified the authorities. After an interview, I eliminated him as a suspect." That brought a murmur of chuckles, then Chief Charlie got serious. "We traced the body through Motor Vehicle Registration to Johnny Kon, a wrestler. He'd wrestled the night before at a country-western night club out on Nebraska Avenue in north Tampa called Outlandish. The barkeeper there gave me the name of a local promoter by the name of..." Chief Charlie checked his notes, "Paul Spiegel. Spiegel identified the body. Well, he said that considering there was no head, it looked like Kon to him. Fingerprints of the corpse matched those all over the car and at the Outlandish and at the victim's home, so it's Johnny Kon.

"This Spiegel guy gives me the names of some of the people he'd seen at the match or around the entrances to the ring. He said these women— he called 'em *arena rats*— usually hung out near the wrestler entrances. We interviewed everybody anybody identified as being at that match, but came up empty-handed. We do know, however, that Kon had been seen leaving the club that night with a blond woman, but nobody knew who she was—

never saw her before. Most people we talked to never noticed anything unusual.

"Checked around the local gyms but didn't find anyone who'd noticed any new, blond female hanging around the wrestlers."

"Question," CID Marco interrupted, "Were there any other marks on the body? Any other mutilations?"

"His fingers were cut in several places, like he was trying to loosen a garrote, which I assume was the weapon, as confirmed by the M.E.. Autopsy showed Kon had sex previous to the murder; traces of cocaine showed up in blood work, but not enough to render the victim unconscious." Chief Charlie sat down. "No blood type other than that of the victim; no other fingerprints— except Kon's wife's on the dashboard," he added.

"Any bruises?" Marco continued.

"Aside from where the corpse's bloat made the steering wheel and seat belt cut into the body, and some superficial bruising about the forearms and shins that appear to have been caused by struggling...which could've happened at the wrestling match," Chief Charlie spread his hands and raised his brow, "nothin, nada, zero. The wrestler just lost his head. Which, by the way, we never found."

"Mr. Marco, what have you got?" Landers asked.

CID Marco rose. A big man, Marco preferred blue plaid shirts and jeans to his industrial green uniform any day. He did insist on wearing lizard boots, regulation or not. Broad shouldered and trim, though not slim, he looked like he spent his weekends chasing cows on the back of a quarter horse— which he did. His southern Spanish heritage tinted his coloring— dark eyes, hair, skin. His face, a wide rectangular shape, bore cystic acne marks along his broad chin. He always wore a serious expression. Smiles on him grew in self-conscious, ragged lines. His voice, moderately deep and as serious as his expression, filled the small conference room.

"Wrestler named Billy Bob, a.k.a. Frank Van Allen, age 28, single, grew up in Tampa's Sulphur Springs and still lived at

The Wrestler Who Lost His Head

home with his parents. No regular girlfriend. From there, I've got the same MO." Marco screwed his mouth around a little as if it weren't on quite right, then continued. "Seen leaving with a tall blond, but nobody could give much of a description of her except that she had a lot of blond hair. Real full, long, you know...kinda kinky-curly and bushy. The traces of cocaine in the victim, the whole bit.

"His manager or agent or whatever you call 'em, Harry Francesco, who's the big promo here in Florida— does the big televised events, stuff like that, said the kid was real talent, that he'd expected great things outta him. Said he was really pushin' the kid. Thought he'd be doing the TV circuit with the big boys in a year or two. Atlanta liked him. Good stage presence. Francesco was real upset this kid bought it." Marco sat back down and folded his arms on the table, leaning forward a little.

Landers picked up a stack of brown manilla envelopes and stood holding them in his hands. "I've got here a set of facts on each of the four murders and a set of police photographs of each of the bodies at the crime sites, plus an autopsy photo close-ups of the areas around the wounds. The victims, in date order, are: Bulldog, a.k.a. Horace Muncy, resident of Los Angeles. He was murdered following a televised event in L.A. at the L.A. Arena. Killed between midnight February 14 and one or two a.m., February 15, 1979.

"Number two: The Psychiatrist, a.k.a. Emmanuel Thornton, a major leaguer like Bulldog, was murdered in Miami on December 6, 1981, following a televised match— both of those wrestlers were championship contenders. I don't know how they work those wrestling deals. Anyway.

"Number three was Chief Charlie's boy, Long Kong Killer, a.k.a. Johnny Kon, a Korean immigrant, who was murdered following a small-time match at Outlandish, a bar in north Tampa. Date of demise June 18, 1982. Apparently, Kon's done a few TV matches right up there with the big boys lately, but still did these small fights in between. He worked days at a machine shop. Details in the folder. Mr. Spiegel, who the chief here put me in touch with, said these matches are kinda like spring training camps for baseball...keeps 'em in practice off-season or something like that.

"And, number four: Billy Bob, a.k.a. Frank Van Allen, fought at the Amherst Lounge, South Dale Mabry and was killed on September 15th— again sometime around midnight the 15th to one or two a.m. the 16th. Yesterday.

"In every single one of these cases I've pointed out: one, no head has ever been found; two, the autopsy showed semen on the penis and in the urethra tube; three, traces of cocaine in the blood in three of them; four, the victims were found in or near their own vehicles; and five, the victims, all but one, may have left the matches with a female, blond groupie. I don't have all the lab reports yet, but when I get them, I'll see that each of you get a copy.

"Motive. Any ideas?" Landers opened the floor.

"Well, for one," Joe O'Leary spoke up, "I don't see how a woman could be strong enough to do that to a wrestler built like that." Joe, an apple-cheeked cherub of an Irishman, adored women and didn't like picturing one with this kind of hobby. He was sorting through the various crime site photographs. "I mean, even surprising him from the back seat of a car, it takes a lot of muscle to slice through a neck and sever a spinal cord. I don't much visualize a guy just sitting there taking it while some broad whittled away. For motive? Professional jealousy? Revenge? Now... maybe it's a groupie's boyfriend or ex or something."

"Oh, I don't know," Marco's voice grumbled like distant thunder, a heavy brow knit in thought, "I bet you an average sized— in good condition— maybe works out in a gym herself— I bet a woman could do it. She jumps up from the back seat, whips a garrote over his head— something like that. I mean, these guys are huge, and they're practically wedged in between the steering wheel and the seat anyway. Plus, if the guy has on a seat belt— he's as good as trapped— he can't maneuver. She probably couldn't crush his trachea, but I bet she could cut off the blood to the brain by closing off the carotid

The Wrestler Who Lost His Head

artery enough to make him faint. Then she could take her time and do her worst."

CID Hatcher of Pinellas spoke. "Frankly, what hits me right off the bat is that if it's not a grudge killing, it's somebody gay." Hatcher leaned back, balancing on the two rear legs of the chair. A veteran in the Pinellas County Sheriff's Department for twenty-five years, Hatcher looked like he was fresh out of Canada. His complexion, blotchy red and white, required maximum sun screen protection at all times. About twenty pounds overweight, most of it in his rump, and with a tendency to retain water, his feet and fingers were perpetually puffy in the Florida heat. Wispy fading blond strands floated above a pink scalp. He tended to lick his faded lips a lot, which kept them chapped and cracked. A lantern jaw below a narrow forehead created a pear-shaped head to match his pear-shaped body.

Landers replied to Hatcher, "Doesn't really fit the usual gay pattern, though. Gay men tend to grossly mutilate when they do these type killings. Aside from decapitation, there are no other signs of mutilation. The men have all been stripped naked and something of their costumes taken *and* part left behind. On one hand, this doesn't look like your typical serial killer, but then it appears that the killer is keeping souvenirs— which is something serial killers do. On the other hand, if it's grudge killings, why keep souvenirs that could connect you to the body?"

Jack Robinson popped up, "In the first place, if these men had finished wrestling, wouldn't they have changed back into their street clothes? I don't see a man going out with a woman on a...date, if you will...dressed in sequins."

Landers studied his charts a moment, then turned to the conference table. "I want every wrestling match in this area covered and filmed on video. I want a picture of everybody there. You may have to pose as a television cameraman, especially on any main events like at the Sun Dome."

"Jesus, how are you going to get the entire audience on film at the Sun Dome?" blurted one of the agents.

"As best you can. An event that big, I'd have four or five men filming. Scan each section of the crowd. But most importantly, get good coverage of the areas by and around the wrestlers' entrances. These smaller events at clubs, though, you're talking maybe a hundred people, so you'd need to hit the entire room. If there's any camera problems, you can work them out with this, ah, Paul Spiegel fella. Then we can pull in some witnesses and see if anybody recognizes the bushy-haired blond."

Marco stated, "Personally, I agree with O'Leary. I don't think a woman could'a done it. I think maybe this is revenge, professional jealousy, that kind of thing. I'm not saying don't check out the broads, but I am saying that, from what this Francesco says, sometimes a wrestler gets heated up because he thinks he ain't getting the breaks. Know what I mean? What motive could some broad have who likes to pick up wrestlers for one night stands? I go with professional jealousy, or a pissed off boyfriend."

"Well, now, Juan," Hatcher called Marco by his first name, "who says it has to be a garrote? We got no heads to prove how these men were done in. Could have been shot execution style."

"No evidence has been found indicating the use of a gun," Special Agent Jesse Hood spoke for the first time. "No gunpowder on the back of the car seats or anywhere, for that matter. No skull or brain material spattered in the vehicles."

"That brings up a matter," Ralph Landers' eyebrows shot up. "These head removals. Aside from the blood bath, the jobs were relatively neat. Could be using surgical blades, plus all the spinal cords had been sawed off neatly with what could be a hack saw. According to the M.E. reports on all these cases, scratches on spinal bone are consistent with those made by a saw. I can't figure out why whoever it is tries to be so neat about it."

"Excuse me? How about some lunch?" Sally waltzed in with a tray of deli sandwiches and three fresh pots of coffee. She felt a bit put off at the lack of enthusiasm.

CHAPTER IV

T.G.I.F. Jack telephoned Ali at The Women's Abuse Center at a quarter to five. "How about you buy me a drink?" he asked. "I deserve one. It's been you-know-what for a day."

"Okay. Where?"

"How about Selena's in Old Hyde Park," he suggested.

"You want to drive all the way over here to Tampa?"

"I am over here. In fact, I'm at Selena's. There's a chilled Rob Roy being made right this minute that has your name on it."

"Tell 'em to hold it for another twenty minutes." Ali's voice smiled.

Jack rang off and returned to his table. The room's population, still small this early, gave him a few minutes of saloon-dark quietness that wrapped around him like a used and favored comforter. He liked this place; he liked the clientele. Folks mostly his age. The Yuppies used to hang out here *en masse* but once the construction of Old Hyde Park's shopping center got well under way, the frisky crowd sought other hunting grounds. Those who remained to persevere through the inconvenience of progress were Hyde Park neighbors who weren't going to let anything or anybody run them off. Selena's owners were pathetically grateful.

Fifteen minutes. Jack saw Ali briskly walking towards the bar's entrance. The door and his smile swung wide as she whipped around the door like a kid on a May Pole, eyed the table, and demanded in a pouty voice, "Well? Where is it?"

Jack called over his shoulder, "Darla!" Darla responded with a quick nod. Magically a Rob Roy in a frosted double martini glass appeared before Ali.

Eyes rolling upwards to greet ever-cheerful Darla, whom Ali thought was the spitting image of Susan Hayward, one of the great movie stars of the '50s, Ali blew her a thank-you kiss. "An angel, you are," she warbled to Darla.

"You're in a good mood," Darla laughed.

"Yeah, how come you're in such a good mood?" Jack asked.

"I had one of those perfect days at work," Ali tilted her head stretching her mouth across her face, lips pressed tightly in a phoney smile.

Darla evaporated. Jack raised his glass to Ali in a silent toast. She responded likewise. "Wanna swap shop or simply drown ourselves in booze?" he asked.

"Drown," Ali twanged. "Actually, today wasn't worse than any other. I really get frustrated with some of those women: the ones who come back over and over again and never get up enough guts to get out. We got this woman, used to be a woman, now she's a hunk of distorted meat. Comes in once a month with her face split open like a busted boil. All the counseling in the world and she still feels sorry for the son-of-a-bitch. 'He cries if I threaten to leave him.' Well, I know that routine. You guys think women can cry on cue? Take a look at these abusive men. Bawl like a two-year-old after they beat their women to a pulp and beg, 'Oh, pwease forgive me; I can't help it.' Either that or they brow-beat the woman into thinking she's done something wrong."

"You did have a good day," Jack twinkled his grays at her. That usually worked. It did again. She twinkled back.

"So, now it's your turn to bitch," she offered.

Jack studied her for a moment, then he deadpanned, "I want to ask you for a date."

Drooping sexy eyelids at him, she puckered lips in a little upturned smile, "So, ask."

"Wanna go to a wrestling match tonight?"

Ali sputtered scotch, slapped a napkin over her mouth to catch the spray, squeezed her eyes shut, then stared wide-eyed at him. "Do I want to do what?"

"Go to a wrestling match."

"You're kidding."

"Nope. Tonight. Starts around eight at the Outlandish. *General Kaos* is taking on *da Brain*."

The Wrestler Who Lost His Head

Ali's face split in half with an open grin and her head bobbed erratically, undecided whether to shake back and forth or up and down. She leaned on the table with her elbows, holding the martini glass with the tips of her fingers, again widening her eyes at him. He broke down and laughed. "*Da Brain?*" she asked. "*Duh Brain* and *General Kaos*. At the where?"

"Outlandish."

"Ho boy, you don't know how relieved I am. For a minute, I was afraid you'd ask me to go to an opera or something sleazy like that."

"Hey," he pretended to be offended, "I only take you to the nicest places. Actually, it isn't sleazy. I mean, folks take their kids to these things."

"Oh, shades of Rambo," she tipped the scotch for a sip. "Teaches kids self defense, I suppose."

"Nah. It's all in good fun. You never saw wrestling on television?"

"Only long enough to change the station," she replied.

"Then this is going to be an experience for you."

"I bet."

"If I buy you dinner here? I hear Selena's makes some really great gumbo and dirty rice."

"You'd stoop to bribery? You? A master fuzz?"

"Look, make a deal with you. You don't like it, you don't have to go to anymore with me. Okay? Just this once? Try it, you'll like it," he drawled.

"Because of these killings you have to cover the matches now?" she asked, though she knew the answer already.

Jack just shook his head yes and pulled on his gin and tonic. "Always nights. Our time together. Until we come up with something hot, why not come with me? We'll make it an evening out. Meet here for din-din and cocktails to lessen the pain if you want. These things are usually somewhere in Tampa. Once in a while they have a major event at the Sun Dome, but most are little local events. You really hate it, you don't have to come."

29

H. Churchill Mallison

She smirked, speaking like a mother to a pouty child, "Otay, otay, I'll come and keep you company." The baby-talk turned tough, "But if I hate it, forget it."

* * * * *

The Outlandish proved to be everything Ali'd imagined. The room, emptied of tables to make space for the fights, had a fog of smoke lingering about six feet from the floor making obscure light even more so. A milling crowd of people had not yet settled down in the chairs that circled the wrestling ring. Jack selected seats on the back row near a deserted bandstand but close to the bar.

Feeling as strange as a foreigner waking up in the wrong country, she studied the restless population. Seated on the front row closest to the bar were two young women with infants in carriers and a boy about six years old. The little boy kept climbing up onto and down off various chairs, unable to sit still. Behind them, seats were reserved by stapled, photocopied programs and a couple of light sweaters. Trying not to stare, she eyed everyone in the place.

Men swarmed the bar like ants on a cookie. Most of them, unshaven and pot-bellied, wore muscle- or T-shirts that hadn't seen soap since they'd been bought at K-Marts and jeans stiff enough to keep them erect in case they swilled too much. Several bearded men wore dark hats with wide brims, mostly the Australian outback style with one side of the brim pinned up, or an occasional western. Three men were dressed in black leathers with pants so tight Ali wondered how they'd ever gotten into them. Their matching vests hung open displaying dirty T-shirts with the sleeves ripped out or hairy chests. Tattooed snakes and Greek crosses squirmed on sweat-glistened arms. Waitresses, in cut-offs so short their smileys showed, pushed their way to and from the bar, talking and laughing, trying to earn a few meager tips for the evening.

The Wrestler Who Lost His Head

A frowsy-haired dirty-blond waitress carrying a tray wove her way toward Jack and Ali. She caught Ali's attention and mouthed Do you want a drink? Ali held up two fingers and yelled "Beer" over the den. The waitress yelled back "Brand?" Ali thought quickly, this place probably didn't carry anything but domestic, so she decided to be patriotic to the town and yelled back, "Busch!" Her eyes met Jack's for approval and he nodded. The waitress, a large-eyed waif who looked to be all of sixteen, wore heavy black eyeliner that accentuated dark circles under her eyes, and bright red lipstick that she'd also used to rouge pale cheeks. For a moment, Ali felt sorry for her. But upon further study of the lanky woman, decided she liked her job and was in her element.

She turned her attention away from the bar, back to the gathering cluster of people who'd begun selecting seats. Some held plates with nachos, cheese and hot dogs in their laps and colas or beers sat on the floor at their feet. Mostly colas or beers, few mixed cocktails in this establishment. They laughed and yelled trying to converse with their companions, which was necessary if one was to be heard. More children trickled in and crowded around the front rows to be closer to the coming action, their mothers lingering within close proximity.

Then, as time neared for the fights to begin, some of the men came away from the bar and joined their spouses or girlfriends by the ring. A microphone squealed from behind and Ali turned to look over her shoulder. An announcer and an aide began setting up on the bandstand. To her surprise, Ali noticed a well dressed middle income couple two seats over and slightly behind her. She smiled at the woman and got a knowing smile back. The man, she assumed her husband, sat with arms crossed studying the room just as she had been doing and seemed to be just as absorbed. He looked like an average Joe who probably worked for General Telephone or Honeywell.

Turning back around, Ali raised her brows and pulled the corners of her mouth down as she recognized something within herself. Jack noticed her expression and asked, "What?"

"You know?" she sang with amazement, "I just realized I'm being a snob." Jack grinned, tipped his bottle of Busch, then went back to his own observations. She looked through more objective eyes at the people around her.

Actually, she decided, the crowd that continued to cling to the bar still looked scuzzy to her. It was the main source of the thickening smog, noise and drinking. But the folks who gathered around the ring, though mostly lower middle income families, seemed like ordinary citizens taking their kids to a circus of sorts. At ringside, popcorn and colas prevailed.

The air began to electrify with anticipation and a flurry of activity began with a sudden swarm of people grabbing seats. Two women, probably in their early to mid-thirties, sat in front of Ali and Jack. Both were fairly attractive, wore dresses and heels, flawless makeup. They engaged in animated conversation with each other while making certain to maintain eye contact with each other and appear disinterested in the men in the room. From the little she picked up of their conversation, this was their first venture into the wrestling world. The claimed chairs behind the young mothers with the babies and the little boy were now taken by women of a different sort.

Ali's jaw dropped, then she shut her mouth and tried to be a little discreet. One of the women wore leathers and metal with a gaping vest over a black mesh tank which stretched over an impressive set of unfettered bosoms. Her hair was divided down the middle: bright blue on one side, screaming orange on the other. Full, soda-pop orange lips sulked and false lashes weighted blue lids to the point that she held her head back to peer through the lashes at a doorway just to the right of the bar. Ali elbowed Jack in the ribs and pulled a mouth and rolled her eyes in "Naugahyde's" direction. She giggled. "Naugahyde," Ali's immediate nickname for the woman, swung a booted foot onto the seat, arched her back to display her best attributes, and raised a surprisingly muscular arm, sweeping long orange and blue locks of hair up to cool her neck. She netted a few catcalls

The Wrestler Who Lost His Head

and whistles and a man yelled, "Don't put my eyes out, Dirty Girty! Button them things up before you start a riot!"

A woman stepped out from the bar and screamed, "You stupid broad! Put your clothes on! Didn't your mama never teach you nothin'!" The woman, a pretty auburn-haired nymph with an enviable complexion the color of cream and big doe eyes, wore a skin-tight white jumpsuit with peach colored sequins designed to display her own proud set of jugs. She planted fists on her hips, elbows splayed, and shook her head in an exaggerated manner shaming Dirty Girty. Ali leaned forward to get a better look; those weren't long sleeves— she wore white gloves all the way up to her arm pits.

"Dirty Girty? 'Naugahyde' is Dirty Girty!" Ali huffed a laugh and began shuffling through her stapled program. "Oh," she sang, "Jack, she's one of the wrestlers! Dirty Girty versus Peachy Keene. I'll bet the one in white is Peachy— the good girl. Yeah, Dirty Girty's the bad girl. Ha! Oh," Ali continued on, more to her self than to him. "But they're not on until later..."

The entertainment had begun.

A small ruckus emitted from around the bar's back door, then the gathering of mostly women wearing breathtakingly tight jeans and Ts and a couple of pubescent boys parted and a bear of a man stalked through. Muscle-bound arms swung at his sides cocked at a slight angle like a cop wearing a holster, ready to go for the gun any minute. He wore fake leopard stretch pants, boots laced with plastic bones. The fur on his chest, back, and arms was his own. He stopped at the edge of the audience, clasped one fist in the other hand, flexed all sorts of arm and neck muscles and let out a roaring growl. Then suddenly leaping, he bounded through the seats, grabbed the ropes and swung himself into the ring. Pounding his chest, flexing this or that to each direction, he grimaced and snarled while the announcer bellowed over the microphone above the boos and cat-calls of the crowd.

H. Churchill Mallison

"At the country-western saloon, Outlandish, this evening we are proud to present to the folks of Tampa... West Florida Wrestling Club's Champion Wrestling! My name is Mister Malice and tonight I will be your announcer. Our referee this evening is Rick Stanley." A man in a black and white striped shirt and black pants trotted towards the ring and climbed inside. He was an average sized man and lean, but next to the pacing wrestler, he looked tiny. "For our first match tonight, already in the ring, we have Leopold the Leper— "

The bearish wrestler yowled and ran at the ropes towards the announcer. Shaking his head like a dog with a rag, he yelled in a gravel voice, "Da's Leo-*pard* you dirt bag! As in C-A-T!" He threatened to jump the ropes and go after the announcer.

But the announcer, feigning great fear, stuttered, "Excuse me! I mis-read...Sir, Leopold the Leopard, *Leopard*. The Leopard has not lost a match this year and I feel for the man that has to face this cunning cat in the ring."

A big man joined the announcer by the mike. Wearing a tuxedo and puffed up like he was ready to take on anything and anybody, he leaned into the mike and articulated, "Donja worry none, *Mister* Malice, I'm right here beside youse and I gar-ron-tee you that no *Leopard* is gonna come up on this stage and mess with the man." He turned his back to the audience and the ring for a second, then spun around and loudly cracked a bullwhip. The Leopard cringed and backed off the ropes, sulking.

The announcer cleared his throat, then continued, "*But* Mister Leopold the Leopard, I think your fur is going to get ruffled tonight! Tonight you are going to meet the lion trainer!" The Leopard roared, shook his black mane at the crowd, and paced the ring making muscle-flexing threats at little kids and skinny husbands. He stopped before a pretty woman and began purring, then continued on strutting.

Applause started up across the room by a door that was out of Jack and Ali's view. Entered a massive blond. He wore orange briefs with a matching cape and white boots with orange wings springing from the ankles. A white, fitted hood covered

The Wrestler Who Lost His Head

the top part of his face and head and corn-silk hair flowed in gentle waves to his shoulders. An orange feather swept back and up from the cap. The crowd began cheering— the baby-face gallantly approached the ring. At his feet was his devoted manager, a wee bit of a man as skinny as he was short. The manager kissed the hem of Citrus Sam's cape. The referee began yelling and waving his arms at The Leopard to force him to his corner. Citrus Sam climbed through the ropes, his manager at his heels. He swung the cape from his shoulders and handed it to the grateful servant. Arms raised and hands clasped above his head, he displayed his sleek body to all and was amply rewarded with more applause and screams and whistles.

The announcer continued, "Introducing Citrus Sam. This boy grew up on Florida grapefruit— *sour* grapefruit— which toughened him and made him grow tall as a tree. Citrus Sam comes from the Okechobee swamp country. So, Leopard, you'd better tip-toe around that cage 'cause this boy cut his teeth on alligator tail."

The referee called both wrestlers to the center of the ring, told them this would be a one fall, ten minute match. He ran his hands over each one's wrists, waists or belts, and boots, then held his arms up signifying that neither one of them hid any weapons and the match could begin.

The men ran at each other from their corners, slinging each other across the ring into the ropes. They bounced off, flying at each other again. The Leopard caught Citrus Sam with a body chop to the chest and knocked him flat. Hitting the ropes and using the spring for momentum, The Leopard leapt, intending to land on Citrus Sam with a foot to his chest. But Citrus Sam rolled. The Leopard hit the ground hard, limping off to the side, grimacing with pain.

Citrus Sam regained his feet and flexed his muscles before walking up to The Leopard, who was still agonizing over his *hurt* ankle. Citrus Sam, with a grip like a vise, grabbed The Leopard by the trapezius muscles of his neck and shoulders. The Leopard tried to elbow punch him and get him off his back,

35

failed, then spun out of the grip. The two men slammed into each other in a hookup.

The crowd hadn't loosened up yet, so the announcer instructed, "Don't be shy. Cheer on your favorite wrestler. Let'em know what you like. Don't be shy."

Tentatively at first, then in full voice, the crowd got into the action. Ali didn't know what to watch, the match or the audience! They began screaming, booing, cheering, coming out of their seats and throwing right and left punches at the air, yelling instructions.

The Leopard caught Citrus Sam in an arm twist and had the sun-kissed king on his knees begging for him to ease up. The cat roared and sneered. Citrus Sam's head was almost to the floor as he yowled. Then suddenly, Citrus Sam twisted out of his grip and spun The Leopard around, getting him in a side headlock. He punched the cat in the chest with his left and the crowd went crazy.

Ali flew to her feet and started yelling, "Kill 'em! Kill 'em!" Jack, astonished, looked embarrassed when Ali shot him a triumphant glance as she sat back down. She burst into laughter at his surprise, then turned back to the ring. She was getting into this thing by now and leaned forward on her elbows.

Citrus Sam grabbed The Leopard around his neck and shoulders with one arm and around a leg with the other and raised the cat over his head. The announcer, giving a blow by blow account of the match, bellowed, "And Citrus Sam is giving The Leopard the airplane spin. Whoa! Body slam. Going airborne, he gets the cat with a right to the midsection. Down, down— Oh! And the cat springs the trap. Don't let 'em get away— Citrus!— Citrus!— Oh for...and The Leopard is going ballistic!"

"Off your duff!" Ali screamed at Citrus Sam. A little old white-haired woman jumped out of her chair and began shaking her purse at The Leopard. Everyone in the room was yelling, except Jack, who was still speechless— Ali was having a ball! The Leopard hit Citrus Sam and knocked him flat on his back.

Leaping up, the cat grabbed one of Citrus Sam's legs and began trying to unscrew his foot.

CHAPTER V

Leopold the Leopard gave Citrus Sam's foot one more grueling twist, then contemptuously threw it away. He circled the ring strutting his stuff, roaring or hissing at the hecklers. "Alligator tail! Dat wimp cut his teeth on alligator tail? Leapin' lizards— must 'a been baby alligators fresh outta da eggs! I tell you who cut his teeth on alligator tail!" He pounded his chest.

Mister Malice blasted over the mike, "It ain't over 'til it's over, Leopard!"

The audience grew wickedly silent as Citrus Sam slowly came to his feet behind The Leopard's back. Citrus Sam shook his long, blond tresses violently as he tried to shake off the agony and clear his mind. He slowly turned his head and fixed his eyes on the cat's back. With a vengeful grin, Citrus Sam stalked the cat. The cat busily heckled his hecklers, unaware of the danger that approached from behind. Citrus Sam lunged, caught The Leopard in a choke hold and twisted him around and over his knee. Citrus Sam scooped up the cat, held him aloft for a moment while he gleefully grinned and yelled to the crowd, "Should I? Should I?" The crowd sent up a mixed bedlam of yeas and nays as the baby-face supporters tried to outshout the bad-guy fans.

Ali jumped out of her seat shouting, "Skin the cat! Kill the sucker!"

Across the room a tall redhead came out of her chair and yelled, "Do 'em big daddy! Gimme some soup! Some *su-plex*! Suplex that fat cat for yo mama, honey!" Ali's eyes widened at the woman's outfit— crimson lycra skin with a deep V to display most of her very adequate breasts, with matching reptile cowgirl boots and hat. She decided the woman must be a wrestler like Dirty Girty...nobody else would dress like that! These thoughts flitted across her mind with the speed of light, ending with a question of how appropriate were these fights for children. But then the action caught her concentration again.

Citrus Sam gave one heave and brought The Leopard down over his knee in a slamming back suplex. The cat rolled to the floor in yowling torment. Citrus Sam finished him off with a flying body chop to the chest. The referee threw himself to the mat and began wildly swinging his arm in a count to three. Citrus Sam leapt to his feet, grinning and pumping the air with clenched fists. The referee grabbed his wrist, holding it high, and pronounced him the winner.

Now Citrus Sam circled the ring with clenched fists held over his head, grinning and boasting. His fans screamed, whistled, and applauded. The redhead ran to ringside, pulled up on the ropes and grabbed him as he strutted by. Latching onto a fistful of blond mane, she gave him a hearty kiss on the mouth and the crowd cheered on.

Citrus Sam left the ring with the redhead in hot pursuit. The cat crawled to the side, pulled himself to his feet by grabbing onto the ropes. He staggered and shook his head, complaining, "Fast count! Fast count!" The baby-facers booed him out of the ring and out of the room as the defeated beast slunk into the backstage darkness.

Ali sat back down, grinning like a kid. This was fun. She shot Jack a look. He rolled his eyes at her.

A brief intermission followed the fight, allowing patrons to purchase food and beverages. Mister Malice thanked all sorts of people: the owner of the Outlandish and various men who'd helped organize the fights. Ali noticed a man in the far corner of the room opposite her with a camcorder who was still filming, even though the fight was over. He wore a Hawaiian shirt, khaki walking shorts and sneakers without socks. Several people had brought cameras and some of them had taken pictures of the fight, but this guy seemed intent on recording everything and everybody. He'd even filmed her once when she'd jumped up shouting at Leopold the Leopard. At first she'd thought he might be an officer, but then decided he was too amateurish and had to be a fan. She watched as the redhead came back to her ringside seat. Ali reviewed the program to see if a female wrestler was listed who might be the red-haired vixen. Nope. Only one female bout tonight— Dirty Girty and Peachy Keene. The redhead made a production of sitting down...leaning over for an unnecessary length of time with arms tight to her sides to swell her already ample cleavage. Ali, glancing down at her own chest, wondered if she was the only woman in the room with average sized breasts.

"She a wrestler?" she asked Jack, pointing the woman out with a quick flash of her eyes.

"I don't know," he replied. "Could be one of the rats. Why?"

Ali rolled her eyes, "That outfit."

"She's not the only one dressed like that," he grinned and nodded towards the bar and the darker reaches around the wrestlers' entrances. There were a number of women near or around the bar dressed in lycra or denim they'd pried themselves into before puberty and then grown into.

"I guess if I'm going to fit in around here I'll have to go shopping at Frederick's of Hollywood. How about one of those jump suits that has holes all the way down the sides?"

"Over my dead body," he replied.

"You see the clown with the camcorder?"

"You mean that guy over there with the orange print shirt?"

"Yeah."

"What about him?"

"Must have just gotten the camera for his birthday or something. He hasn't missed a thing. Even has me when I was yelling at Leopold."

"Oh, great," Jack groaned. "Bad enough I have to watch you making an idiot of yourself..."

"I beg your pardon?" Ali feigned hurt.

"Now everybody's gonna see you acting like Rosy the Ringside Rowdy."

The Wrestler Who Lost His Head

She burst out laughing. "'Rosy the Ringside Rowdy.' I like that." She leaned into him and whispered, "You mean he's...?"

"Yeah." He knew she'd realized the cameraman was one of his team after all.

"Know how to blackmail him to shut his mouth, don't you? Take a picture of him in that ridiculous outfit," she snorted.

"We get you a stretch jumpsuit with holes in it and match you up with him, and you two'd fit right in," Jack remarked, pushing his chair back on its hind legs. He intertwined his fingers behind his head and resumed his silent watching.

The next match was about to begin. Mister Malice announced, "Ladies and gentlemen, presenting our second match this evening, I have to say that I hope this one doesn't turn out to be a grudge match. This is a sport, folks, and this is a place for professional athletes. I hope these two wrestlers remember that there are children here and stick to the rules of wrestling and fair play. Referee, you be sure to make doubly certain that neither one of these anima— ahem— men, have weapons hidden about their persons. Okay. Announcing, from Madrid, that's Madrid, Spain, folks, not Madrid, Oklahoma!...*Spanish Fly!*" A roar of protests rose from the crowd as Spanish Fly swung into the ring. He wore a headpiece that resembled a mosquito head and an elaborate black and silver sequined, winged cape. "And here defending his middle-weight championship, *Enchilada Jones!*" Cheers greeted a muscular African-American built like a mythological god. He wore a Mexican sombrero, a beaded vest embroidered with encliladas and toreodor pants.

Jack touched Ali's arm and leaned towards her. "I'll be back after a while. Don't miss me." He got up and walked toward the bar.

Ali tried not to follow him with her eyes but couldn't resist until she saw that he was working his way into the mob around the bar, relieved that he hadn't left the building. She turned her attention back to the entertainment.

* * * * *

Jack shouldered his way to the bar, squeezing between a Lycra doll's back and a leatherette jock's. The jock turned slightly and looked at Jack over his shoulder. The doll just shuffled a bit to make more room. Jack held up a finger to signal the bartender. Over the din of noise he yelled that he wanted a bourbon on the rocks. Jack couldn't stand bourbon, but he figured this to be more of a bourbon crowd than a scotch one. He didn't plan on drinking it, just looking like he drank it.

The jock turned a little, there wasn't a whole lot of room for moving, to glare at Jack. His breath mingled cigar and beer. Jack contained his revulsion.

Jack smiled into his face. "Bit crowded."

"Yeah. Wudn't too bad 'til some inconsiderate slob shoved his way in here." The man gave him a yellow fake grin.

Jack looked him over. He was Jack's height, very muscular, and looked mean as a homeless New York alley cat. "You ought to be in that ring fighting," Jack said, complimenting the man's physique with an approving glance. "You wrestle?"

"Been rasslin' since I wuz born. Obviously, you ain't," the man rotated his shoulders. He had a couple days' growth of beard and was one of the *naugahyde* crowd. Shirtless, his hairy chest bulged spreading the black leather vest wide. An acre of grass stretched from one side of the vest to the other and it grew as thick as his shoulder-length, died-to-match-his-suit hair.

"Nah, I'm just a fan. Love the fights."

"Yeah?" That pleased him and he turned a bit more to the side to size up Jack. A woman laid her hand on his massive shoulder and made complaining noises. He shrugged her off and looked Jack in the eye. "Seen any of my fights?"

Jack hesitated. Should he lie and say yes or admit that he hadn't. "I'm new in town. This is my first local..."

"Name's Dice," the wrestler said. "Now, you want to see some real fighting, you come to the fight next month. Ain't that right," Dice spun his head to include his group of leathers who

The Wrestler Who Lost His Head

packed around him. A flurry of "Goddamn rights" and back slaps.

The possessive woman, a petite blond with heavily coaled eyelids and matching dark eyebrows, purred, "Ain't nobody can beat my Dice. Ain't that right, honey?" She leaned around Dice to get a better look at Jack and gave him her prettiest smile. Also poured into black leather, the woman looked like a fountain pen with hair.

Dice turned his back to her and faced Jack, interested.

Jack grinned and looked sincere, "Wouldn't miss it. Who you fighting?"

"Ain't firm yet, but I think I'm gonna fight the A-rab. He's from out of Atlanta. Thirteenth. Down at the Amherst Lounge. Know it?"

"Amherst? Don't believe I do."

"It's South Dale Mabry. Near MacDill."

"MacDill?" Jack queried, although he knew full well where MacDill was, and the lounge for that matter. But he decided to keep up the pretense that he was new in town.

"Holy Jesus," Dice split with a wide yellow grin that almost turned Jack's stomach, "yew are new in town!" To his surrounding friends, he said, "Ain't never heard of MacDill! Ho!-boy." To Jack he said, "MacDill Air Force Base. Occupies the south end of the peninsula— you know, Westshore and Interbay?" When Jack still looked confused, Dice continued, "Hell, just get on Dale Mabry and drive south. Can't miss it, it's right outside the base with a big pink neon sign."

"I'll find it. And I'll be there looking for you," Jack said. He tipped the bourbon to his lips, started to take a sip, but the smell of the bourbon put him off— cheap bourbon, cigarette and cigar smoke, stale beer and sweat. "Hey, you know," Jack leaned towards Dice conspiratorially, "what about these chicks?" He nodded his head indicating the general collection of women who made up about half the crowd gathered in the dark recesses of the room.

H. Churchill Mallison

Dice gave him a knowing smirk and leaned towards him trying to whisper low enough so that nobody else could hear, "Weren't for my old lady bein' here... Easy pickins."

Jack evilly squinted at him. "Yeah?"

"Shoo," Dice said cockily, "I reckon I done practically everbody in this here room."

"Yeah?"

"Man, these broads crawl all over the wrestlers. Can't beat 'em off with a stick. Not that I do!— beat 'em off, that is. Ha!" He elbowed Jack in the stomach almost knocking the wind out of him. "Now a guy like you? You ain't no rassler, but you could do alright for yersef in here. Sheee-it. Take your pick." Dice turned his back to the bar and surveyed the crop. "More fuckin' arena rats in here than there are fighters. Them women rasslers, too. Now you want a wild ride...saddle up one of them!"

Dice's woman clamped a claw on his arm. "*Hon-ey!*" she whined. Dice turned to her and put a meaty arm around her and started talking with his friends again.

Jack started to leave but the chick who'd been standing with her back to him turned around suddenly— knockers to beat all hell pressed flat against Jack's arm and side.

"Oh," she giggled, "Excuse me, hon. Who are yew? I don't believe we've had the pleasure!" Ginger-hair and big blue eyes, patched jeans and a polka-dotted blouse unbuttoned almost to her belt. "My name's Rhonda. What's yours?"

"Uh..." Jack looked for Ali. "Next time, honey. I'm here with a date." He hurried toward the lights and safety of the bar's ring side.

CHAPTER VI

The FDLE set up a task force room in an office complex just off the Gandy bridge on the Pinellas County side of Tampa Bay. The owner let them use the space rent-free since the building was only a third occupied and nobody was exactly fighting to get space there. The location was about as central as they could hope for; Gandy Boulevard ran from south Tampa's Bayshore Boulevard on Hillsborough Bay straight west across Tampa's southern-most peninsula and the wide, shallow Tampa Bay. There it connected with I-275, which, when completed, would make St. Petersburg and Clearwater easily accessible.

From the air, the three major cities and their surrounding bedroom communities looked like one huge horseshoe-shaped city. Three bridges crossed the bay; Gandy at the south end, the *The Frankenstein* at the middle, and the northernmost bridge, the Courtney Campbell Causeway, which was near the Tampa International Airport and led directly to Clearwater. No matter how you sliced it, with the killings in north and south Tampa and Madeira Beach, which lay about halfway between St. Petersburg's beaches and Clearwater's, there were a lot of miles to cover.

Communications and furnishings had been set up quickly and the task force moved into its new home. FDLE Supervisor Ralph Landers had immediately split the forces into groups to handle various aspects of the investigations.

Special Agent Allen Tolliver was placed in charge of a group of officers and agents provided by various law enforcement agencies from each sector to handle most of the footwork. He chose Jack to coordinate investigative assignments and report back to him. Tolliver worked directly with other team leaders forming groups who would compile information and handle computer research and communications with the FBI and other law enforcement organizations and laboratories. Team leaders reported directly to Landers.

Jack's team consisted of himself; Chief Charlie Daniels of Madeira Beach; Pinellas County Sheriff's Deputy, Det. Maurice Downey; Hillsborough County Sheriff's Deputy, Det. Rick Casey; Det. Maddy Ulner of Tampa PD; and Det. Joe O'Leary of TPD, who also served as the chief liaison between TPD and the Task Force. Other personnel was available on an *as needed* basis.

Jack assigned each of his people a section of the two-county area, plus fringes of Pasco and Manatee, soliciting help from the other teams and community police forces when they could spare the manpower. A list of every body-building, health, sports gym or spa was drawn and assigned. Jack and Det. Maddy Ulner covered the list of witnesses from the two Tampa wrestling matches. Det. Rick Casey started on the gyms in south Tampa, and Det. Joe O'Leary started with a wrestling school in the city's northwest side. The other team members were instructed to cover the gyms in assigned territories. Chief Charlie drew the beaches from St. Petersburg Beach north to Clearwater. Det. Downey organized a small group of policemen from various Pinellas County communities to cover their gyms. Everyone was looking for a woman fitting the description: medium build, muscular, five-six to five-ten tall, long, probably very curly, dirty-blond hair possibly into body building, martial arts, and wrestling.

The team groaned. Every gym? God.

* * * * *

Jack parked in front of the Spiegel Towing Company. A huge truck with a disabled city bus still in tow blocked the wide gate entrance to its yard. Several men hurried about waving arms and shouting instructions. Jack made his way around the confusion and entered a small gate to the side of the wide one.

The Wrestler Who Lost His Head

The office building, quite small, wasn't much larger than a security gate house. He knocked on the door jamb as he stepped inside. The room was literally stuffed with overflowing shelves and smelled like oil, dust and old paper. Behind a desk piled high with office miscellanea sat a man intensely studying a form.

"Excuse me," Jack said. "I'm looking for Paul Spiegel."

The man looked up. "You got 'em."

Paul Spiegel, a sturdy figure dressed in dingy work clothes, looked like he probably had wrestled at one time. His biceps put Jack's to shame. Dark hair with pecan-colored sun streaks complimented a darkly tanned olive complexion. Though he was dingy from working in the yard, his face and hands were clean, as if he washed them frequently. He didn't have the ingrained grime associated with garage mechanics.

Jack withdrew his badge from his jacket, flashed it, and put it back. "Special Agent Jack Robinson, Florida Department of Law Enforcement. If you've got a few minutes I'd like to go over the recent wrestling matches. I believe you set them up? In the Outlandish and the Amherst Lounge?"

"Oh. Yeah. Well, I told the cops all I know..."

"Yes, but I'd like to, well, go over it with you again. See if you remember anything else. Is this a convenient..."

"— Sure, sure. No problem, but," he kind of bolted in his seat, shot a look out the window overlooking the front, then turned back to Jack, "could you give me a few minutes and let me get this bus business cleared up? Then I'm all yours. In fact, why don't we go down the street to McDonald's and get a cup of coffee. We can sit and talk easier there. I can meet you there in...say...fifteen minutes?"

Jack brought coffee over to the booth. Paul Spiegel had declined an offer of anything to eat.

"I've been over the reports of your interview. You said you know quite a few of the people who frequent these affairs."

"Oh, yeah. Well, I don't, like, know them, but I see them as regular attendees. I mean, I know some of their names but I don't go to bed with 'em. An expression," he added, just in case Jack thought he meant it literally.

"First, just out of curiosity, what do you...*do*?" Jack asked.

Spiegel understood that he meant what did he do in the wrestling business. "I just...well, I organize these small local fights. You know, find places to hold the matches. You wouldn't believe how difficult that can be. Not too many places have enough room, or if they do, they don't want to be associated with wrestling for one reason or the other. Line up...actually me and some other guys...line up the fights. You know, contact this one to fight that one."

"Other guys?"

"Yeah, like Manny Malice, for instance. He runs a school. Used to fight. And there are others like that. Most of us are retired wrestlers who just want to stay involved even though we don't fight anymore."

"I take it you know about everybody in town who trains or represents wrestlers? And all the wrestlers?" Jack thought for a moment things might get considerably easier.

"Oh, sure. It's like a community, sort of. You know. Everybody knows everybody else."

"These people work out at any particular gym?"

"Well, they can work out in any gym, but...most of the wrestlers kind of frequent the same places. There's a couple of camps in town, too."

"Camps?"

"You know, rings. Where they work on their techniques. A lot of the guys work out in Malice's camp. Gimme some paper, I'll make you a list. It won't be, like, everything, but I can list the main places if you want."

"Groupies ever hang out at these gyms and camps?"

"Arena rats? You kiddin'? Of course they do. Malice runs 'em off. But if it's a gym and they're paid members, well..." Spiegel took a sheet from Jack's note pad and started writing a list.

The Wrestler Who Lost His Head

Jack watched while he wrote. The man had an open, friendly face and manner. Jack thought he might be Italian, but he didn't know what origins the name *Spiegel* had, though he wouldn't have thought it Italian.

Spiegel finished writing and handed over the list. He said, "You coming to the next fight? Friday the 13th of March? Ha! Should be a good show, gotta great card that night. Bring the kids, they love these things."

"As a matter of fact, I'd like to discuss these fights with you. I'm going to have to have officers at these fights. Undercover, of course. We'll be doing a lot of filming. That going to be any problem?"

"Nah," Spiegel pulled a frown that said no problem and waggled his head. "In fact, there was a guy taping with his camcorder at the last match. Some of the boys'll have a friend tape his match sometimes...especially if it's a good setup. We'll cooperate in every way possible with you guys. You just tell us what to do or what not to do. We'll be eternally grateful if you can stop these horrible murders. You know, Mister Robinson, that's the damnedest thing." He shook his head sadly, "The damnedest thing. Good boys, both of 'em."

* * * * *

Jack drove to the Outlandish. Dark of night hid a lot of flaws. Harsh mid-morning glare from a cloudless sky baked cement stuccoed buildings and asphalt; its heat combined with breathless air. Paint cringed, cracked and peeled on all but the newest buildings. The Outlandish had been around a long time, and like an old whore, her flaws ran deeper than the exterior paint. Termite damage rendered one slender column beneath its six-foot overhang useless— it literally dangled from the overhead structure. The heavy front entrance, a solid fir door with deeply cut panels, once had been a rich mahogany color, but now was as grayed as a twelve-year-old dog. Jack tried the door. Locked.

He walked down along the front and rounded the corner. A delivery truck was backed up to the rear entrance, but nobody was in sight. A three inch thick slab stepped up to the opened doorway. One average bay area thunderstorm would put this floor under water in about two minutes. Jack leaned inside the door. Voices. He followed them.

"Hey!" a voice barked from the shadowy recesses. "We don't open for another hour."

Jack asked, "Fred Henry here?"

A big man emerged from the gloom. Jack recognized him as the bartender. Out from behind the bar, he was bigger than Jack remembered.

"I'm Fred Henry. What do you want?" The barrel-chested man wore a striped, cotton, short-sleeved shirt opened at the neck and jeans that bagged in the seat. Carrying a dish towel, he wiped his hands and suspiciously eyed the intruder. His features were as dark as his disposition seemed to be at present.

Jack introduced himself and showed his ID. Another man emerged from the darkened interior, talking loudly. "That should do it Mister Henry. Say you wanna increase the order next time? Oh, I didn't know somebody was out here..."

Henry excused himself and turned to the delivery man. They exchanged a few words, Henry signed the invoice, and the man climbed back into his truck and drove off. Henry turned and motioned for Jack to follow.

It took a few seconds for Jack's eyes to adjust to the dimly lit interior. He went around and climbed up on a stool while Fred Henry went behind the bar and continued cleaning up. "So, what can I do for you?" Henry's voice said he was reluctantly trying to be civil.

"Want to go over the night Johnny Kon fought here..."

"Look, how many times I gotta tell you guys the same fuckin' story? I've been patient, but I gotta tell you, this ain't good for business. That Kong Dong guy— "

"— Johnny Kon. His fighting name was Long Kong Killer," Jack reminded him.

The Wrestler Who Lost His Head

"Whatever. Anyhow, he didn't get killed here, so why do you keep buggin' me? I mean, this keeps up, no more fuckin' wrestling matches here!" He slapped the edge of the sink with the towel and puffed up his considerable chest, jutting a chin forward.

"Mister Henry, I came by early just so we could talk without customers around. Now, I know you've cooperated with the police, and I want you to know we appreciate that. But, fact is, you might be telling your story a few more times. You see, sometimes you suddenly remember something you overlooked or forgot..."

"I ain't forgot nothin'. I tol the man— the policeman— that I didn't notice whether or not Kon left with anybody. I'm up here waiting on a hundred-fuckin'-customers and you think I notice if some dame tries to pick up some guy. Hell, man, everybody in here's tryin' to pick up somebody. Look, some of the wrestlers come in this back door where we came in, and some of them use the exit over there." He pointed towards a door at the opposite end of the bar. "That's the toilets and another door to the supply room."

"Where do the wrestler's dress?"

"They bring a trailer in here. Park it out back. They come into the supply room, and some of 'em— the baby-faces, go around and come in from the door back there where the toilets are. The heels come in the way we did. Or vice-versa. I don't pay no attention. Anyway, there's always arena rats or wives hanging around the entrances."

"Regular customers?"

"Some. Some not."

"Names?"

"Names? Well, Margie Hendricks comes in here all the time. She's one of my regular customers, though, not just around when there's wrestling. Broad they call Tish the Dish, but I don't know what her last name is. Margie might. Rest of 'em... I don't know. I told the other cop to talk to Paul Spiegel. He knows more of 'em than I do."

51

H. Churchill Mallison

"Know where I can find this Margie Hendricks?"

"Try the phone book. How the hell do I know where these people live? They come in here and order a beer, for chrissake." He paused, looking down at the work counter he was wiping, his lips moving like he was still barking. "Best way I know to find her is come in here at six-thirty. But, listen bub, you want to come in here and talk to her? You do it nice and quietly. I don't want my customers upset...that includes Margie, too. You understand?"

Jack gave him a lopsided grin, nodded his head affirmatively, and rose. "You got it. Thanks a lot, Mister Henry. 'Preciate the help. Oh, and one more thing...I'd appreciate it if when I come in here?— you don't know me from Adam. Right?"

"Never saw you before."

CHAPTER VII

The warehouse-sized room echoed every time a phone rang or when anybody spoke above normal level. Metal desks sat in irregular rows. At the front, near the entrance, several utility tables were drawn together to form a larger work area. Two-thirds of the room had the drywall installed, but the rest remained skeletal. Telephone cables snaked across the floor, taped in traffic areas with duct tape, connecting every desk phone to the outside world. Along the east wall windows cast long bright rectangles across the room at regular intervals. Along the west wall, a slide screen had been installed, and maps and charts tacked up. The Task Force headquarters. Nobody worried about the lack of paint or the unfinished walls. It didn't cost the taxpayer a dime and it would suffice for the time being.

A secretary on loan from the St. Pete PD covered the phones when no one else was there and handled clerical tasks, including data input into the computer's Lead Tracker Database. Most desks were furnished with desk-top computers so that when the investigators came into the office, they could scan the information; sometimes they input info, too. The supervisor saw to it that each basic lead was prioritized and given an ID number. It was also his job to make certain all the investigative personnel stayed up-to-date on the case status. Usually several people milled about the room or worked at their desks, or shared desks, either catching up on paperwork or making endless telephone calls trying to track some person or thing.

The FDLE had fit both doors to this section of the third floor's vacant space with security locks that required cards to open. All personnel had their own. Only official staff entered this room without special permission and an escort.

Jack sat on the corner of a desk, one leg dangling, while Tolliver gave the team a pep talk. Some of the detectives sat on desks, some on chairs gathered together in front of the slide screen. Tolliver had just gone through the collection of police photographic slides of all of the murdered victims. He'd clearly been disappointed that checking out the gyms wasn't going along as quickly as he'd hoped, and was still in the process of complaining about it.

Jack had brought in Margie Hendricks and she'd looked at photographs of known female offenders, but hadn't recognized anyone. Jack showed her stills taken from the film made at the Outlandish and she provided a few names, but they'd turned out to be dead ends, too. The most common crack he heard was that the description fitted a couple million broads.

Joe O'Leary walked like he was on wet tile, carrying two overly-filled styrofoams of coffee. Reaching Jack successfully, without spilling a drop, he extended the offering. "So, how's it going, Jack, ole buddy?"

He shrugged. "You?"

"Checked out Manny Malice's camp. No girls hanging around. Malice doesn't allow it. Not even wives. Talked to some of the guys who were sittin' 'round. Mostly young kids there, you know, kids straight off the farm or out of the slums, thinking because they're good at street fightin' they'd make good wrestlers." He started chuckling at a memory and his apple-cheeks grew rosier.

Joe O'Leary was one of Jack's favorite people. He drank a bit too much Irish brew and looked like he was going to deliver a ten-pounder any minute, but he loved folks— ladies in particular.

"There's this one guy in the ring. Tooth missing right up front. Looks like he ain't bathed in a fuckin' month of Sundays. Redneck as all hell. He's big enough, but he's all flab. Puffin' like a smoke stack. The trainer is trying to teach him this move, see, where you get the guy from the side, kick a leg under and around while you grab him around the chest and swing him to the floor. This hold, see, the attacker has to go down, too. He goes down, all right! Not only does he land underneath, he's slap on the bottom and gets elbowed in the mouth. Haw! Comes

The Wrestler Who Lost His Head

up spittin' blood. Tries the move a dozen times and only gets worse. Clumsy as a bull on ice skates.

"These wrestling schools...take anybody's got a dime. I asks this Malice if he's got anybody that's half decent. He looks all offended. Then he informs me that he has the best shoot fighters in the southeast. Yeah, sure."

"What's a shoot fighter?" Jack asked.

"Beats the shit out of me. What am I all of a sudden?— a wrestling expert? Anyhow, I asked him who else handled wrestlers and he gave me a couple of names. One's a..." O'Leary started rummaging around in the inside pockets of his suit jacket, then the front pockets, then back again. He finally located a crumpled piece of paper and unfolded it. "Harry Francesco. Says you want to know anything, ask him. So I ask him about the women that hang on these guys and he gives me this *look*, like he ain't got much to say about women. He says he don't know nothing about 'em, don't have nothing to do with 'em. I got a list of the men he coaches and some of the phone numbers. I'm tellin' ya, getting anything out of Malice is like pullin' hen's teeth."

"Let's compare notes." Jack pulled out a small spiral pad from his jacket and they began checking off names and deciding who would catch whom.

Jack decided to locate Harry Francesco right off the bat. From everything he was hearing, he was Mister Big in wrestling promo in Florida.

* * * * *

Harry Francesco and his father were partners in an athletic club on Kennedy Boulevard near downtown Tampa. Not the usual health club brimming with males and females exercising their libidos, the gym had three rings, boxing equipment, exercise pads on the floors, and weight lifting equipment to one side of the room. Boxers sparred in one ring; another healthy specimen pounded the hell out of a tackling bag. Some kid was

H. Churchill Mallison

losing the battle with a punching bag and that brought a smile of appreciation to Jack's lips.

Jack had called ahead and made an appointment with Francesco, which proved to be a good move, since Francesco unpredictably popped in and out of the facility. A burly man in sweat-stained T-back and shorts sauntered towards Jack, who looked around the room expectantly while he stood by a battered wooden desk that sufficed as a reception center.

"Can I do something for you?" the man asked as he approached.

"Jack Robinson. Have an appointment with Harry Francesco."

"He's not in at the moment, but if you had an appointment, he should show any minute. He's usually punctual for appointments. You here to register or something?" His eyes took Jack in appraisingly and Jack recognized a fleeting expression about the man's mouth that said he thought Jack could use a good program.

"No. Business."

"Well, have a seat. Should be here soon," he said and then turned away. Jack watched him walk toward the ring where the boxers were working out. His thighs were so muscular that they affected his gait.

Jack caught himself looking at his own thighs which were, of course, clothed in suit pants. All of a sudden he felt skinny. He hadn't felt skinny in a long time, not until he wound up on this assignment. His sudden reappraisal of his body was interrupted by a booming voice.

"Jack Robinson? Harry Francesco." If Jack felt undersized before, this man made him feel like the old Charles Atlas commercials where this skinny, puny dude gets sand kicked in his face and his girl stolen by a hunk. A six-three— four?— wedge with arms bigger than Jack's body approached. The man had cauliflower ears, a nose obviously broken a few times, a jaw that could intimidate a shark. Despite the well-pounded look, the

The Wrestler Who Lost His Head

man was handsome in a *very* rugged way. Jack wondered what his opponents looked like.

He rose and the men shook hands across the battle-scarred desk. Jack went through the usual introductory routine. Mister Francesco sat back, crossed an ankle over a knee, laced his fingers behind his head, and listened intently.

"I know less than nothing about wrestling or how it works," Jack said. "What I'm looking for is possible enemies these men may have had— you know, professional jealousies. You have much of that in this business or is it so...planned?— that it wouldn't be a problem?"

Francesco thought for a few minutes before answering. "Well, sure, you're going to have some jealousies. I mean, you may have a guy who's really a great wrestler, but he's just not large enough to make the big time, so he never makes it to the big money. I mean, today...the world championship material...you're looking at men well over six feet tall. Hell, today, six-three isn't that tall. You can have the most skilled wrestler on earth who's five-eleven and he hasn't got a chance against a wrestler of comparable skill who's six-three. Men today come bigger and bigger. Another thing. You might have a guy who's a good fighter but has zero personality, you know, stage presence. In big time wrestling, stage presence counts almost as much as talent. And, let's face it...like everything else, there's politics.

"A smart guy with a good personality and talent promotes his promoters so he'll get the best fights. The most exposure." Francesco pushed back to balance on the chair's hind legs. He took his arms down and crossed them over his chest. His chest and arms were so muscular that crossing his arms was almost awkward, and apparently, not very comfortable. Soon he had elbows splayed and fingers laced behind his head again.

"Know of anyone who may have been jealous of these two men? Johnny Kon or Frank Van Allen?"

"Frankly, I didn't know either one of those boys. I think Van Allen was one of Malice's boys, but I'm not sure. I heard about Kon lately, but I wasn't, you know, I didn't know the man. I kind of had it in the back of my mind to check him out. Rumor was that he was Atlanta material."

"Atlanta material?"

"Yeah. See, I work with the UCW a lot. They're headquartered in Atlanta. When I have good talent that I think will make it on nationwide television, I send my boy up to Atlanta. If they like him, they'll put him in touch with a booker and get him started."

"The booker schedules his fights?" Jack asked.

"Yeah, the booker is the guy who sets him up after Atlanta has decided whether or not to change his image. You know, get him a stage name if he isn't using one, or they don't like his own name for some reason. Put him with a designer to get him outfitted. Decide if he's gonna be a baby or a heel. Work him.

"He has to pay his dues; go through the ranks. You know, these men don't make a lot of money until they hit the major televised events."

"What are you looking at?"

Francesco knew he meant dollar-wise. "These kids that come in here? If they're any good, they get on a card somewhere, they get maybe $15 to $30 dollars for a night's work. Sometimes a guy will have to drive 250 miles for a $30 gig. It's a hard business. But, now, if you're *talent*, you make the ranks in good time. It takes, oh, six years to get to the real money."

"What about the good ones who aren't big enough? What do they do?"

"Some of them do television, too. Fill-ins before the main event. There's a decent middle-weight circuit."

"So you got some kid comes in off the street. He's got his heart set on making a career out of wrestling. He's just under six feet but he's a good fighter. He isn't going to make the big time?"

Francesco pulled a mouth and slowly shook a negative. "Competition out there is murder."

The Wrestler Who Lost His Head

"How do you find 'em?"

"I don't. They find me. I tell 'em right up front that I don't run a wrestling school; I'm not looking for anybody to represent, and it's a tough ride."

"So there's plenty of room for jealousy. How about revenge? I mean, suppose you get a couple of guys in the ring who really get down and mad and lose their cool? Maybe blow the fight."

"I've had that happen. Once I had a man get pissed and he went for blood. Fired him. There's no room here for temper tantrums. This is a sport. In fact, what we're doing here is what we call *sports entertainment*."

"Let me ask you something," Jack's smile said he was going to ask for tales out of school. "This one you don't have to answer, but... Well, my impression is that it's kind of like a soap opera. Good guys against the bad guys. Sometimes the bad guy has to win to keep the tension up. Am I right?"

Francesco grinned. "You're not wrong. But we don't just promote good guys. Sometimes we have a bad guy that is just so damned *bad* that the audience loves 'em! We listen to our audiences. We give 'em what they want."

"Let me ask you this. You have any ideas who might have murdered those two wrestlers?"

Francesco grimaced and leaned forward, bringing the chair back on all fours. He propped his elbows on the table and thought. Shaking his head, he finally responded, "Can't imagine. I wouldn't count out revenge, but I don't know of any particular feuds right at this minute. I'll think about it. Could be a jealous husband or boyfriend. Women go after these guys like you wouldn't believe."

"What about that? What do you think about that?"

"Listen, what I tell my boys. They want me to represent 'em. After I size them up for personality and talent, I ask them if they're married. I tell them I like married men who are faithful to their wives and live clean lives. Now that don't mean I won't promote somebody single, but you can run into problems there.

Once, years back, had one wrestler's wife take off with another one of my boys. God. I don't need that crap."

"What happened?"

"Well, the two bulls collided, of course. And she didn't help, either. She used to manage the husband— you know, part of the act. When she hooks up with the new guy, I tell her, no more. Stay off stage and out of sight. You retired when you left...number one. I don't want to go into names here. You get into a situation like that, yes, you might end up with a killing. But I can't imagine it'd go like these. And I can't imagine that happening twice so close together either. I run a tight ship. I want my men happily married and no drugs. This is a family oriented entertainment business and I want to keep it that way."

Jack rose. "Got any questions, can I give you a ring?"

"Sure," Francesco reached behind and withdrew his billfold. He pulled out a business card and handed it to Jack. "Use the second number; you can always reach me at that number, day or night."

They shook hands. Francesco's shake was firm, but he made it a point not to be bone-crushing.

"Oh!" Jack remembered something. "By the way, what is shoot fighting?"

Francesco grinned, "That's a form of wrestling that's very popular in Japan. Starting to do it in the U.S., too. It's kind of a combination of kicking, boxing, wrestling— anything goes fight. Mean. Mister Malice handles a team. Sends 'em on Japanese tours. It's really a good area for middle-weights."

"Well, I won't keep you any longer. Thanks. You think of anything," Jack retrieved a calling card and handed it to Francesco. "Like you— you think of *anything*, even if you don't think it's particularly important, day or night, give me a call."

CHAPTER VIII

Ali huffed and puffed up the deck stairs to the second floor apartment. The French doors were open, so she knew Jack had beat her home. "I'm home!" she yelled in two musical notes. "Early!" she sang.

"Back in the bedroom," came his reply.

She joined him. He stood in front of the full-length mirror in his Jockeys. After giving him a quick hello kiss, she began stripping off her work clothes. Pulling on a pair of white duck shorts and a light-weight casual cotton blouse the color of hearts of daisy, she observed that he still stood in front of the mirror.

"Like what you see or what?" she teased.

"You think I'm skinny?" Jack questioned her, eye contact through their mirrored reflections.

"Skinny? No. I think you're perfect, sugarfoot."

"No, really."

"Yeah. Really," she laughed and shot him a curious glance. "Why? What brought that on?"

"Oh, I don't know. Maybe I ought to start working out again. Haven't worked out in over a year."

"You look fine to me. Want to take a walk before or after supper?" she asked.

"I've put on a couple of pounds," he stated.

"So have I. It's because we're living together, eating regularly, and we're happy. Haven't made the adjustment yet. As a matter of fact," she continued, now staring down at her hips and legs," I need to go on a diet. Think maybe we ought to join a gym or something?"

"You are the one who's perfect," he said, turning away from his disappointing image. He took her in her arms. "If being happy makes us fat, once we're married, we'll turn into tubs of lard."

"Maybe we should take up running down the beach instead of walking," Ali suggested.

"Yeah. Could."

"But I hate running," her voice fell. "Makes my boobs jiggle and it hurts."

"Get one of those sports bras?"

"I tried one. They still jiggle too much. And my butt jiggles, too. You ever watch some of these women running by? Even the skinny ones? All the wrong things flap and jiggle. It's hideous. We could walk harder."

"Walk harder and work out in a gym," he suggested. "Two or three nights a week, go by on the way home."

"Yeah. Well, that's settled. Before or after supper?"

"I'm starved. Let's eat, then we'll walk," he decided.

During a light supper of tuna-stuffed tomatoes on a bed of lettuce, a lethal combination of virtue and determination had set in for both of them, he brought the subject up again.

"You don't think I'm too skinny?"

"Oh, for Pete's sake, Jack. What's with you? A minute ago you were complaining that you'd put on a couple of pounds, and now you're worried you're too skinny! Make up your mind."

He grinned sheepishly. "You should'a seen this guy I interviewed today. Jesus. Size of a building. His freakin' forearms were as big around as my leg! His biceps..." Jack rolled his eyes and curled his upper lip. "Found out he used to be World Heavy Weight Champion. Was for years. Retired now and he's a big cheese in the UCW out of Atlanta. Puts on these major wrestling matches and those nationally televised events. I sure as hell wouldn't want to face him in a dark alley."

Alley grinned. "I don't know if this is any comfort to you or not, Jack, but I don't go for the muscle-bound type. You have a gorgeous body. Long, slim muscles...cute fanny. I prefer muscles up here," she pointed to her brain.

"Aw— you *do* think I'm too skinny!"

Singing in four frustrated notes, she drawled, "Jack!"

Shaking his head and frowning resolutely, he stated, "I'm going to start working out. Tomorrow. I'll be a few minutes later getting home evenings. I figure thirty minutes is enough to

The Wrestler Who Lost His Head

kill me." He studiously folded a ragged piece of ice-burg lettuce with his fork. "Tell you what. Soon as I get clear of this wrestler business, we can get a family membership somewhere convenient."

"Why 'soon as'? Why not now?"

"Well, I'm thinking about working out in some of these gyms while I'm hunting for that mysterious blond. Get a look at the clientele."

"This has the ear-markings of a bad idea," Ali teased.

"Why don't you find us a nice club and go ahead and sign us up? When I can, I'll join you."

"Okay," she agreed. "For now, let's clear up this mess and take our evening stroll."

The night was beautiful. A soft breeze kept the humidity from feeling sticky, and the days were growing noticeably shorter with the approach of October. Their enthusiastic gait held for one direction, but on the return, they slowed to a stroll.

* * * * *

Third gym in as many days. Most of the other detectives were doing the same thing— setting it up with the management for fake memberships so they could come and go, work out, get a good look at the customers. Ask questions on the Q-T. The busiest time of day was from five-thirty until ten after the normal work day.

Jack sat on a bench in the dressing room staring at his untied shoe strings. He didn't know if he could reach them, he was so sore. A youth with more muscles than brains came strutting through, giving Jack a contemptuous look. Or so Jack imagined. Groaning, he leaned down, tied the laces, and then stood up. Each night took longer to warm up. His muscles were slabs of torn, raw meat. He wanted to go home and go to bed and not move for a week.

Determined not to limp, he moved into the gym. He couldn't face the bicycle tonight. Instead, he grabbed onto a handrail against the wall and started swinging his legs to loosen them up a little. Then a few squats. God that hurt. He felt like a ballerina warming up at the bar. He eyed men pumping tons of iron, accordioning themselves on the *Crunch*, doing rapid-fire sit-ups at a 45 degree angle. He'd had no idea he'd gotten so out-of-shape! Never again! *They* say the first three days following muscle soreness are the worst. Hopefully, that meant tomorrow he'd crawl out of bed feeling a little less ripped apart from limb to limb. Even his fingers hurt!

He eased into the warm-ups. It was the second time he'd hit this gym. It was on Spiegel's list of favored places and had a huge female membership as well as a number of wrestler clients. In fact, not ten feet away, one of the wrestlers was bench-pressing a bar with so many weights on it that he had little more than enough bar left to grip. There was an empty bench next to him. Jack limped over. He put ten pounds on each end of a bar and lay down on the bench. This was embarrassing. But...he had to start somewhere. Actually, it was so light that Jack almost threw it when he heaved. He got up and added ten more pounds at each end. Yeah, he could have added more, but his biceps were already sore as hell.

The wrestler's puffs sounded like a train's steam engine starting up. Jack did twenty presses and looked over at the man. He still pumped and puffed like a locomotive. Jack placed the bar in its rack and sat up on the bench. Jaw a little slack, Jack couldn't take his eyes off the man. Finally the guy stopped pumping and sat up. He glistened with sweat.

"You're Citrus Sam, right?" Jack asked.

The man turned his head slowly toward Jack and stared at him, undecided whether or not to acknowledge him.

Jack continued, "Caught your fight the other night at the Outlandish."

Still no encouragement.

"I'm a friend of Harry Francesco's," a wild exaggeration, but it got his attention.

"Yeah? How you know Mister Francesco?"

The Wrestler Who Lost His Head

"We do business together."

"Yeah?" More interest.

"You in his stable?"

"Plan to be."

"Think you're ready?" Jack asked. "You sure as hell looked good to me."

"You a scout?" Citrus Sam riveted his attention on Jack.

"Maybe." Jack rose from the bench to move on. Then, as if on second thought, he turned back. "Interested in a cup of coffee when you get done here?"

"Maybe," Citrus Sam apparently didn't want to appear too eager. "Name's Bill Cahill. Yours?"

"Jack Robinson."

"Mister Robinson," now even a smile, "I'll be done here in about twenty, thirty minutes."

"Okay. That's about how long it will take for me to finish, too. By then I won't be able to walk."

Citrus-Sam-Bill-Cahill shot him a knowing look and grinned. "Don't overdo. You might hurt yourself."

Jack felt like telling him to do something unnatural and impossible to himself, but resisted the urge. Instead he smiled and limped over to the leg press.

Jack studied everyone in the room while he sat on the bench with his feet hooked under the padded, weighted lift. An aerobics class was in full swing in the middle of the floor at the far end of the room. From his position, he had a great view of everyone's vibrating derriere. He decided to work out on the *Crunch*, which was positioned perfectly to see most of the people in the room from a frontal perspective in one collected group.

Between excruciating curls on the Crunch, a machine with weights pulled down with the arms and another set of weights raised with the thighs— simultaneously— that did an incredible number on all the torso muscles at once, Jack tried to look at the sea of faces in front of him. He was in such perfect agony, however, that he saw little more than colorful stars. Not many minutes passed before he hung there like a crucified victim, panting, sweating, and silently cursing. As he hung there in limp repose, he finally had a chance to look at each individual. Did they all have to make it look so easy?

Ten minutes later Jack stood in a scalding shower hoping that somehow the cascade would ease his distress. He was slipping into his loafers when Bill Cahill came into the dressing room. Cahill had already cleaned up. In clothes, he looked like a handsome, normal, everyday sort of guy, with an exceptional build. He'd pulled his blond mane back in a ponytail, wore a racing green Polo shirt and stylish tan sports pants with all kinds of pockets up and down the legs.

"Ready to do that coffee?" Cahill asked.

"How about a drink instead?" Jack suggested, grinning sheepishly. "I could use a painkiller right about now."

They met at Malio's.

"So, you know Harry Francesco?" Cahill hunched over a draft beer.

Jack gave him an apologetic smile, reached into his jacket pocket and withdrew his badge. "I do know Mister Francesco. He's cooperating with us trying to solve these wrestler killings. Sorry to deceive you back there." A series of emotions flickered across Cahill's face. First disappointment, then anger, the realization that these killings were bigger than his feelings at this moment. Jack replaced the badge and then wrapped both hands around a scotch on the rocks. "I can offer a little advice...that doesn't sound right. What I mean is, when I was talking with Francesco, he told me he didn't go looking for talent. Said it comes looking for him. You tried contacting him?"

Cahill studied him for a minute, then replied, "No. Guess I figured I'd work my way up the ranks, then... I know Paul Spiegel. I guess I figured you get good enough, word gets around."

"Frankly, I don't know jack shit about your business," Jack said. "But if it was me and I had your talent, I'd walk right into his office and say 'here I am.'"

The Wrestler Who Lost His Head

"Yeah?"

"What he told me, boys who want to wrestle for him do just that. He looks 'em over. Said he's not interested in managing anybody, but if real talent comes through the door, he isn't going to turn him away.

"Anyway, Mister Cahill— "

"— Bill."

"Bill. Both these local killings. It's thought that a tall blond picked these men up after the matches at the Outlandish and the Amherst Lounge. I've had one woman say she saw a blond leave with Johnny Kon, but she couldn't identify anyone by the crime photos. It's thought she's one of the women who hangs around the wrestlers."

"An arena rat?"

"...Probably." Jack really hated that term. "About five-seven to five-ten. Muscular. Might be a female wrestler. Long, frizzy blond hair. You know, kind'a dirty-blond."

"That could be about anybody."

"This one's supposed to look like one of those female body-builders."

"Seems like...I don't know. I could have seen someone like that. Me, I don't get off on arena rats. Like there was this fuckin' redhead at the Outlandish who wouldn't leave me alone. Bitch followed me clear out to the trailer. I told her to get lost." He took a pull on the beer. The way he drank it, Jack didn't think he was much of a drinker. "Told her I was married and not interested."

"You married?"

"No. But I am choosey."

"How about at the gyms? Any women come on to you at the gym that might fit the description?"

Bill put his fist to his lips and began rubbing the fleshy part bunched between his thumb and forefinger back and forth. His eyes unfocused while he searched his memory. "Now that you mention it. A woman came in there once who worked out on the equipment pressing some pretty impressive weights. Yeah, and she'd fit that description. Come to think of it, we struck up a conversation about body-building contests. Said she'd been runner-up... Where'd she say that was? ...I don't remember what state she said. Wasn't Florida."

"California?"

"California. California. ...Could'a been."

"Seen her here since?"

"No, I don't think so. If she has been in again, I haven't noticed. I come here to work out, not chase women. Frankly, I like my dolls sweet, petite, and in the kitchen. These broads in here forgot how to be feminine, think they gotta compete with men all the time."

"Look, do me a favor. You see anybody at any of the matches or working out, please contact me. And, I were you?—I'd continue to avoid...arena rats...until this mess is cleared up." Jack gave him a card. "Do me another favor, too. You don't know me. You don't know I'm an agent. Right?"

"You really think I ought to just drop in on Mister Francesco?"

"What's to lose?"

CHAPTER IX

Maddy Ulner strode into the gym. Maddy never simply *walked*. She moved with little feminine affectation and loads of determination. Working out was an established habit for her. Being a female detective and frequently in precarious situations, she dared not let herself get out of shape.

This was her third night here. Since Jack had assigned her to cover this gym until further notice, she'd struck up a casual relationship with several other women who were here every night. Unlike Jack, Maddy had a well established routine and never got sore muscles anymore.

She smiled to herself when Jack entered her mind. Poor guy. After a week, he was just now getting back to normal. Good thing, too. How much fun could it be going on a honeymoon with a shiny new bride if you were so sore you couldn't do a few push-ups?

How much freedom did he have left? She thought of being married as serving time. He was on the countdown. Two days? Three? Maddy smirked. She'd had another fight with Dave. So she told him, come down and work out with me. Would he? And act a little cooperative? Hell no.

Maddy wore hot pink tights with a black French-cut brief pulled over her ass. She supposed women layered the lycra to hide their cellulose dimples; she wore it to be stylish. Silly, yes, but something they all eventually were suckered into. As for cellulose, at 28 and being an avid athlete, her thighs and buttocks were tight as a teenager's.

She started out with ten laps around the jogging path. As she trotted around and around, she scanned the room. Some of the roommates scanned her, too. She saw the wrestler Jack called Citrus Sam arm curling a gawdawful amount of weight. He was the only man in the room who looked like a wrestler to her, so she assumed it must be him. There were a number of bodybuilders, but nobody in his league.

At the moment, all but one woman aside from herself exercised in the aerobics group. Aerobics wasn't her thing. She liked jogging and lifting weights, but you could have the sissy stuff. The one other woman working out on the equipment was a tiny brunette pumping away on the leg press.

What the hell did Jack say Citrus Sam's real name was? Anyway, he'd started watching her. She ignored him. The more she ignored him, the more he watched. Maddy liked her men well muscled, but wasn't really into Mister Universe types. Still, he was good looking. The color of his hair actually was the color of corn silk, and his eyes were startling blue. He wasn't ghostly white like most people with hair that pale, but had a moderate, even, golden tan. There ought to be a law against men wearing those stretch pants lying down on their backs pumping iron in public. Nothing about this guy appeared to be average!

She did a respectable fifty curls on the Crunch with eighty pounds. Jack called it the torture chamber. Inhale, exhale, inhale, exhale. She saw feet standing nearby and looked up. It was *Wonder Man*. He watched her.

"Just a few more," she puffed.

"No hurry."

"Forty-three," exhale, inhale, "Forty-four," exhale, inhale. "Forty-five," she announced. Glancing up again, the blond still stared at her.

"Very impressive for a woman," he remarked.

Her look said what she wouldn't say: fuck you. She climbed down off the machine, sagged for just a second, then went over to a leg press. Unable to resist, she looked back. He'd already started crunching— and she couldn't believe the number of weights he'd loaded on the thing. She huffed at the flash thought that invariably went through her mind when she saw these muscle men: probably stupid as hell— brains of an ox.

She laced fingers behind her head and closed her eyes. The top half of her remained quite relaxed. The length of the stretch,

The Wrestler Who Lost His Head

adjusted for the length of her legs, pressed the small of her back firmly against the padded seat. She pumped eighty pounds with ease. Fifty pushes was enough. When she finished, he was still crunching at a rhythmic pace.

A woman named Dot saw her and came over. "How's it going?" Dot asked.

"Fine. You?"

"Tired tonight. You seen that blond wrestler that comes in here?"

Maddy could tell by the tone of Dot's voice that Dot had observed her observing the blond.

"Hard to miss him," she grinned.

"Know who he is?"

"Isn't he Citrus Sam or something like that?" Maddy asked.

"Yes." Dot's eyebrows did a little dance on her forehead.

"What's his real name?"

"All I know is Bill. Heard the instructor call him that. I thought maybe you knew him and would introduce us," Dot said.

"Never met the guy."

"Oh. Way he was following you around, I thought you were friends." Dot sounded a little disappointed.

"I've got a *friend*, thank you. One at a time is more than I can handle."

Dot brightened. "Well, listen, if he starts talking to you and you get a charitable feeling, introduce me. He generally ignores the women in here."

"Yeah, sure." Maddy shot her a polite smile and walked over to a four-sided machine with a vast number of tortures attached to it. She started doing behind-the-head pull-downs on the shoulder bar.

The low stress of this exercise gave her plenty of time to observe others in the room. The only kinky-haired blond in the place at the moment was a teenage boy desperately trying to get some meat on his angular shoulder bones. The kid was about six-five and had apparently shot straight through any pre-pubescent fat. A few women clustered around the sit-up boards.

H. Churchill Mallison

They were engaged in conversation and an occasional head would turn and seek out Citrus Sam the Wonder Man. Maddy smiled. They sure did flock to wrestlers.

She gently lowered the shoulder bar and walked around to another side of the machine where there were two padded thirty-inch high bars. She hiked up on one, stomach to the bar, and caught her knees under the back bar and started doing mid-air back raises. Thirty of those and she flipped over and did thirty mid-air situps. Following those, Maddy stretched out on a vacant space of floor and closed her eyes. Time for a touch of rest.

"I think you're the only serious woman in this place," a voice remarked. She knew it was him before she even opened her eyes.

"Gotta keep in shape," she smiled prettily and opened her eyes, connecting with those intense blues.

"Mind sharing the floor with me?" he asked.

"Not at all."

"Name's Bill. Yours?"

"Maddy."

He stretched out beside her and folded his arms behind his head. "You a model or something?"

"Or something," she replied. "I hear you wrestle."

"Where do you hear that?"

"You pulling my leg?" she shot him a look. "One of the women just asked me to introduce you. I said I don't know you."

"Well, pretend you don't. If I want to meet somebody, I will. You're not a model, what do you do?"

"I'm a cop."

"You're kidding!" He rose to sitting position and grinned. "No kidding. I thought lady cops were butchy."

"Yeah?" She rolled her head to the side and locked her silver grays on his sapphires. "And I thought all muscle men were borderline retards."

The Wrestler Who Lost His Head

Taken aback, the first emotion that flickered across his face was indignation. Apparently, the thought mechanism kicked in, though, and he paled, then reddened with recognition. He took a deep breath. "I'm sorry. I deserved that. That was a very insensitive remark and...maybe I am a borderline retard. I meant to be complimentary."

"You might try reading *How to Win Friends and Influence People*." She turned her eyes to the ceiling, then deliberately, slowly, closed them, signifying that she'd erased his existence.

Chagrined, he continued to stare at her, silently wishing for absolution. After being studiously ignored for a full minute, he added softly. "What I meant is that I didn't know the police had such beautiful women on the force. I hope you excuse my *faux pas*." When she didn't respond, he got to his feet and went on about his routine.

* * * * *

Maddy sat on one of three leg roll machines swinging weights. Dot lay on her stomach doing fanny presses to Maddy's left and Camile sat to her right resting between sets. Dot and Camile held a conversation around Maddy about the virtues of various hunks in the room.

"Know what blows my mind?" Dot asked Camile, begging an opening. "Maddy, here, turns down Bill the wrestler! Every freaking woman in the place wants a shot at that guy and she treats him like he doesn't even exist!"

"I don't get what you women see in these guys," Maddy interrupted. "Besides, how many times I gotta tell you, I'm living with a boyfriend who doesn't like pets."

"What's pets got to do with anything?" Camile asked.

Maddy just rolled her eyes. "It's a joke, Camile."

"Well, I don't get it."

Maddy rolled her eyes with more exaggeration, huffed, and explained bluntly, "I mean he won't let me have other boyfriends. You know? Boyfriends? Pets?"

"If you don't like the guy, why don't you introduce us?" Dot demanded.

"If you must know," Maddy lowered her voice out of consideration, because what she was going to say they wouldn't like. "I told him...a woman here asked me to introduce her and he told me 'no thanks.' Okay? He says he wants to meet somebody, he'll take care of it himself. Or words to that effect. Besides, what am I? A matchmaker? Anyway, Dot, I thought you were married."

"What's that got to do with anything? Citrus Sam can put his slippers under my bed any day of the week. Except Sunday. My old man's home Sundays." She followed that with a hearty laugh.

"Speaking of wrestlers," Maddy's voice announced a new topic. "I heard there's a lady wrestler works out in here sometimes. Tall blond woman? I heard she's one of those professional body-builders. Y'all ever seen anybody in here like that?"

"Yeah," Camile drawled. "I bet I saw her once. Muscles like you wouldn't believe. I think that's freakish on a woman, myself. Wasn't too long ago, either. Only saw her that one time, though, so I figure she must have changed gyms. She's another one who made a play for Citrus Sam."

"I think it's gross for a woman to try to build up like a man," Dot curled her upper lip like she smelled something. "Makes 'em look like dikes."

"Oh yeah? Well, that dike was sure as hell putting the moves on Citrus Sam. I tried to talk to her but she didn't have no time for no women," Camile replied. "Rude bitch."

"Excuse me, girls," Maddy smiled at each in turn and climbed off the bench. "Gotta get finished and get out of here sometime tonight. Y'all take care."

Maddy worked out on several other pieces of equipment before she managed to inconspicuously finagle her way next to Cahill. He was pressing weights on the four-sided center. She climbed upon the double bars and started doing suspended back raises. He tried to pretend he didn't notice her, so apparently, he was still embarrassed. She flipped over and began the suspended sit-ups. She fixed her eyes on his face and waited until he noticed her staring. He glanced away the instant their eyes met.

"Hey, Cahill, no hard feelings? Okay?"

His responsive glance was icy. She gave him another few seconds. "So I responded to your insult with one of my own. Maybe we should both forget it. You seem like a nice enough guy."

This time when he looked at her, he maintained eye contact and nodded a curt affirmative. None of this interrupted his steam-engine puffing. She gave him a friendly smile, then hopped down off the bars. Finding a large enough space on the floor to spread out, she sat down, placing her feet wide apart and began doing side stretches. She always cooled down with Yoga stretches.

From behind her, "I graduated from FSU with a degree in marine biology and I work for the State of Florida's Environmental Department checking out waste hazards. I was on the U.S. Army's wrestling team when I did my bit for the country and I like it."

She rolled her head and looked up at the giant standing over her. "Gee, so I'm not a butch and you aren't a retard." Her voice was softened and her smile sweet.

He knelt down beside her. "And I still think you are one hell of a beautiful woman." He openly admired her spectacular body: nice bust— not huge, but certainly *va-va-voom*, tiny waist, softly rounded hips, and positively gorgeous legs. She had an oval face, sultry almond-shaped eyes of smokey gray— and he loved women with a slight overbite and adorable, pouty lips.

H. Churchill Mallison

CHAPTER X

Ali's eyes popped open at four-thirty a.m. on Saturday, October 1, 1982: the hour verified as she fumbled for the clock radio. The tall, bright green numbers told her to go back to sleep, but she knew that would be impossible. Quietly slipping out of bed, she pulled into a robe and padded to the kitchen. Cautiously taking the coffee pot apart, trying hard not to make any noise, she cringed at every tiny clink that seemed to echo through the predawn stillness. The water from the faucet sounded like Niagara Falls drumming into the stainless steel pot.

While she waited for the coffee to finish perking, she opened the French doors and stepped out into the cool morning air. The Gulf of Mexico shimmered beneath a bright moon; the sea, calm and quiet, seemed to hold its breath, anticipating the first light of day.

She shivered and pulled the robe more tightly about her. The tantalizing aroma of fresh coffee called her back into the kitchen. With a steaming mug, she returned to the deck and stretched out on a lounge. Ali didn't mind waking up early mornings because then she could be there when dawn paled the sky and the sea awoke. Sometimes she'd see dolphin rolling, or even playing, and once she'd seen an enormous sting ray fly through the air in a mighty leap just off the reef.

This morning, however, her thoughts were full and she failed to notice the paling sky. Graham would be arriving in time for a late breakfast, and from there it would be hectic. She mentally ran over the list of things to do, trying to make sure she hadn't forgotten anything.

Finally she admitted to herself why she'd been unable to sleep. She hadn't just awakened at four-thirty. She'd also awakened at one o'clock, one-thirty, then two-thirty. She'd just given up by four-thirty. She was getting married again. The first

The Wrestler Who Lost His Head

marriage hadn't worked out, and God only knew the troubles she'd had with men over the years.

The first wedding was supposed to have lasted a lifetime. They did all the right things: got married in the church; had a son two years later. It lasted seven years, and then only because she was too stubborn to admit she'd made a ghastly mistake. Graham loved his father and his father loved him, so she'd tried making the sacrifice. The utter boredom with the man had been bad enough, but he also tended to get drunk every now and then. When he did, he'd start hitting her.

Her mother used to say: The secret to a good marriage is to learn how to fight. You never strike each other, you never say I don't love you, and you never go to bed mad. And you don't cheat on each other. Ali had believed that was all there was to making a great marriage. So much for that. Max finally struck her one time too many.

The few affairs she had after that withered upon extended contact. It seemed that the first month of a relationship was always perfect, then it started on a roller-coaster ride from there on, going mostly downhill. The icing on the cake was Sam.

Ali shook thoughts of Sam from her mind. That horror was well in the past and she was tired of reliving that final scene when he'd attacked her and she'd struck back and killed him. If that wasn't enough, several years later she'd been attacked by a psychotic killer. Ali had no intentions of ever taking abuse from a man again. She'd been through too much.

But Jack was different. That's what made her so nervous. Was he really? Would he still be sweet, funny...kind...two years from now? Would he remain faithful? ...Why didn't his other marriage work?...

Stop it. This is supposed to be the happiest day of my life. Or the first day of the happiest of my life.

"Oh, for god sake! I knew I forgot something! I forgot to pick up the flowers from the florist!"

H. Churchill Mallison

Six o'clock. Jack came out onto the deck with a steaming mug. Ali didn't hear him. She'd dozed off. When he sat on the lounge next to her, it scraped the floor and she woke.

"What are you doing up so early?" she asked.

"Me! What time did you get up?"

"God. Four-thirty. Couldn't sleep."

"Not nervous, are you?" Jack asked.

She stopped to think about her answer. "...Maybe I am a little." Why tell him she'd been going through the holy terrors. "Trying to make sure I've remembered everything. And guess what. I forgot to pick up the flowers last night."

"Honey, all you've got to remember is to say 'I do.' You don't even have to remember to get to the church on time because I'm taking you there, even if I have to do it in handcuffs. I'll run down and get the flowers after Graham gets in. That'll give you two a few minutes alone." He leaned down and gave her an extra enthusiastic good morning kiss. "You hungry?" he asked.

"Yes, but we can't eat," she said.

"What do you mean we can't eat?"

"Graham's going to be here for a late breakfast. Remember?"

"That's fine, but I can't wait that long! How about a little tied-me-over? Maybe some toast?" Jack brightened, "I'll even make it. You sit right there. Okay?"

"Well...just toast. I've got a big breakfast planned because we won't eat again until the reception at seven-thirty."

* * * * *

Graham pulled into the driveway at ten o'clock. Ali heard him crunching along the gravel path that ran beside the house to the gulf-side deck and ran down to greet him. They embraced in a long hug and he kissed his mother on the cheek.

"Hey, mom! You look like a bride!" He gave her another hug. "Before I go up, why don't I get my stuff?" She followed

The Wrestler Who Lost His Head

him back to the car and they chattered like wild canaries. He told her about college and said he finally had a girlfriend. Nothing serious, but he really liked her. She told him to finish college before he got too involved with anyone. He told her she sounded like a mother. He carried a suit bag and an over night case and gave her the wedding present. Jack met them at the base of the deck stairs. Graham gave Jack a one-arm hug around his neck.

"I can't tell you how pleased I am that you two are getting married," Graham beamed at his about-to-be stepfather. "You're getting the best looking mom in the world."

"No, I'm getting the best looking wife in the world. She's your mom," Jack teased.

Ali cooked enough breakfast to feed the Army. Spanish omelet, hash browns, bialys from a Jewish bakery, bacon and ham, coffee and juice.

"Good Lord, Mom. You expect us to eat all that?"

"Well, you're not getting anything else until the wedding reception," she explained.

"I'll be so bloated I won't be able to get into my suit," Jack ogled the food.

"You'll get in it if I have to use a shoe horn," Ali replied. "Besides, we have until around two this afternoon to goof off. We can get in a nice walk and maybe go swimming."

They browsed through the meal, taking their time and enjoyed catching up on the family news. Then the phone started ringing off the wall. First her sister who couldn't make it down from Maine for the wedding. Then her Aunt Bea who was older than God and couldn't make it. Various friends from the Crises Center and the FDLE called even though they were coming.

Ali started handing out jobs. Jack, go get the flowers and deliver them to the Methodist Church. Graham, why don't you come with me while I check on the caterers and make sure everything is set up at the reception hall behind the church. Somehow the day got away from them and by five-thirty Ali was

H. Churchill Mallison

in a total state of panic because none of them had showered and started to dress and they only had one bathroom!

She ordered Graham into the shower first. He had to dry off and dress in the living room while Jack took his turn. At last the men were out of the way and Ali could get her hair washed and her make-up on. Twice she had to remove the eye makeup and start all over again!

Graham drove his mother to the Church and Jack rode over with Joe O'Leary, his best man. For good luck, they wouldn't see each other for a whole twenty minutes before the service. She laughed. "Times have changed."

She felt like she stumbled breathlessly into the vespers room. A few brief last-minute instructions from the Minister and the organist. Hank Grisham's wife, Teresa, pitched in and helped by pinning the pink roses on the men's lapels. Teresa and Ali had become good friends since Jack had gone to work for the FDLE, and she was Ali's Matron of Honor. Graham was to give her away.

* * * * *

Jack stood with Joe and the Minister at the alter. They turned towards the back of the church. The pews were about a quarter full. Just about everyone from their work places had come. Neither Jack nor Ali had parents any longer, so Graham was the only relative present.

Jack felt fine. Wasn't nervous a bit. He smiled as he caught the eye of this person or that in the congregation. Then the music began. The Wedding March. Ali and Graham came through the anteroom's double doors and down the aisle.

Ali wore an off-white dress of lace tiers and a wide satin and lace bow atop her cropped, curly dark hair. A single strand of pearls at the neck with matching earrings. Three pink roses with lace and ribbons were attached to a small, white Bible that she held in lace-gloved hands. Those tiny hands he loved so much. Jack's throat constricted with emotion and he almost panicked at

The Wrestler Who Lost His Head

the thought that he might cry. Ali beamed; Graham, so tall and handsome, escorted her so proudly. It was then Jack realized how much like Ali Graham was. As she drew nearer, Jack's eyes watered and his nose began to run! Embarrassed, he pulled out a handkerchief, trying to quietly and gracefully dispose of the mis-routed tears. She met his eyes and beamed.

*****

"Oh, what a lovely wedding! And that Jack of yours! He's so sweet!" The women loved that Jack had teared up so much he had to blow his nose! What a lucky girl Ali was to catch such a dear man!

The men gave him a hard time, whacking him on the back and telling him it wasn't such a bad deal getting married. He'd get over it! Cheer up!

The buffet was abundant and well done. Ali had been careful in her menu selections so that there would be no soggy or wilted hors d'oeuvres. A small band provided music.

Jack lead her to the floor for the first dance. "I'm the happiest person in the world today," he said and kissed her. Applause from the guests.

"No, I am," she whispered.

"No, I am," he insisted.

"No, I am," she grinned. "Our first disagreement and we've only been married thirty minutes."

CHAPTER XI

Selena's again. Another Rob Roy, chilled, straight up with a twist of lemon awaiting. The standard bribery. Jack sat at one of the darkly stained round tables, an ankle crossed over one knee, chatting with Darla, the Susan Hayward look-alike. The usual crowd hadn't started coming in yet, it was Wednesday night, not a particularly busy. Darla had just remarried, too, and they were comparing notes on how great married life was treating them. Darla saw Ali first and called to her to get her attention.

"Hey, Mrs. Robinson! Over here!" Darla waved.

Ali approached, beaming. She'd done a lot of that the last two weeks— beaming. "So, you two tied the knot! Congratulations! Your first one's on the house, and it's ready and chilling on ice. Be right with you."

Darla dashed off. Jack said, "She just got married, too. Think it's contagious?"

"May be. It certainly hasn't been the rage the last few years." She leaned toward him and they kissed. "So how was your day?"

"Busy," he shrugged. "Yours?"

"Actually, pretty quiet for a change. I'm glad, since we're in for another adventurous night at the wrestling matches. Which gladiator arena are we going to tonight? The Outlandish or the Vancouver."

"Amherst," he corrected, "Not Vancouver. Lucky for you, it's the Amherst."

"Why lucky?"

"It's a little...less...shall we say, earthy."

She eyed him suspiciously, "Like, how much less?"

"Like they sweep the floors sometimes."

"Oh, *well*," she tossed her head and gestured great relief, "then that's different." Nodding her head and raising her brow,

The Wrestler Who Lost His Head

she continued hamming it up. "I'm glad to see we're finally moving up in the world."

Darla arrived with a frosted glass of golden liquid.

Ali said, "Oh, thank you Darla. You've probably saved the evening. Did Jack tell you he's taking me out on the town tonight? Aside from here, that is. After imbibing lots of antiseptic and healthful food stuffs?"

"Where to?" Darla asked.

"The Amherst Lounge."

"Where's that?" Darla's brow drew together. "A new place?"

Ali laughed. "No, it was here back when there were still Florida natives running around in fig leaves. Back when MacDill was lizard land and there was no Air Force."

"Oh?" Darla's tone said something sounded strange and she wanted to know more.

"...To the wrestling matches!" Ali's eyes widened and she plastered an evil grin across her face. "Who's fighting tonight, anyway, Jack?"

"The word is..." he paused to create suspense, "...who the hell is it? Wait a minute." From his back pocket he withdrew a photocopied, stapled program that Paul Spiegel had mailed to him at the office. Dramatically, he opened it. "Dice versus The Arabian Knight— that's K-N-I-G-H-T— for openers. Peachy Keene, again, honey, fighting Mean Milly. Ali really digs the women's matches. But the big one's between Prince Albert and Mama's Boy."

"Y'all really go to those things?" Darla's grin said she didn't believe it.

"Oh, yes," Jack said. "I can't keep Ali away from them."

* * * * *

On the way over, Jack gave instructions. "Honey, tonight...we have to go in separately."

"What do you mean?"

"As if we aren't together. If you look cuter than anybody else in there, maybe I'll work my way over and make a pass at you later on."

She fell silent for a few minutes. "Okay. I'm guessing this is so you can be freed up to move around." He smiled at her and twinked his nose, all of which said to her that she'd hit the nail on the head. "Just please keep an eye on me? I mean, if somebody starts bothering me..."

"— I'll hang the bastard up by the balls. Just sit near the ring. You know, sort of near the mothers and kids. Nobody'll mess with you."

"Anything I can do? You know, like look for somebody?"

"Sure. If you happen to see a tall woman who looks like a body-builder with blond kinky hair..." Jack fully described the female they were looking for. "However, honey, if you do see such a person, just signal me and stay clear. Oh, and should we luck out, I may have to go with one of the officers and you may have to go home by yourself. But this goes for any time you go to these fights with me. You know that."

"You mean you won't let me go on a chase with you?" she pouted. For a split second he thought she meant it, then he laughed. "Yeah. Sure. No, babe, we want this one alive."

"Oh, you," she slapped his thigh. The *Sam situation* must be fading, now he could tease her about it and she could tease right back.

* * * * *

Ali went inside first; Jack watched her, but stayed back for a couple of minutes. She paid for her ticket and they stamped her hand with a luminescent stamp. Puffing up her courage, she strode into the room, trying to appear casual. In fact, she hated going into any bar alone, always thinking that anyone who saw her would think she was up for grabs.

In this club, an elongated oval-shaped bar divided the vast room. To the right of the huge bar individual tables were set up

The Wrestler Who Lost His Head

and crowded with boisterous men and women who looked to be anywhere from early twenties to eighties. There were so many short haircuts, Ali figured a lot of the young men were from MacDill Air Force Base.

The left side of the room had been cleared for the match. The ring took up most of the width, with just enough space for people to get around it to the other side. Folding chairs were jammed in tight rows along the east and west walls. It was a tight fit, but with the bar separating most of the drinking crowd from the ringside, the air was a little clearer of cigarette and cigar smoke than it had been at the Outlandish, and Ali could breathe better.

She decided to cross over to the other side of the ring. Once over on the west side, she noticed a curtained- off square in front of what probably was the back door to the place. This curtain allowed separate entrances of a sort for the wrestlers. She sat on the back wall near the center. A waitress caught her eye and Ali nodded. The woman wove her way through the gathering throngs.

"Kin I git'cha a beer or somethin' honey?" she asked.

"Busch," Ali said. "And do you have any popcorn?"

"Shore do, honey. Be right back." Ali watched her leave. She was a back-slapping, never-saw-a-stranger country girl who was having as much fun as the customers. The type that likes what she does and is perfectly content to keep right on doing it forever. She wore comfortable, ugly jogging shoes with socks, tight jeans, and a flowered blouse. Though she looked a badly-aged forties in the face, her ass was small and tight and her waist slim. Ali noticed she called a lot of people by their first names.

She saw Jack enter. He stood near the entrance end of the bar looking into the ringside of the room. He spotted her. Then he wandered over to a thicket of men at the bar and worked his way into the crowd. Every now and then she'd search for him, spot his position, then go back to people watching.

Most of the mothers with children stayed on the east side of the ring, nearer the entrance to the club. The announcer began setting up. Ali recognized him from Outlandish: Mister Malice. For lack of space, he had to set up in the corner near the curtained back entrance near the west end of the bar. There were no stools at that end since that was egress to the bar and the waitress' station.

The *arena rats*, as Ali'd heard they were called in the wrestling circle, began filtering in from the drinking side of the bar. They clustered at the end of the rows of seats nearest the wrestlers' entrance. Again the bone-crushing jeans and lycra tights. Ali wondered how anyone could sit down in jeans that tight. She'd never been comfortable even standing up in tight pants. The crotch seams divided those women as far as the divide could allow, and they indeed looked like they were split all the way up to their bulging, implanted breasts.

A raven-haired woman with tresses almost to her waist came in and sat down in front of Ali on the first row. She wore electric-blue lycra tights with a matching blue sequined blouse cut in a deep V both front and back. The woman looked familiar to Ali, but she couldn't place her. *The Raven*. Ali pinned nicknames on every character who caught her attention.

There was *Madam Crotch* on the sidelines wearing jeans that would have to be surgically removed from the recesses of her body. *Misty,* a dewy-eyed, petite creature dressed in an expensive gingham and jeans outfit, with lots of crinkly, bright-yellow hair that all but hid a small face with a tiny, thin-lipped mouth. She looked like a waif.

Fountain-Pen— Jack got credit for that name. He said she was Dice's woman. She wore black leather skin over bones and had no bosom nor ass. The woman should be dipped in ink and someone should scribble a note to her about anorexia nervosa using her spare form as the writing instrument. Pencil slim— literally.

Mister Malice began testing the microphone, signaling the folks that the matches were about to begin.

After watching the crowd for a few minutes, Ali began recognizing a number of the people she'd seen at the match at

The Wrestler Who Lost His Head

the Outlandish. She saw Dirty Girty at the bar surrounded by men. Same tight black leathers, same opened vest displaying her attributes through black mesh. Ali checked the program. Dirty Girty wasn't playing tonight, but she still wore her professional costume. She wondered if it was customary for the wrestlers to wear their outfits even when they weren't on the program.

Mister Malice interrupted her reverie. "Ladies and gentlemen, please take your seats ringside if you're going to watch the matches. The first event on the card this evening will begin in exactly three minutes."

A short, round granny came huffing and puffing around the ring's corner to sit on the western-most wall. She took a seat on the front row as close to the center as she could manage, next to The Raven. Ali recognized her as the little old lady who'd given Leopold the Leopard a thrashing with her purse as he'd left the ring after losing the match the last time.

The mike squealed, everyone grimaced, then Mister Malice started his pitch. "West Florida Wrestling Club wants to extend it's appreciation to The Amherst Lounge..."

Fountain Pen left the bar and vanished behind the black curtains.

"The opening match this evening, ladies and gentlemen, is between Dice and The Arabian Knight. Now, I know there's strong feeling about this match. There's been a lot of off-stage animosity between these two men, between Dice's wife and Bella Prunella— who's in love with the A-rab— even though he doesn't know she exists. Now I'm telling you, Dice, and you, too, Arabian Knight, I want a good, clean match in this ring tonight. And Lucy Mangione, Dice's bride and manager, I expect you to behave tonight. I see Bella Prunella up there at the bar. I just want you two women to remember there are children in this room. You're supposed to be role models of society..."

— Ali almost sprayed the Raven with beer over that one! She moved up a row and sat so that she was behind and one seat to the right of the Raven and the little old white-haired lady.

H. Churchill Mallison

A scattered applause rose and Ali swung her head to the left. Dice entered. Big, bad, outfitted in black leathers— or faux-leathers. A bit barrel-chested and very hairy, with a day's growth of beard, he created the perfect bad-guy image. Bouncing along beside him, whooping it up, arms raised clapping, was Fountain Pen, trying to encourage an enthusiastic reception. He swung into the ring and she followed by scrambling beneath the ropes. She climbed all over him, petting him. He slings her aside with one arm and she meekly crawled outside the ropes, but stayed up on the platform by his corner. Most of the room boos him.

Lucy Mangione starts screaming at the crowd. "Shaddup! Who ya think ya booin'! Hey! How'd you like a bust in the mouth!" she screams at one of the sideliners.

Bella Prunella strutts from the bar and comes around the ring booing and waving her arms to encourage others to join her. She makes her way around to where Ali and The Raven are sitting, shouting. "Ha! Wrestler! That hair-ball couldn't beat a dog. He can't even control that skinny broad he's married to!"

"Ladies, ladies," Mister Malice scolds, "both of you sit down and shut up and let's get this show..."

Both women turn on Mister Malice, shouting almost simultaneously, "Who you think you're tellin' to shut up!"

"I'm telling you both to shut up and sit down," Mister Malice barks.

Bella Prunella lunges in his direction and stumbles over a chair. As she is untangling from the collapsed folding chair, Lucy swings from the ring, runs at her and pushes, and then runs at Mister Malice. Bella untangles herself and runs after both of them. Mister Malice frantically backs away, bellowing into the mike that if Dice doesn't get his wife off him, he is going to be fined.

Meanwhile, Bella is swinging at Lucy and Mister Malice. Dice vaults over the ropes, striding over casually, and plucks Lucy from the melee by her leather belt and carts her off with all fours flailing at the air. He plunks her down at the end of the

The Wrestler Who Lost His Head

front row and with wide gestures, instructs her to sit down and not get up again.

Mister Malice screams into the mike as he's trying to fend Bella off, "What about her! Get her off me!"

Dice sneers, "She ain't my problem, Mister Malice. You can't fine me for what that stupid Bella Prunella does." To the audience he complains, "That Bella Prunella is a professional wrestler and she attacked my poor little Lucy. That is a mean woman, let me tell you!"

A tuxedoed muscle man, Mister Malice's body guard, rushs from around the bar to his rescue. He grabs Bella around the waist and drags her away. She screams, "Let me at the little worm!"

Mister Malice straightens up his bow tie, slicks his mussed hair back, and clears his throat into the mike. "Now, let's see if we can get on with the first event on the card." He turns toward the curtain to see if all is ready. The bodyguard disappears behind the curtains with Bella in tow. He waits for just a second, then the curtain is swept aside. "Entering the arena is *The Arabian Knight*!" Cheers almost raise the roof.

Posing in front of the black backdrop stands a dazzling white hero. His kaffiyeh a silk-sheen cotton, its agel pearled sequins. The matching tobe has sequins covering the shoulders and flowing down the hems of the front and back in an intricate design which billows around him as he marches towards the ring. The only thing missing is a shimmering Arabian horse.

On his heels comes Bella Prunella, weeping and worshiping him, trying to grab his arm. He studiously ignored her.

When The Arabian Knight reaches ringside with weeping Bella in tow, The Raven, sitting in front of Ali, leaps to her feet. She reaches for Bella, grabbing her wrist. "Sit down!" The Raven screams in her face. Bella swings around and faces the woman. Ali notices that Bella is startled, then confused. She shakes free of the stranger's grip and gives her a look that says, hey, lady, this is only an act! Don't get your bowels in an uproar!

H. Churchill Mallison

All eyes in the room turn on Bella and the tall, black-haired woman. It is then that Ali notices the cameraman—person, a woman manning a camcorder. The photographer zooms in on the confrontation.

"Get out of here," The Raven enunciates.

Trying to keep her voice down to a loud whisper, Bella says: "Look, why don't you just sit down and enjoy the matches. Don't take this so seriously."

"I'm takin' over from here," The Raven replies in a no-nonsense voice.

"Who the fuck are you?" Bella whispers. "Get your fuckin' mitts off my arm or I'll fix your ass."

"Think so? I'll take you on anytime, sugar tits."

The bodyguard rushes over. "Hey, hey!" He pulls the women apart. "We're here to see Dike and The Arabian, not you two broads. Now break it up. Bella, get back over there at the bar where you belong." He shoves Bella in that direction. She sulkily returns to her crowd, turns around, and continued to stare back at the electric-blue intruder. From here, Ali could see that Bella is genuinely confused. In front of her, the bodyguard talks quietly with The Raven. Now Ali wishes she'd stayed on the other side of the ring so she could see the woman's face. This is better than the fight. "I don't know who you are, lady, but any more trouble out of you, it's out you go. Got that?"

The Raven turns sideways and Ali studies her profile. She has a faintly hooked nose, sharp cheekbones, and full lips. Her most notable feature is very long, mink lashes that obviously are not real. The Raven puts her hands on her hips and stares the bouncer down. Loudly she announces, "The A-rab is mine! You got that *Miss Prunella*! M-I-N-E." Her eyes tells the bodyguard to get lost, she is making herself part of the act, like it or not..

The Arabian Knight, by now in the center of the ring, turns and looks at her. His eyes fix on hers for a moment, then he turns back to his audience and begins ceremoniously removing his headgear and cape. A roar of approval rises when suddenly, all eyes riveting onto the two wrestlers again, the sideline skirmish forgotten.

Ali studied the Knight. He had a head of thick auburn hair with darkly tanned golden skin of a natural redhead who didn't freckle. His eyes, though, were such a pale blue they were almost white. There was something almost beautiful and very strange about his sculptured features. A granite statute come to life. Ali understood how women could be drawn to this one. Like a fine horse, he was to be looked upon and admired.

She leans forward and touches The Raven's shoulder. "Excuse me, you know him?"

"What's it to you?" speaking as The Raven slowly turns around and fixes her eyes on Ali's.

"Just that...what a gorgeous man." Ali rolls her eyes appreciatively, and smiles. "I can see why you'd want to stake your claim. You a wrestler?"

"Fuck off," the woman sneers and turns abruptly away.

Ali flushed with embarrassment; her attempt at playing cop and trying to worm her way into the woman's confidence a miserable failure. She turns her focus on the match.

CHAPTER XII

Maddy Ulner trained the camcorder on each person sitting along the far wall, zooming in on every face. Then she zeroed in on the people concentrated at the ring-side of the bar. Trying to get everyone at the bar's face would be tricky without it appearing obvious, so she moved around the room a lot, always with the ring between her and whomever she photographed. No one paid any attention to her. She wore skinny pants and a loud, oversized T-shirt in shocking pink with a big alligator on the front, one leering eye exactly on her nipple. A smaller gator road on her back left shoulder. Both glittered with sprinkles. She'd pulled her dark hair back into a pony tail and wore a lot of makeup, so she fit right in with the arena rats.

She also wanted to film the patrons on the other side of the bar so she'd have everyone at the club, but hadn't figured out how to do that without being conspicuous. Besides, it was very dark on the other side.

Jack leaned against the bar on his elbows watching the wrestling. Dice, airborne off the ropes, hit The Arabian with a cross-body chop, slamming The Arabian to the floor. Dice threw his torso over The Arabian's and the referee dove to the floor and swung his arm high counting. "One! Two!" The Arabian kicked and jolted free, rolled, and came up on his feet. He staggered over to the ropes in front of Ali, the old woman, and The Raven.

The Raven came out of her seat shouting, "I love you, dahlin'!" The Arabian Knight captured her gaze, pretending to be surprised, even shocked, and slowly shook his head negatively, silently mouthing a question to her, "Who are you?"

Dice, who'd been strutting around the ring, now came up behind The Arabian and grabbed him by the hair. "Hair! Hair!" the crowd shouted. "No pulling hair!"

The Wrestler Who Lost His Head

The Arabian turned around slowly and fixed Dice with a menacing stare. They locked arms in a hook-up.

Jack studied the electric-blue clad nymph from across the room. He turned to the man to his right. "You go to a lot of these matches?"

The man, a long limbed, skinny fellow decked out in a western shirt, western jeans, fake snake boots, and a cowboy hat, grinned, showing that one of his front teeth was missing. "Yeah, nevah miss 'em. Love this stuff. Funny as all hail." Jack almost smiled at his distortion of *hell*. "Know who that woman is over there? The woman in blue who went for Bella?"

The cowboy studied the woman for a few minutes. "No, don't reckon I ever seen 'er before. Purdy thang, though, ain't she."

"I thought maybe she's a wrestler," Jack added.

"Could be. Looks like one, don't she. Way she's dressed. Looks strong as a fuckin' ox, too. I wouldn't like to be on the losing end of an argument with 'er. Takin' on Bella lak thet. Bella ain't no lush in the ring, let me tell ya. She kin hold her own with the best of 'em. That lady could be new, though. Meybe she come down from Et-lanta or sommerselse."

"Bella work with The Arabian?"

"Nah. These broads— wimmen rasslers?— they always trying to git in on somebody's act. They's bad as the arena rats. You ever catch yersef a rat?"

"Nah," Jack curled his lip. "You?"

"Yeah, time or two. Them's that's left over. They'll go with anybody with a fuckin' doller."

Dice had the Arab down on his knees torquing his wrist and arm. The Arab grimaced with pain and pounded the canvas with a fist.

Maddy wormed her way to the bar and started joking around with some of the patrons. "Smile purdy for the camera," she flirted with a cluster of grinning men who openly ogled her.

"Wha-chew shooting us for? We ain't fighters. Fight's that'a way, sweet thang."

H. Churchill Mallison

"I can't pass up a good looking hunk like you," she'd grin and then turned back to the ring.

"Buy you a beer?" one of the men offered.

"Sure. But if I drink much more, I'll plumb be drunker'n a skunk!" She pretended to be tipsy. "Hey, look at all them folks on the other side of the bar. I bet they can't see much from there! Hey! You over there!" Maddy called over to the other side of the bar. When she caught some of their attentions, she scanned them with the camcorder. One of the women on the dark side yelled back, "What you wasting your film for, honey. It's too dark over here and ain't none of these bums worth takin' a picher of!" Maddy lowered the camera and laughed heartily. Then the beer was passed to her, so she joined the fringe of the group that was so accommodating.

Jack sidled over to Maddy and grinned in her face. "Well, hell-o there, sweetie pie," he said, eyebrows shooting up and down.

She grinned back in his face. "Hello there yourself," she answered. He leaned into her and whispered something. She swung her free arm up on his shoulder and snuggled her ear to his moving mouth. She pressed her body against Jack's, hooking the free arm about his neck, pulling his face down closer to hers, and began whispering in his ear.

From Ali's perspective across the room, they appeared a little friendlier than working relations required. Her heart skipped a beat, then she caught herself. Ali knew who the woman was, a detective from TPD who worked with Jack. She'd come to the wedding. As far as Ali was concerned, she'd seemed mighty friendly with Jack at the time, now that she thought about it, and very indifferent to her. Despite an effort not to, Ali felt a tinge of jealousy. Pulling her eyes away from the detectives' *conference*, she forced herself to watch the contest in the ring.

The Arabian Knight grabbed Dice and slung him into the ropes in the corner. He pounced on him and started banging Dice's head on the turnbuckle. The crowd screamed wildly.

The Wrestler Who Lost His Head

Jack and Maddy had gone off to a corner by themselves in what appeared to be an intimate huddle. Ali couldn't keep her eyes on the match and her heart began thumping against her ribs.

The Arabian scooped Dice up and raised him high over his head. He spiraled in wide loops until they were about center ring. The audience leapt out of their seats and chanted "Roll the Dice! Roll the Dice!" Lucy stormed the outer ring alternating between pleads for mercy and outrage. The Raven kept jumping up and sitting down and jumping up again, throwing punches at the air. The little old lady next to her got excited, too, and began barking "Ack-ack-ack!" and thumping her purse with a fist.

Maddy jumped up out of her seat and started filming again. Jack got up and disappeared behind the dark side of the bar.

Ali calmed down and felt ashamed that she'd reacted with jealousy. What was the matter with her anyway. That detective looked like a damned hooker. Well, she did tonight, anyway. Ali recalled to mind what she'd looked like at the wedding. If she remembered correctly, the woman was a goddamned knockout when she dressed normally. Whatever Jack was doing, Ali didn't see him for another forty-five minutes. Meanwhile, back at the circus, the match had turned again.

The crowd went insane. Dice had gotten The Arabian in a headlock and was pounding the hell out of his face with his fist. Then he locked elbows with The Arabian and sent him sailing over his head in a finely executed double-arm suplex. The A-rab slammed to the canvas. Dice flew to his feet, ran to the ropes at the ring post and scrambled to position. With all the force he could muscle, he flew at the Arabian, hitting the floor with a knee drop to his arm. He continued to knee drop while the Arabian Knight screamed in agony. Then Dice spun around, scurried up the ropes again, and hit The Arab with a Flying Guillotine!

The referee flung himself to the canvas and began counting. "One! Two! Three!" He leapt to his feet yelling, "And the winner of this match is Dice!" By now Dice pranced around the

H. Churchill Mallison

ring punching the air and exploding, "Dice! Dice! Dice!" The referee grabbed his wrist in the victory salute.

The Arabian Knight lay inert for a few moments, then began flailing his arms. Slowly, he dragged to his feet. Dejected. Dice's woman, Lucy the fountain pen, ran up and kicked him, then skittered away through the ropes, trailing after her hero. The crowd booed as Dice strutted. The little old lady with the white hair rose to her feet and began shaking her purse at him. He ignored her. She ran after him and whacked him with it. Lucy spun on her and made all kinds of threatening noises before the old woman quit. Granny stomped back to her seat complaining that the count was too fast and somebody ought to hang the damned referee.

The women fought next: Peachy Keene versus Mean Millie. Mean Millie entered first. She was a husky woman with the face of a junk-yard dog, and a tire around her waist. Stomping to the ring, she sneered at everyone in the audience, and flung herself into the ring like a pit bull bitch ready to kill. The female counterpart of Leopold the Leopard. Orange, mangy hair, scowling eyes, and puffy greased lips. Stalking the ropes, she barked at little kids telling them they'd better get with their mama's because she ate kids for breakfast. The kids loved it. Dressed in wall to wall purple tights, she looked like the world's ugliest grape. Mean Millie was appropriately booed.

Then Mister Malice announced Peachy Keene's arrival. Peachy Keene was the exact opposite of the other redhead. Her mane a glimmering halo of gold highlighted auburn, her flawless complexion creamy, her figure outstanding. Adorned in white tights and peach sequins, gloves up to her armpits. As she strutted the ring smiling beautifully for everyone, she pealed the gloves off like a stripper getting ready to disrobe. While Mean Millie snarled and slashed at her with claws, the referee fended her off yelling at her to go back to her corner. Peachy complained to the audience with innocent wide-eyed amazement, "See how mean Mean Millie is!"

The Wrestler Who Lost His Head

The referee signaled the women to the center of the ring. He checked their waists and boots for weapons, then held up his arms to signify that the fight can continue. "This is one fall, fifteen minute time!"

Jack observed a couple of the arena rats deserting for the bar during the women's event. The petite blond in the expensive country outfit came around to the less crowded, dark side of the bar and found a stool. Jack slipped in between her and the man on the next stool. He held up a finger to catch the bartender's attention. "Two over here. Beer, and," he smiled down into her upturned eyes, "what would the lady like?"

"Who says I want you to buy me a drink?" she asked. Her voice was as petite as the rest of her.

"Would you accept a drink if I go away?" he asked.

She thought about it. "What's the catch?"

Jack laughed, "Catch! I'm just saying I think you're cute as a button and I'd like to have a conversation with you and buy you a drink. However, if you don't want to have a conversation, I'll still buy you a drink and be polite and go away."

She gave him a bored look, but said, "Gin and tonic."

"Gin and tonic," he repeated to the waiting bartender. The bartender set about his task. "You a wrestling fan or do you just like The Amherst?"

"Both," she said. "But I particularly like the wrestling. I know a lot of them personally," she added to impress him.

"You know the lady wrestlers, too?"

"I know some of them. Most of them are kinda snotty. Really," she said in a voice that asked if he could believe it. "I mean, getting down on the ground wrestling around with another woman certainly don't turn me on."

"I don't know," Jack grinned. "Might be fun!"

"You men are all alike."

"Not quite. For instance, I'm not a wrestler."

"So tell me something I don't know," voice sarcastic.

He sipped his beer and stared into her eyes. He couldn't tell what color they were, the room was too dark on this side. Her soft curls hid all but her very large eyes, petite nose, and tiny little pink mouth. Her chin looked like a child's. "You old enough to drink?" he asked.

Rolling her eyes up at him again, she pursed her lips and shook her head. He could tell she was flattered, though, even though she tried to act tough. "You want to see my driver's license?"

"Yeah," he continued grinning.

"You a cop?"

"Me? You crazy?"

"Then why should I show you my driver's license?"

"Then I'll know what your name is and where you live."

"Boy oh boy, is that ever a good reason not to show somebody my driver's license! You could be some kind of wacko for all I know."

"My name's Jack. You can tell me your first name, then I couldn't find you again unless you want me to."

She turned her head away from him and said something to the man on the other side of her. Jack shrugged and picked up his drink. He started walking away. She spun around on the stool and called after him, "Boy, you sure give up easy. My name's Sandra."

Jack nodded and said, "So, I think I'll go over here and find myself a comfortable table. Join me if you'd like."

She slipped down off the stool and followed him. All of the tables were full, but it looked like a couple were getting ready to leave one. He slouched against the wall at a discreet distance and waited for the availability. She joined him, leaning against the wall beside him.

Jack rolled and propped himself against the wall with one hand above her head. She looked up at him and smiled. He stooped so his face was right in her upturned one. With his other hand he fingered the tips of her curls, pulling one out straight and watching it sproing back in place. "You are cute as a puppy."

The Wrestler Who Lost His Head

"Know what? I always wondered why men tell women they're cute as a puppy. That's the same damned thing as callin' her a dog, ain't it?"

"You know that isn't what I meant."

She fluttered her lashes and dropped her jaw giving him a look that said she was too cool for the same old dumb crap. "Pul-lease." She drooped her eyelids dramatically, then rolled her big what-ever-color-they-were eyes up to meet his again. She knew these tall guys liked little women who looked *up* to them all wide-eyed and childlike. Just like she knew they all liked to pretend every woman they took to bed was a virgin.

He backed up a little, though he still kept her between him and the wall. "I used to know a lady wrestler. Big damn woman. I don't mean fat, I mean tall. How tall are you? Five-one?"

"I'm five-two."

"Get out of here."

"I am!"

"Well, anyway, this lady I used to date? She was about five-ten. She put on those three-inch spikes?— practically as tall as I am. She had muscles like you wouldn't believe. Into body-building. Stuff like that."

"And she dated you?"

Jack found her tone insulting but kept the smile plastered on his mug. "Yeah. Why?"

"Well, you obviously aren't into body-building."

Offended, he drew back a little further and asked, "What's wrong with my build?"

"Oh, I don't mean there's anything wrong with your build. Just that you obviously don't go in for steroids and pumped up muscles. Actually, I think you're kinda cute."

He turned his head from side to side as if looking to see if anyone overheard this conversation, then turned back to her. "Well, that lady wrestler thought I was built good enough to suit her. Maybe you know her? Like I said, tall? Muscular? Long

H. Churchill Mallison

blond hair— real curly, like yours. Only yours is softer." He smiled.

"No. Besides, it's the men wrestlers I'm interested in, not those over-stuffed broads. Lookit, I gotta go."

"Hey," he crooned, "don't rush off."

"Jack...that is your name, ain't it? I ain't interested, okay? You're a nice guy and all that, but I really...prefer wrestlers."

"Well, then, do you know somebody else I could...you know..."

"*What!*" she shrieked and half the damned people in the bar turned around to see what was wrong. "*What do you think I am! A whore?*"

In shushing tones: "Hey, hey, cool it. No, that's not what—"

A huge brute in a shirt unbuttoned to his waist swung off the bar and was on Jack like a dog on a raw steak. He literally grabbed Jack by the scruff of the neck and slung him away from Sandra, then jacked him up on the wall. Now it was Jack with his back to the wall pinned in by somebody a whole lot bigger than him.

"Yo, cool it man," Jack said into a mad bull's face, holding up both palms in front of him. "Misunderstanding, that's all."

"Lady don't think so, you prissy-assed jerk!" Hot beer breath slapped Jack in the face and almost gagged him. The brute turned to Sandy, "He bothering you little lady?"

"He implied that I was some kind of pick-up or worse!" Sandy fumed, fists on hips.

"Maybe I ought to just teach you some manners. You city boys are all alike; ain't none of you got no manners." He jammed Jack, bouncing him higher up the wall none too gently, and drew back a fist.

CHAPTER XIII

Jack pleaded with Sandy, hoping to calm down this redneck hero of damsels in distress, "Sandy! That's not true and you know it,".

The bull looked from Sandy to Jack and back to Sandy again. "What ever you want little lady," he said gallantly.

Maddy Ulner came over with the camcorder. "Jack, honey, there you are! Hey, mister, you put my brother down!"

"Get out of the way," the bull warned Maddy.

Maddy pulled the camcorder up to her eye. "Go ahead you fuckin' ape. I'll have it on tape and I'll go straight down to the State Attorney's office and file a complaint for assault."

The bull huffed a laugh, "Yeah, sure. In the fuckin' dark."

"This is no ordinary camcorder, sonny, and it's loaded with special film for night recording. I'm a professional photographer. Trust me, I'm not kidding. Put him down."

Just about everyone on the dark side had closed in to watch what was going down. The bull reassessed his position and let Jack slide down the wall until his feet once again touch *ferma terra*. Mister Malice's bodyguard waded through the crowd. He came in close and waved for the foursome to gather around.

"Listen, folks. Is this a weird night or what? Break it up, or I'll break it up, and if I can't break it up, the cops can. The fighting is on the other side inside the ring."

"Well, he started it," Sandra complained, pointing at Jack.

"Sandra?" the bodyguard said in a voice that implied she'd been in this situation before, "You gotta...listen, how come is it every time I see you at a fight you almost start one?"

Maddy latched onto Jack and pulled him away. "Good job, big shot." She hauled his butt back onto the lighted side and took him over to a corner where they could talk. "What the hell was that all about?"

"Hey, she thought I thought she was a hooker." He grinned. "Actually..."

H. Churchill Mallison

"You keep harking at me not to blow our cover and you almost get the shit kicked out of you."

"I beg your pardon," he tucked his chin and scowled at her. "For your information, I can hold my own against some overweight hick who thinks he's tough shit. I just didn't want to have to. Thanks for saving me, sis."

Maddy sighed. "Did you find out anything?"

"Yeah. She doesn't like women wrestlers, just giant male ones. And she thinks I'm too skinny."

Maddy burst out laughing.

* * * * *

Ali had heard the scuffle on the other side of the bar, but couldn't see anything of what happened. Then she saw Maddy dragging Jack back into the room, go to a corner, and now they were both laughing it up. The unmentionable stabbed her heart again and she forcibly turned her attention back to the ring.

Peachy had a handful of ratty hair and had closed in tight to Mean Milly so Milly couldn't pull any stomach punches. Both women were snarling. Then Mean Milly got a leg hooked behind Peachy and shoved. Peachy slammed to the mat taking Milly with her, refusing to let go of her hair. But Peachy was on the bottom. Mean Milly proceeded to sit right down in the middle of Peachy's abdomen and started whopping nose-slaps on her.

The crowd screamed for Peachy to throw off Mean Milly, but Milly was too heavy to budge. She sat there admiring her fingernails while Peachy yelled and thrashed her legs about. Then suddenly, Peachy managed to hook a leg over Milly's head. Peachy grabbed her ankle and pulled her leg down further, then with a roar, slammed Mean Milly down on the mat. Using her legs, Peachy got a good grip and Mean Milly was trapped.

With considerable ruckus, the petite blond came swishing around the rear end of the bar and stumbled along the row of seats, working between onlookers, until she could get a good

The Wrestler Who Lost His Head

center view. She sat in a vacant chair next to Ali. Ali noticed the woman was flushed with anger.

Ali asked, "You in there when the fight broke out?"

"Was I," not a question, a statement. The woman pouted.

"What happened? If you don't mind my asking."

"Some creep implies I'm...you know," she whispered "...an easy mark." A little louder, growing excited by the rapt attention this woman was giving her: "A whore! So I tell him to ...ef off...and this nice guy from the bar comes over, you know? Anyway, he's going to fix the son-of-a-bitch good. Then mister big shot, you know, Mister Malice's bodyguard comes over and blames the whole thing on *me*. What's a woman gonna do?"

Not knowing what else to say, Ali said, "Oh, my."

"That's him over there with his *sister*. Little boy has to have his fuckin' *sister* come rescue him. Jerk." Ali looked where she stared and it was Jack she was glaring at.

"You mean that man over there with the girl with the camcorder?"

"Yeah, that *pussy*."

"He called you a whore?" Ali couldn't believe her ears.

"Not exactly. But when I told him I like wrestlers, he asked me if I knew any other girls he could pick up. The nerve. The ef-fuckin' nerve."

Ali closed her eyes and pulled her fist to her mouth. She took a deep breath and turned back to the fight. Irresistibly, her eyes pulled over to the corner. Maddy had her hand on his knee! All of a sudden, Ali was furious. The longer she sat there trying to hide her feelings, the madder she became. By the time Mean Milly was through making mincemeat out of Peachy Keene, Ali was ready to do a little meat tenderizing on Jack!

With supreme effort, Ali managed to get her anger under control. After all, Jack was on the job and she knew damned well that whatever had happened was just part of the job. To get information, sometimes you had to do weird things to gain people's confidences. He and Maddy were partners, sort of, and she figured that sometimes maybe they had to pretend to be sister and brother, maybe even sometimes...lovers. Still, it grew harder and harder to concentrate on the wrestling matches.

The crowd really was mad when Peachy lost the fight and even some of the kids were running up to the canvas and yelling "No fair! No fair!" The men at the bar made catcalls when Mean Millie stomped around the ring victoriously. She invited one of her hecklers into the ring and he acted like he was going to take her up on it. Then at the last minute, he turned around, waving off her threats, laughing.

* * * * *

Crossing the Gandy Bridge, heading back to the beaches taking Highway 684 to 688, then north to Indian Rocks on Gulf Boulevard, Jack drove in front, Ali following in her car. The fine sliver of a new moon on the wane, barely visible since it lay dead center between the last quarter and the dark, new moon, winked from behind blowing drifts of thin stratospheric clouds. Ali sulked. Jack, completely unaware of Ali's disposition, drove home deeply buried in his own thoughts, trying to sort through events looking for some enlightenment of this puzzling case.

Ali continued to build up a head of steam. Just couldn't help it. *I mean, there he was so damned cozy with that damn Maddy Ulner! A woman knows when another woman wants her man. And Maddy Ulner wants Jack.* She remembered how Maddy had danced so close to him at the wedding reception. Steam started puffing out Ali's ears.

So, okay, so on the job sometimes he has to maybe flirt a little with a woman to get information out of her, *but to the point that she starts yelling and some bully decides to teach Jack some manners?*

They parked side by side and headed up the steps to their apartment. Jack made the mistake of breaking the silence. "You're awfully quiet. Didn't you enjoy the matches? I thought you were having a grand old time. I saw you jumping up and down rooting for the good guys."

The Wrestler Who Lost His Head

She didn't answer; she turned towards the deck balustrade, staring out at the gulf.

He reached over, laying his hand over hers on the railing.

"I guess I'm pissed," she admitted quietly.

"Yeah? What about, honey?"

She remained silent for a few minutes, trying to decide whether to keep her stupid jealousy to herself and work it out, or come clean and tell him what was bugging her. All the counseling manuals said it was better to get it out before it grew out of proportion, to discuss your grievances, to communicate. She knew she was being silly, but she still felt this burning anger. He squeezed her hand, encouraging her to speak up— at least, that's how she interpreted the gesture. Finally, she decided to express her feelings.

"Well, for one. You know the little blond in the Jordash jeans outfit? The one with the big eyes and lots of blond Shirley Temple curls?" Ali saw Jack shoot her a glance in her peripheral vision. "The one that *caused* the fight to break out on the other side during the women's match?" Watch your tone of voice, she thought to herself. She tried to sound causal, but bitterness sharpened the edges of her words. "She came over and sat beside me and told me all about this jerk who called her a *whore* because she wouldn't go out with him."

"In the first place," Jack, immediately alert to thunder clouds gathering over her head, carefully kept his voice modulation soft, "I did not call her a whore, nor did I insinuate she was a whore. Sandy didn't let me finish saying what I was going to say before she started yelling that I'd insulted her. In the second place, Ali, I did not ask her to go anywhere. Nor did I intend to. I am a conscientious detective, honey, but there are limits to what I will do to get information. If I think someone's got info I need and isn't coming across, I'll pull my badge. I didn't want to do that." He fell silent a moment. "I find it hard to believe you'd believe..."

"I didn't say I believed her, I just said it pissed me off that you'd put yourself in such a situation. You could have gotten hurt."

"I can protect myself."

"And in the second place, what's with this Maddy Ulner stuff?"

Another side glance in her peripheral vision. Jack's voiced tensed a little, "What does that mean?"

"Nothing."

"No, out with it. Just what bothers you about Detective Ulner?"

"Oh? Now it's *Detective Ulner*? It certainly looked friendlier than that." Ali shut up, took a deep breath, and decided to try this again. She was letting her temper get the best of her and making implications that she knew damned well weren't true.

"Ali, Maddy Ulner and I were working as a team. If we have to play brother and sister to cover each other's ass, then we'll do it."

"Jack, I've seen a lot of brothers and sisters together, and for one thing, when they whisper to each other, they don't press their bodies together. For another, they don't caress each others thighs!"

"Who's pressing their bodies together and feeling each others thighs?" Jack didn't exactly yell, he emoted— loud enough to be heard in the next county. "Listen, I don't know what the hell you're talking about, but if you can't mind your own business and let me do my job, you can just stay the hell home the next time!"

Sarcasm thick as swamp mud, Ali oozed, "Oh, don't worry honey-chile, I'll stay at home and you can just *investigate* all over hell and back with your *Detective* Maddy Ulner." Out of the mud and into deeper water, she barked, "Let me tell you something, Jack. I know when a woman sets her sights on a man and that bitch has hers on you!"

The Wrestler Who Lost His Head

Thoroughly frosted, Jack clamped his mouth shut, gripped the railing with both hands, and glared at the gulf with enough intensity to create waves. God only knew, it had been a bad enough night! Ali, knowing that if she'd ever mishandled anything in her whole life, she'd done it now. She turned about, staring but seeing nothing, towards the French doors. Half ashamed and half convinced she was right about Maddy Ulner's attentions, she wasn't at all sure what to do at the moment but shut the hell up.

An eternity passed. Neither moved from the rail..

Ali finally said meekly, "I'm sorry. I know you were trying to get information out of Sandy and just doing your job. That really didn't bother me. It's really Maddy Ulner that got under my skin."

"Give me a fucking break, Ali!" Jack, still infuriated, wasn't having any of it.

"Are you so naive you don't know when a woman's trying to move on you?" Ali asked.

His stare could melt sand.

"Even at the wedding, for God sake." Like a dog with a rag, Ali couldn't let it go. "No other woman there danced pressed up against you like she did, or lay their heads on your shoulder. At a wedding, no less! — with the groom! She was all over you."

"Ali, I'm warning you..."

"You're what? You're warning me? Of what? No, babe, I'm warning you. Don't play games with me because I won't take it!"

Another eon of screaming silence.

Jack pushed back from the railing, shot her a withering stare, then went straight back to the bedroom and started changing his clothes. Ali threw herself onto a deck lounge chair despite the fact that the evening was growing a little chilly. She crossed her arms beneath her bosom, boring a new black hole through the ozone layer, on through the heavens with rays of burning frustration.

H. Churchill Mallison

* * * * *

Jack almost popped a button on his favorite plaid shirt before he regained control over his emotions. He stared at himself in the mirror and saw more fury there in his face than he'd seen since that morning when he'd thrown Susan out of the bed and against the wall back in the most miserable era of his unhappy marriage to the wannabe socialite. The expression stunned him. He watched his reflection as this sudden revelation drained the power from his out-of-control anger. At last coherent thought broke through the wall of anger. *I'm not reacting to Ali, I'm reacting to all those years of frustration with Susan. Just stop a minute and think this through.*

* * * * *

Ali sat huddled, knees drawn up, numb. She blew it; she knew it. She'd wanted to get some kind of message across, but at this point, she wasn't even sure what that was. A good cry would help, but she felt too scrambled to do anything at all. All she knew was that she hurt like hell.

Jack came to the door in his robe and stood there for a moment watching the fluff of blowing hair that showed above the back of the lounge chair. He ran his fingers through his own hair, took a deep breath, and tried to figure out what to say.

"Look," he began. "This thing got out of hand."

Silence.

"Ali, I love you to death. I wouldn't hurt you for anything on this green earth. Maybe those lines are cliches, but I can't think of a better way to put it. I don't think either one of us is responding to the other. I think you're responding to...bad experiences in your past...your ex, maybe Sam. I think I responded to past anger with Susan..."

* * * * *

The Wrestler Who Lost His Head

Ali started to say something, but froze, her lips forming a word that never made it to the surface. It hit. Not in word-formed thought, but in a sudden insight that flashed through her mind too fast to break down in simple terms. She shook her head and slowly blinked her eyes. She sat up straight in the lounge and turned toward Jack. His silhouette, back-lit in the frame of the French door by the kitchen light, stood breathlessly still. Slowly she rose from the lounge and stood facing him.

"You're right," she whispered.

"Come here," he held his arms out to her. She entered them. Jack held her closely for a long time. "Want to kiss and make up?" he asked, smiling sweetly as he lifted her chin. He gave her a little peck on the lips. She leaned into his chest.

In a cautious, tiny voice, she said, "Jack, I don't doubt you. But I do mean it when I say Maddy Ulner wants you for herself."

"You're not going to start that again," his voice firmer.

She leaned back and looked him straight in the eye. "Listen, I know I was...how do I say wrong?...feelings are feelings and there is no right or wrong about how you feel. I handled my feelings badly. But honey, I'm a female and females protect their nests. A female knows a dangerous female when she sees one. No, you let me finish," she quickly added when he looked like he would get mad all over again. "I'm not saying that you have done anything to deliberately attract her. Honey, I'm not accusing you. I'm just telling you that Maddy has the hots for you. And I'll kill the bitch if she messes with my man." No, she shouldn't say kill, she suddenly thought— cops took that literally! She hastily added, "I don't...Oh, you know what I mean."

Jack took her by the shoulders and held her away from him so he could make good eye contact. "Ali, I promise you, Maddy Ulner doesn't appeal to me in the least. Hell, I don't even see another woman! You're all I want, Mrs. Robinson." Once again, he grabbed her to his bosom and held her tightly. "But I think you're freaking nuts; Maddy Ulner isn't remotely after my body."

H. Churchill Mallison

Ali pulled her head back and gave him a look that said he was blind as hell, released a sigh, and said, "Let's go to bed, honey."

CHAPTER XIV

Ralph Landers called a general meeting of the Task Force at seven-thirty in the morning. Men and women sat on anything available, even window sills, all eyes on him.

"The news media has latched onto these wrestler killings like an alligator to a fat duck and they're blowing this thing up for all it's worth. Furthermore, now the Universal Championship Wrestling Corporation out of Atlanta, and the Federated Champions International out of Indiana, are getting all hot about this business and starting to put a choke hold"— a patter of chuckles at his pun— "on the politicians and law enforcement agencies. Even threatening to pull out of Florida all together, which has the Chamber of Commerce all bent out of shape. They want this investigation to go nationwide. FBI's cooperating on that level, and is going to lend us their local support when they can. Of course, at this minute, the murders still have been limited to California and Florida. As far as we know.

"I have a schedule here. Make a note of it. The next major event in Florida is going to be at the *Sun Dome* on February the twelfth, nineteen hundred and eighty-three. Following that, the year's biggest event in wrestling takes place in Indianapolis in April. Twelfth, then, too. This doesn't even include the little local matches we have around here. There is a lot of pressure to make damn good and sure that these fights are safe and nobody else is killed. We will send a team to Indianapolis assist the locals if necessary.

"Now. Covering the Sun Dome is going to be a job and a half. I've been in touch with UCW and FCI officials. We can expect full cooperation from those people. Anything we want, including a lot of extra manpower for those events. Tolliver will have a detailed map of the Dome's layout and will be getting in touch with all of you for duty that night.

"Now, I know it's not even Thanksgiving yet, but I'm expecting a slowdown on assistance during the upcoming holiday seasons. I'm telling my crew right now: don't expect time off until we get this mess under control. I sincerely hope the local law enforcement agencies will also continue to give us all the assistance they can.

"Now, I know you're all out there busting your ass, but please...let's get this perp wrapped up before Christmas. Okay? Okay. Back to work."

Everyone seemed to sag a little, look from one to another, then rose in mass. Business as usual.

* * * * *

The holidays passed with an irritable, fluctuating crew. The Sheriff's Departments had pulled back some of their staff. The usual criminal activity in the growing metropolitan area of the west central Florida coast had been on a steady rise, right along with the population. The police force detectives from the surrounding cities had to fit their Task Force investigations in along with their usual local assignments from their Captains. About the only consistent help from outside the FDLE was Chief Charlie. Madeira Beach— well, all the small beach communities— seemed like the only peaceful spots on earth at times.

Chief Charlie Daniels and Jack became good friends and Jack frequently met him at Moe's Beach Shack for breakfast. Charlie had decided to quit smoking and now ate too much. If he wasn't eating, he was smacking the hell out of a wad of gum. A divorced man who'd been on the loose for about five years, Chief Charlie also had to deal with Ali, who was on a crusade trying to fix him up with somebody. On occasion, Charlie, with any female Ali could scrape up, and Joe O'Leary and his wife, Martha, would come over to Jack's and Ali's for cookouts. But mostly, for the Task Force, it was endless tracking down of

The Wrestler Who Lost His Head

minute bits of information about an animal who left no trail, no scent.

* * * * *

The three gyms Jack worked regularly were the three most popular with the wrestling community. By now he was on first name basis with a few of the better wrestlers who fought in the local circuit. Each thought he was the only wrestler Jack had taken into his confidence; each kept an eye out for the mysterious woman, or an ear out for any interesting gossip about feuds. These men had been carefully scrutinized before being taken into confidence. Maddy Ulner, usually too busy with her regular load from the Tampa Police Department, did her bit by working out in the three gyms nights, so between the two of them, they kept them pretty well covered.

The new year rang in with an escalating drug problem that spread through the country like an epidemic. The Task Force dwindled down to a skeleton crew. Even Maddy found it harder to make it to the gyms after work.

She met Jack at Malio's for lunch.

"I'm sorry, Jack. I just can't help this week. I got two dead kids in Sulphur Springs. This business of shooting up cocaine and heroine mixed is spreading like the fourteenth century black plague and it's just about as deadly. God, it's depressing."

"Hey, I understand."

"When I can get a minute, I will. Promise." She smiled sweetly, elbows on the table, hunching her shoulders defensively about her head, staring into his pewter eyes. She reached out and laid her hand on his. The darkened booth provided an intimate setting. She began stroking the back of his hand and there was no mistaking the look in her eyes. Jack withdrew his hand and picked up his coffee. When he set the cup down in its saucer again, he put the hand safely in his lap. She straightened up, then excused herself for a minute.

Maddy headed for the Women's Room. Jack sipped his coffee again and dismissed the incident. A few minutes later she returned. She slid into the booth next to Jack instead of across from him, pulling herself up against him. Her skirt rose above her knees; a bared thigh pressed against his. Ample breasts brushed against his left arm, and not by accident. She'd worn a low-cut blouse and her position exaggerated an already ample cleavage. His eyes automatically fell to her heaving bosom, then shot back up to meet her sultry, heated hazels. A hand deftly slipped into Jack's lap.

Jack drew back a little, took his free hand and removed hers. "Maddy..."

"Oh, come on Jack. God..."

He turned towards her, hiking a knee up onto the booth seat, forcing a separation. "Look, you're a beautiful woman and a fine detective, but I am not interested."

"Jack..."

He took a deep breath. In a flash he remembered Ali's accusation that he'd thought so absurd. She'd been right, though he'd probably never let her know. Why make waves for nothing? He almost laughed. "Maddy, look," he got a hold of both her busy hands and held them up in front of her face, "get on your side of the table and stop this right now. I mean it." He frowned, looking a whole lot more upset than he actually felt. "You want to continue on this investigation working with me, knock it off. I'm not just a married man, I'm a happily married man."

Pouting prettily, she leaned back. "What? No time for play?"

Jack's eyes went cold and he stared her down. "Don't get cute, Maddy. I don't need somebody trying to rock my boat."

"You afraid?"

"I'm just not interested." His pressure on her arms encouraged her to slide backwards, out of the booth.

In a flash, she changed her mind and bounced to her feet. She plopped back down on the other side where she belonged.

The Wrestler Who Lost His Head

"Oh, well. Nothing ventured and all that." The way she sucked her teeth said she thought he was a wimp.

"I get the feeling you think this is all a joke," incensed, Jack said evenly. "Grow up, Maddy. Excuse me," he rose.

"Hey, don't go away mad. I didn't mean anything by it." Her face dropped all coyness and sobered. "I think you're a hunk so I thought I'd try."

"I'm flattered." He didn't mean it. He picked up the check and left.

* * * * *

Jack pressed a respectable one-seventy-five from the bench. If nothing else, this investigation certainly had gotten him back in shape!

Tonight there were two wrestlers in the gym who were gaining pretty good reputations around town and had been booked a number of times for the local televised matches. One was Citrus Sam and the other was a new man on the scene who called himself Alligator. His real name was Alan Lee Gaits, so Alligator fit.

The man, a natural comedian, became very popular very quickly, even though he basically played the heel role. Sometimes they'd pit him against another bad-guy, which cast him in a kind of baby-face position. This gator was well over six feet long, solidly built, agile, had personality oozing out his pores, and probably had a good shot at the majors. To make it even better, his exceptionally handsome features made him too good looking. When he was bad, he strutted and let the world know that he was Mister Irresistible and would preen and blow kisses or brutally reject adoring women. On the occasion that he played the underdog, he'd act intimidated, vulnerable, woo the ladies and seek sympathy, then pull comical stunts on his opponents.

Jack had found him extremely cooperative and likeable. Citrus Sam was so adverse to women coming onto him that any of them with previous contact gave up on him after one shot and looked for more willing prey. This guy adored women as much as they adored him, and he wasn't currently attached to any one female. Jack kept him in sight all night.

Jack puffed as he rose out of a squat with two hundred pounds of discs on a bar across his shoulders. "Pfew! Nine," he straightened his knees to take the load off this screaming thighs, then started (Svvvp!-sucked air) into the final squat. First day of One-hundred and it was a twenty pound increase.

First he saw the legs as they trotted past his downward cast eyes. Muscular legs. Shaved legs all the way up to French-cut iridescent chartreuse green tights. No second skin of beige-colored lycra to make her legs look better than they were. She didn't need 'em. He watched the firm, muscular ass jogging around the bend. Jack placed the weighted bar into its rack and walked over to the leg press machine and stood in line. Two people waited ahead of him. His eyes flicked around the room, catching stretches of the jogging path between clusters of machines or people. There. Frizzy blond past her shoulders. Chiseled face. Etched body.

He noticed Alan the Alligator across the room showing a kid how to do something and joined him.

"Got a minute, Allen?" he asked quietly.

"Yeah, sure. Minute, though." Alan turned to the kid and further instructed him, then turned back to Jack.

"What's up, Robinson?"

He took him a little to the side. "Know the big blond who's doing the laps?" He waited while Alan located her and watched her for a few minutes.

"Nah, can't say that I've seen her before. Think that's the woman you've been looking for?"

Jack pulled a face. "The one we're looking for is apparently very attracted to wrestlers. I don't mean to intrude, but you know, if she— "

"— comes over and makes a move," Alan nodded, indicating that he'd cooperate should the woman come on to him. "Boy,

The Wrestler Who Lost His Head

I'll say one thing. Lookit 'er. No cellulose, no sagging, no stretch marks. Talk about an ass. Betch'a that's not all that's tight."

Jack moved away from Alan for the rest of the night, giving blondie lots of room to make any moves. For a while, he thought he'd made a mistake. Then he saw her take a machine next to him and start working. She turned her head and stared at Alan. He acknowledged her attention with a smile. They started talking.

Jack stalled around until almost closing time. Once blondie had latched onto the Alligator, he hadn't been able to shake her loose. Jack wondered which was the most aggressive— the bitch or the alligator.

He stood in the shadows by the portico near a scraggly, unkempt hedge and waited for the woman to leave. Hearing the door swing open and voices coming through, he swung a foot up onto a cement bench and pretended to be tying his shoe. Alan and the woman came out and walked to the edge of the driveway. From there you either turned left or right, depending on where you'd parked. Jack overheard them.

"Well, if I can't talk you into a cup of coffee," she sounded cheerful, if disappointed, "then, maybe next time?"

"Maybe we can do that. You come here regularly? I don't remember seeing you before."

"No. I came here once before, but it's been a while. Busy. Bustin' my ass trying to get a job. When you coming back?" she asked.

"I usually get here Wednesdays. Some nights I work out at Larry's Place. Hey, I see you around next Wednesday, maybe I'll take you up on the coffee or something later."

"You this way?" The woman's question asked if he'd parked on her side of the building.

"Sorry, I'm that-a-way. Good night." Alan raised his hand in a waving gesture and took off in the opposite direction.

Jack finished tying his shoe and then casually walked to the parking lot behind the woman. Pretending he'd momentarily lost his car, he came up behind hers, quickly memorized the license tag number, then moved on. She backed out of the space and drove out. He pulled his pad and pencil and wrote down the number. As Jack unlocked his Skylark, a set of headlights swung into the lot, driving slowly. The silhouetted car pulled up to Jack and stopped and the electric window slid away.

"Jack!" Alan.

He leaned down to peer into Alan's late model Z.

Alan grinned, "Belinda Gianconni. Didn't get the address, but she lives in Tampa."

"Thanks, buddy," Jack punched Alan's shoulder. It felt like punching a rock.

CHAPTER XV

It's very *uncool* for a cop— Jack referred to himself as a cop when thinking over his actions and reactions, *uncool and naive, to get excited over a little breakthrough.* So when he strode into the Task Force and ambled over to the computer, he acted like it was just another other day. His insides were in turmoil, though, because he just flat knew he'd found her!

Sitting down at the computer, he punched up Motor Vehicle Registration and entered the tag number. A few seconds passed, then up popped the registration. Belinda Gianconni: address 4105 Riverside, Tampa. Automobile, Chevy Impala, '79. Next he ran her name through all the available police records and sent it to the FBI for a check. An hour later Jack studied an immaculate list of reports. Not so much as a parking ticket.

He drove to 4105 Riverside. Parking across the street, Jack studied the place. A duplex. High bushes outlined the property and were repeated around the base of the building. The bushes needed a trim and the mangy lawn needed weeding and mowing. From the shoddy looks of side wings off each unit, the closed-in carports probably had been a do-it-yourself garage project without proper building permits. The cement-block structure needed a paint job and mold grew beneath the eaves. The duplex sat in a neighborhood of mostly pricey middle-income homes. The overgrown bushes that effectively hid the place may have been a compromise between the landlord and irritated neighbors. A rental sign said the other side of the two-story townhouse-style duplex was up for rent. He made note of the phone number.

The real estate agent reluctantly decided to give out the information. "Listen, I don't want Ms. Gianconni to know I told you anything. I don't need bad relations with the renters. Especially ones who pay on time, which she does." The agent glared up at him from behind the desk. She was as round as she was tall and dyed her hair that pale red a lot of older women used to cover a head full of white. It didn't make her look younger; it made her look rusted. Her flabby face rubbered into a sagging frown, weak, faded green eyes shot darts at him.

Jack nodded, applying years of practice at being patient with a generally disgruntled citizenry.

She hefted herself from a groaning swivel chair and waddled over to a corner file cabinet in the back of the office. Making an ordeal of it, she poked a flabby finger at each drawer's label as if she had difficulty finding the drawer containing the Gs. Pulling out a file, she returned to the desk, dramatically flopped it onto a scattering of papers, and seated herself upon the unhappy chair. She flipped open the folder.

"So waddya wanna know?"

"Previous addresses."

"Mizeres"— that's how she pronounced Misses.— "D-U-F-F-E-L, pronounced *Doo-fell*," she'd emphasized lest someone call her *duffle* as in bag, ran a long red artificial fingernail down an application form. "Only one listed. We only require the last five years. It's— are you ready?" She looked up to see if he was ready to write it down, her scowl implying she didn't want to have to read it twice. "Number 2-B, Crescent Hills Apartments, 149763 Crescent Drive, Hollywood, California. She don't list no zip. Want the phone number?" Jack nodded, she read it off.

"Say when she left there?"

"April 30, 1979. No address from then until she moved in here on February 3, 1982."

"You didn't ask her where she'd lived between April, '79 and February, '82?"

"Of course I did. I made a note here that she said she'd lived with her mother for a while and drifted around a couple of years. Lived with a girlfriend some. She helped the girlfriend out with money but there ain't no record of that. Seemed nice enough, so I ran a credit check on her. Clean. No claims against her, so I let her have the place."

"Where was the mother?"

The Wrestler Who Lost His Head

"How should I know? I din ask."
Jack thanked her and left elated.

* * * * *

Landers told Jack "No go," on his request to place Gianconni under twenty-four hour surveillance. "Until you got a whole lot more solid evidence this woman is involved, you're just going to have to cover her yourself. I can't supply extra manpower for hunches this vague." Jack telephoned Joe O'Leary. He said he doubted seriously if TPD would cover her either at the moment, but he was free to continue to use Maddy Ulner when she could fit it in, and that he'd help when he could. Jack caught Maddy at her TPD desk cursing a typewriter as she tried to fill out a report with two fingers. Eyebrows rising seemed to lift her head like a puppet's on a string. She waited for him to open.

"Change of plans," he said. His face split with a happy grin and she got her hopes up, misinterpreting his eagerness.

"Oh?" ladened with innuendum.

"I think I've found her."

"Oh?" a split expletive. One note acknowledged disappointment, and the second expressed surprise, then curiosity.

"Her name is Belinda Gianconni. *And* she lived in Hollywood, California on February 15, 1979. Unaccounted for between April '79 and February '82 when she lived with her mother and friends for a while. Got to find out where her mother lives. I want Miami-Fort Lauderdale checked out. We can probably trace Gianconni's movements through credit cards. Maybe we can get that info from a check with the credit bureaus down there. February '82, she moved into a duplex here. We know she was in most of areas at the times of the murders, and I'm betting she made it one-hundred percent."

"Get a tail on 'er," Maddy suggested.

"All we got is us. Landers can't spare anybody. O'Leary said you're all he can spare."

"Shit."

"Way I figure it, we can work it out between the two of us. Drop the gyms for the time being and see if we get anything solid. Then we can expect some support."

* * * * *

Nine-thirty a.m. The pale blue Impala backed out of the garage, swung around in an arc, pulled onto the rutted drive, and came out to the street cautiously. The overgrown viburnum blocked her view, so she had to nose out carefully and lean over the wheel to see if any cars were coming. Maddy had parked right in front of her driveway on the other side of the narrow, two-lane street, making Gianconni cut the wheel hard. Twisting around, she tossed the detective a bird, then drove on.

Maddy waited until the Impala turned at the corner, then she pulled out and followed. That was the problem with watching that damned duplex, she had to park right in front of the driveway to see anything. At night you could hide in the bushes, but certainly not in broad daylight.

Gianconni pulled into a Shell service station on Armenia, pumped gas at a self-service unit, paid, and drove back onto the street heading in the direction of downtown. With all the traffic, following her proved to be easy enough. Gianconni pulled into an attended laundromat. She carried in a plastic basket of laundry. Maddy could see fragments of her through the street reflections in the darkened window glass. She talked with the attendant, then returned to her car. Pulling back onto Armenia, she continued on to Kennedy Boulevard, then turned east. Maddy followed her to an old stuccoed building with boarded up windows near the University of Tampa. Gianconni pulled into a side parking lot. She locked her car and walked back to the Kennedy Boulevard sidewalk. Maddy parked her car across the side street from the Impala and followed.

The Wrestler Who Lost His Head

Gianconni stopped at several doors, searching for numbers. Finally, she found the address she wanted and disappeared through the entrance.

Maddy caught up. The building, a windowless, faded green, warehouse-looking structure, had two-inch letters on the door announcing Mitsui School of Judo, Inc. She waited a few minutes, then pushed the door open.

In the middle of the huge room were rows upon rows of padded mats. In the center of the mats stood two lines of students in bare feet wearing white, heavy-cotton judo suits. The instructor stood in their midst, but Maddy couldn't hear what he said. She quietly walked over to folding chairs on the sidelines and sat down to watch. The big blond stood at the end of one of the lines of students. The instructor and Gianconni wore the only black belts on the mats.

A tall, muscular, male Caucasian, also a black belt, walked up to Maddy. Standing very erect in his bare feet and startling-white Judo suit, looking so serious that Maddy almost grinned, he asked if he could be of assistance. She found his stiff formality comical, but maintained a straight face.

"Uh...I'm thinking about taking a class."

"You will need to speak with Professor Mitsui. He sets all the class schedules and he's busy at the moment teaching. It would probably be best if you telephoned and made an appointment."

"Any problem with my sitting here to watch?" she asked.

"That is fine. Perhaps if the Professor has time, he can talk to you between classes. Understand, please, that I cannot speak for the Professor."

She nodded to indicate she understood. Maddy noticed that the man spoke the word *Professor* with great respect, bordering on awe. She also observed that Professor Mitsui was Japanese; and though the man addressing her was an American male, his speech pattern sounded short and choppy, as if he'd been around Professor Mitsui so long he'd picked up his affectations.

About a fourth of Mitsui's students were Oriental, the remainder a mix of Caucasians and blacks. The age range appeared to be from late teens through mid-thirties. What she found surprising was the number of women in the group— they made up a third of the class, give or take one or two.

Mitsui stood quite still and silent until he had everyone's full attention. Then in a little louder voice, which Maddy could overhear, he made an announcement.

"It is honor to present to jis crass *sensei*," he bowed to Gianconni, placing his flattened hands to his thighs and bending from the waist. She, in turn, bowed to him using all the correct mannerisms. To his students, he said, "You remember, *sensei* is teacher. *Sensei Gianconni* accept position with school. *Sensei* Gianconni come with excellent skills and is Women's Champion *Jire Jitsutsu* for California, 1977.

"*Sensei* Gianconni agreed to demonstrate ability to fight *shia*. Challenger is Thomas Hulling, who is man of great ability fighting the *shia*." He raised his hands above his head and brought them together silently, then bowed and scooted backwards out of the field.

Hulling and Gianconni stepped from the line of students and faced each other. Both bent from the waist in a *rey* to each other. Poised, blade-like hands in ready position, the challengers locked eyes only for an acknowledging second.

"Hi!— Hi!" Gianconni barked a *ki ai* to startle her opponent. She struck with a slashing chop toward his throat, then recoiled to her first position as quickly as a striking rattlesnake.

* * * * *

Professor Mitsui politely fit Maddy in between classes. "I have just retain new instructor, *Sensei* Gianconni, so you are lucky. You start class starting tomorrow. Is this satisfactory?"

Maddy nodded.

"As student you will be expected to forrow rues, to speak proper terms, be punctua'. We expect you work hard. Takes bery hard work to become even a beginner in Judo. The fee incrudes my book of instruction, which also incrudes the forty basic Judo throws. A'so, I have video which you may check out once to view..."

Well, why not, Maddy thought. I'd always intended taking up Judo, so now's as good a time as any.

* * * * *

Jack and Maddy cornered Landers at the weekly gathering of the Task Force.

Jack's voice insistent: "Ralph, for God sake, except for Miami, we place her in the area of each crime, and we're working on Miami right now. She's strong as an ox and capable of committing the crime."

"But to date, you still haven't placed her at a single one of the matches, Jack."

"Let's do a line-up. Get Spiegel in here, and that female witness, Margie what-s-'er-name."

"I don't know, Jack. If it is her, right now we don't have enough to book her, and I don't want to spook her, either. Let's not give away our hand yet. Let's just keep an eye on her for now. You keep doing what you're doing. If you prove she was in Miami at the right time, we'll go round-the-clock on her before, during and after the next match. How's that grab ya?"

Jack shrugged and spread his hands palms up.

CHAPTER XVI

Maddy slumped against the fender of her gleaming white '80 6000LE, "I'm sorry, Jack. I just can't do it right now. I've got a Hyde Park rapist on the loose; I've still got those kids' deaths... I just can't. I mean, sometimes I just plain gotta get in a little sleep." .

"Hey, I appreciate your help. Believe me, I understand."

"I feel real bad about this, but..." Maddy stroked the fender of the Pontiac as if comforting it.

"Boom! Idea strikes like a thunderbolt!" Jack grinned. "You dropped out yet?"

"No. Thought I'd go tonight and then tell her I can't continue on at the moment. Find out if I can join another class later on without having to go back to square one. I really do want to continue. I've learned a lot under her. — Ha!— Literally! ...She doesn't know I'm a detective, so I've got to think up some feasible excuse: my grandmother's dying, something like that. So, what's your great idea?"

"I'll stop by there today; ask to join her class. They'll tell me it's booked up? Call me tonight and tell me they got an opening?"

"There's a waiting list."

He frowned. "Any suggestions?"

Maddy thought for a few seconds. "Could take Professor Mitsui into your confidence? You can trust him, I'd stake my badge on it."

"Then why didn't you?"

"Didn't need to. I lucked in and got there the day Gianconni started and the Professor still had room on her schedule. Apparently he carries a long waiting list all the time, so he really needed another pro to help out. She started with a full load. That caught 'em up for about two days, then word got around he's got a new instructor and it's back to the waiting list again. Mitsui has a hell of a reputation locally, and a lot of people going

The Wrestler Who Lost His Head

to other Judo schools are just biding time until they can get on at his school."

Jack thought over what she said.

She added: "Oh, I suggest you telephone him for an appointment. You do a drop-in, you're going to have to show your badge to get his cooperation and then you've blown your cover."

* * * * *

"You sink Sensei Gianconni is criminar?" Professor Mitsui stretched his Japanese eyes as wide as they would go, which wasn't much. "Cannot berieve zat."

"No, Professor Mitsui, I am not saying Miss Gianconni is suspected of being guilty of a crime. I am saying that I need to be allowed in that class and I prefer no one know I am a law enforcement agent. I'm sorry, I really cannot divulge further information."

"But hab number of po-reece-men in courses. You just be one more."

"But those officers aren't working on the investigation and they were here before she came. No, I have to handle this my way, Professor Mitsui."

Professor Mitsui appeared to go into a trance. Jack waited patiently for what seemed like five minutes. Then Mitsui's eyes focused on Jack's and Jack knew he was *back*. "I run bery crean schooh, Speciah Agent Robinson. Inform students zat if I find out zey take drugs, zat it!— zey out! I discourage smoking *tabako* and partaking riquor. I teach martial arts and diciprine. Zey no room in my schooh for questionaber teacher. Usuary, I good judge of character, but now wonder if I make mistake hiring *Sensei* Gianconni."

Jack closed his eyes, frustrated, and tried to think how to impress upon this gentleman that he shouldn't lose faith in Gianconni yet. His mouth indicated several false starts before he finally spoke, measuring each word: "Sir...I ask you to keep Miss

Gianconni on as instructor and let me into her class, not because she is guilty of a crime, but because..." He started over again, "In the United States, a person is innocent until proven guilty. It would be a shame if you fired Miss Gianconni and she turned out to be the wrong person. She would suffer an injustice for no good reason."

Mitsui vanished inside his head again and Jack waited patiently for him to return. The eyes once again centered on Jack's. "I assign you to one of her crasses." He glanced at his watch and added, "Prease excuse me, I hab class in two minutes." Mitsui rose and *reyed* Jack signifying an end to the interview. Jack returned the bow. The master left the small office, leaving Jack standing there.

* * * * *

The students arrived *en masse*. Jack stepped through the entrance to the *Do Jo*, paused, bowed a *rey*, and walked to the edge of the mats. He removed his shoes, *reyed* again, then joined the lineup to one side of the room. Professor Mitsui had a group working on the other side. After all the students had gathered, *Sensei* Gianconni entered. She *reyed* at the edge of the mat, removed her slippers, then walked over to her class. She stood at the head of the two lines of students and bowed a *rey*. The group *reyed* in return.

"We have lost one of our students due to an illness in the family, and have gained a replacement. Would you introduce yourself?" Her gaze fell upon Jack.

"Jack Robinson. I am honored to be accepted into your class." A little bow.

"I understand you have some experience?" Gianconni continued.

"I studied Judo before 'Nam. I know some of the basics, but it's been a long time."

"Care to show me what you can do?"

The Wrestler Who Lost His Head

They faced off in the center between the two lines of students. Jack made a fatal mistake: he fixed his eyes on hers. "*Ki ai!*" she barked and kicked him in the shin.

Then one of the first rules to remember came back to him— if you maintain eye contact, you can't see what's happening below the belt! His shin screamed.

Defenses up, he danced about the floor. His eyes kept drawing back to hers all the while he tried to resist that hypnotic gaze and watch all fours at once. "*Ki ai!*" another bark. As fast as a magician's sleight of hand, she came into him with an *og oshi*, slinging him over her hip onto his back. Automatic reflex rolled him onto his stomach so he could get up. The instant he rolled, she pounced on his back, sat astride him, dug her heels beneath his pelvis, and clamped a *hadaka jime* around his neck. Jack Robinson passed out almost immediately.

She swung her leg as if dismounting a dead horse and raised her arms in victory. No smiles. This was serious business. She rolled Jack onto his back, gave him a strong push to his breastplate to restart his heart and wake him up. While he lay there coming to, she explained all her moves to the class, emphasizing that this particular maneuver could be fatal. The push to the chest could be vital to revive the downed fighter since there was always a possibility the heart wouldn't start back up on its own.

Jack, speechless, regained his feet. Student and teacher squared off, *reyed* each other, and Jack humbly returned to the line. Rule number two he'd forgotten: don't roll onto your stomach.

The moves came back to him rapidly, but the years gone by without ever practicing Judo had left him rusty as a salt water tackle box. He changed into street clothes in the men's locker feeling a little stiff. At least he'd already regained good muscle tone and had increased his strength from all the workouts at the gyms, but he sure had forgotten a lot of Judo. If nothing else, this murder case had shaped his act up considerably. He smirked and shook his head a little.

H. Churchill Mallison

One of the other students, a man about his age, slapped him on the back. "Know what you're going through, old buddy. I just went through the same thing. Hell, back before 'Nam, I was pretty damned good. I come in here a month ago and got myself humiliated right off the bat. Comes back, though. Like riding a bicycle. Name's Hank."

Jack raised a quizzical eyebrow and gave Hank a lopsided grin. "Man, she doesn't fool around, does she. My number one error was misjudging her capability."

"Yeah," Hank grunted, "she does a fucking number on the male macho image, doesn't she? She's okay, though. Good teacher. No nonsense."

Jack crossed the *do jo* with his gym bag in hand. Gianconni stood near the entrance/exit. She caught his eye and jerked her head back, signaling him over. In street clothes, and with that kinky blond mess tied back from her face, she looked sexy. Wearing an oversized purple T and black skinny pants, her muscular biceps were hidden by sleeves almost to the elbows. With the hair out of the way, she had killer bedroom eyes. Drooping lids, smokey hazels, black lashes a foot long. High cheekbones gave her eyes a cat-like slant, and her slim, bony, slightly aquiline nose added to the tigress look. Full, pouty lips, now outlined with vermillion and filled in with tangerine, curled in a mocking, closed-mouth smile, bunching her cheeks, making her high bones fuller.

Voice now a purr, Gianconni said, "Sorry I was so rough on you back there."

He shot her a look that said he had enough sense of humor to survive her attempts to humiliate him.

"You're in good physical shape, though," she added, slowly lowering the shades on those heavily lidded eyes, then opening them again and fixing on his. "I figure you'll be back in the swing of things in no time. Hey, you in a rush?"

"No," his voice matter-of-fact.

"I'm going down the street for a break. Want to join me? We can discuss your progress plan."

The Wrestler Who Lost His Head

He gave her a slit-eyed grin, "Sure, why not."

Over herbal tea— coffee isn't good for you— she studied him silently for a few minutes. "How come you got bumped ahead of everybody else to get in my class?"

"Who told you that?"

"I have access to the schedules and the backup list. Your name wasn't even on it and *voilá*, here you are." Before he could think up an answer, she continued, "I confess it was wrong of me to do it, but to be perfectly honest, that's why I got so rough with you. I don't like it when somebody tries to break in line in front of me."

For a couple of seconds he tried to think of some plausible reason for being given the special treatment, then decided that would be another wrong move in a day of wrong moves. Instead, he hardened his gaze and replied: "I got bumped up because I said I wanted to get in a class. I didn't ask to be bumped ahead of anybody. If I was, it was somebody else's decision and who are you to question it?"

She thought that over for a minute and, he figured, decided maybe he was somebody important and she'd better back off before she got herself in trouble. From what he'd gathered, she needed the job. Her tone of voice turned sultry again, "You just interested in Judo or are you planning to go further?"

He knew she meant go on to *karate* or *Jitsut Su*. He shrugged and returned her stare. "I here you're a former champion? California? What?— *Jitsut Su?*"

"*Jire Jitsut Su*," she corrected.

"What's the difference?"

"*Jire Jitsut Su* is a no-holds-barred contest. Judo, karate, kicking, punching, wrestling. Whatever it takes."

"You're tough."

"You got it." Another pouty smile, this time all on one side of her face in a smirk that could out-smirk a world class cynic.

"You ever thought of pro-wrestling?" he asked. "That's where the money is, I hear."

"For men, maybe. Yeah, I thought about getting into that. Frankly, though, those matches with the women are too silly. Hell, I'd rather take on a middle-weight for real than get into that game. There's not a woman can beat me and I'm not interested in entertainment."

"So you don't like wrestling."

"Oh, I love wrestling. I just don't dig female wrestling. I wanna wrestle?" this time the pouty smile pure invitational, "I'll take on a man any day."

"Yeah?" Jack's tone said he might be interested.

"Not you, cream-puff," she laughed heartily, then added in a velvety purr, "At least not until your game improves. I like...competition." She sipped the rose hips, "Figure, though, you'll get there. Frankly, I prefer...bulkier muscles, but you're strong. Get to work on those moves, sugar, and I'll teach you some you never thought of before."

Jack sat back, squaring his shoulders, and looked very interested, indeed. Then he glanced at his watch. Maybe for once, he could get home at a decent hour. She caught his glance and then hopped up from the booth.

"Hate to break this up, Jackie-boy, but I've got another engagement and I'd better get on the...," honey dripped, "...stick. See you on the...," even thicker honey, "mat."

Belinda Gianconni left. Jack deftly pocketed her tea cup. He left an extra large tip on the counter, feeling guilty about stealing the cup— this rundown joint wasn't doing such great trade these days and probably wasn't much longer for this earth. At least now they had her fingerprints, just in case some ever showed up.

* * * * *

It took about fifteen minutes to emotionally shift gears out of the investigative mode and back into husband. He looked forward to spending a few uninterrupted hours with his bride. This case had played hell with their time together and this was his first early night in two weeks. He smiled: had some wrestling of his own in mind...and this time, he would end up on top! ...Well, he'd win, anyway.

When this case is a wrap, Ali my love, we're going on a honeymoon. Go to the islands, or maybe take one of those cruises to Mexico. That would be nice.

CHAPTER XVII

February 12th. Cars started arriving two and a half hours before the event, filing into the parking lots surrounding the Sun Dome at the University of South Florida in north Tampa.

The facility crawled with undercover police and agents, University of South Florida's security police, and maintenance crews. Every available law enforcement personnel in the FDLE and Hillsborough and Pinellas Counties patrolled the grounds and the enormous stadium.

FDLE's agent, Marilyn Sneed, and TPD's detective, Maddy Ulner, jointly commanded a team of officers disguised as maintenance. Sneed supervised the male unit, Maddy the female. These teams, paired off by two's, patrolled the toilet facilities keeping an eye out for anyone or anything suspicious.

"Jesus, look at 'em, and it's only six-thirty," Officer Eleanor Haddly remarked to her partner as they retrieved push-brooms from a maintenance closet off a main thoroughfare. A steady stream of people trickled through the gates and lines were already backed up in front of the refreshment stands.

JoAnne Brooks widened her eyes, giving Haddly a would-you-believe-it stare, "Somebody said campers started coming in at three a.m. and the people spent the whole freaking night waiting in line to get tickets. You believe that?"

"That's nothing unusual," another officer replied. "You never worked any concerts?"

"Let's get one more check." Sneed waved her arms, signaling everyone to gather around before heading out to their assigned territories. "Everyone's got a photocopy of the Gianconni woman?" Sneed and Maddy scanned the group. Sneed continued: "Okay. Walkie-talkie contact every fifteen to thirty minutes. Male officers to me; females to Detective Ulner. If you see Gianconni, contact your team leader and say there's no toilet paper and state your position, and do not lose sight of

The Wrestler Who Lost His Head

her. I repeat— do not pick her up, we want her under surveillance only. And for God sake, if there is no toilet paper in your position, send a regular maintenance person to get it and don't say nothing about it on the walkie-talkie. Okay, let's go."

Every gate, every entrance-way was manned. All eyes scanned the arriving hoards of people for Gianconni or any suspicious or highly unusual character.

Allen Tolliver, Jesse Hood, Jaime Cortez, and Hank Grisham were attached to television crews and were checking out their equipment. Each television station had its battle station and the agents were sent to the floor as roaming cameramen, which made a good cover for them to shoot the audience while the real cameramen filmed the fights. Grisham's job was to cover the wrestlers' entrance. Both the baby-faces and the heels would use the same ramp. Another pair of officers covered the locker rooms, one in each, using standard camcorders, in the guise of taping locker-room interviews before and after matches.

Jack slapped his thigh with a rolled Program and scanned the vast passages. Joe O'Leary stood next to him feeling like hell. It'd been his man who'd lost her when she'd left her duplex earlier..

* * * * *

Belinda Gianconni couldn't help but notice yet another fucking car parked right in front of her driveway. Was somebody having her followed? Her heart began pounding; her eyes kept darting to the rear view mirror watching. Sure enough, he followed her about two cars back. She played it cool and drove over to Westshore Plaza Shopping Center. She parked her car in the covered garage at the Mall entrance by Robinson's Department store. Getting out, she locked the car, and turned around. She pretended not to notice the man parking in a space one lane over and three cars down. Hurrying, she almost trotted to the double entrance. Once inside the Mall, she ran through the entrance to Robinson's, made some quick maneuvers through crowded aisles of clothing racks, found a dressing room in a corner, and stepped inside. Peeking through a crack in the swinging doors of the stall, she could see through the open archway to the main floor. The man was nowhere to be seen.

She stayed there until a pesky saleswoman came by the second time asking if she could be of help. Thinking fast, Gianconni said, "My period started. Can you get me a tampon or something, anything, from the ladies room?" The salesperson made unwilling noises until Gianconni yelled at her, "Well, what the hell do you expect me to do! You don't want me in your fucking dressing room, then go get me the fucking tampon like I asked!" The irritating saleswoman left in a huff.

As soon as the woman left, Gianconni cautiously opened the door. It seemed safe. She slipped out and continued weaving her way through what seemed like miles of racks. Then she faced the Mall entrance. Go for it and see if anyone followed?

She spent the next hour darting from store to store. Finally, Gianconni worked up enough courage to take a look in the parking garage to see if all was clear. The son-of-a-bitch's car was still parked down from hers. She hadn't seen him well enough to tell what he looked like, his face had been nothing more than a white circle with sunglasses and a shadow of hair. She didn't even know if his hair was long or short, dark or light. What the hell was going on? She began feeling creepy again, like she had in Los Angeles, and then again in Miami.

She retreated to the ladies room in Maas Brothers and called a cab. She met the cab at the back entrance to Wolf Brothers. Now that she'd rid herself of whomever was following her, she relaxed. "Take me to...Tampa Square Mall," she smiled. What the hell. She'd have a great time shopping and then take a cab home, get her old junker she'd parked out back, and still make the fights in plenty of time. The Impala was perfectly safe where it was, just a few minor adjustments to her routine. She'd managed to shake her tail.

* * * * *

Since the argument she'd had with Jack following the matches at The Amherst Lounge, Ali'd stayed home when he had to work a fight. Not because she was pouting, but because it did bother her every time she thought about Maddy Ulner knee to knee with her husband and putting her arm around him. Yes, she knew they had to put up a front. Yes, she knew her anger interfered with Jack's ability to do his job. No, she didn't want that! So she'd cheerfully stayed home and had done her best to assure Jack that everything was fine and dandy. And it was.

But this was the big match. A real one. The Sun Dome. And she wanted to go. Because she was Jack's wife, he'd been able to get her a seat right on the wrestlers' runway, down close to the ring. Fantastic seat! She felt so excited, even if wrestling was tacky as hell. Not wanting to miss a thing, she'd arrived an hour and a half before the first match and was relieved she'd come so early. The parking lots were rapidly filling up. Before finding her seat, she bought a bucket of popcorn. A whole bucket! Eat your heart out, Jack, I've got the whole greasy mess all to my little old self! Ha! If anyone was a worse popcornaholic than she was, it was Jack. She wished he could join her and enjoy the entertainment for a change.

Eyes gleaming, munching like a half-starved waif, Ali sat on the edge of her seat, head swiveling, taking in everything. She'd never seen so many six- to twelve-year-olds in one place. And there were so many grandmas and grandpas, there was enough polyester in this hall to cover the earth. Only the arena rats dressed to beat all hell for the wrestling matches, and there were plenty of those, too, crowding the wrestlers' ramp just like Ali.

The seats began to fill; the sheer numbers surprised her. Later she'd hear on the news that over nine thousand people had flocked to the fights.

* * * * *

H. Churchill Mallison

I smile to myself. Check out that body. Check out those muscles.

Flexing, turning to study the reflected image from every angle, a hand smoothed the tight, gleaming lycra bodysuit over a form of perfection. *Enough daydreaming, get a change of clothes for later.* The dark, baggy shirt would hide the fantastic build that always drew attention. Old jeans that were ready to be trashed. Running shoes. A smile trembled at the corners of those full, flushed lips and sparks danced in those haunted eyes. Into the large, glossy Burdines shopping bag went a new plastic raincoat and fresh disposable paint rags acquired from a hardware store. Already loaded were the garrotte— made with a fine, high C piano wire, the perfectly honed hacksaw, the old shower curtains, and the oversized rubber boots.

Dreamily, the heavily-lidded eyes studied the card. Good line-up tonight. Of course, preferably, that one, but if he didn't work out...well, as a second choice, and the other sucker was a pushover... Of course, the more challenge to the hunt, the more thrill to the kill. Now, too, the additional charge— teasing, outwitting the cops— and the F-fucking-BI!

* * * * *

Lights dimmed over the bleachers; spotlights focused on the ring. A hush fell over the thousands of spectators. Two former World Heavy-weight Champions manned the microphones in the press box and their conversational coverage of the events was both televised and heard over the Sun Dome's speaker system.

Mic Spalding, a six-foot-seven, muscular, still impressive sixty-two year-old grandfather of eight, leaned into the mike and asked the other announcer: "Have you ever seen a meaner, nastier, fighter than *Alligator?*"

"Than Alligator?" Mullet Dosier laughed sourly. "Well, now, Mic, I gotta tell ya the truth." Mullet hauled himself up straighter in his chair, took a breath, then leaned into the mike and enunciated, "An alligator may be one tough critter, and he

The Wrestler Who Lost His Head

may have the hide of a tank, but there is one thing that can penetrate the armor of even a Russian tank."

"I can't imagine anything that tough," Mic shook his head negatively.

"You obviously haven't seen *The Lawyer* in action. Get a rotten, no-good, hittin'-below-the-belt lawyer on the scene, Mic, and you got a weapon that'll blow the lid off a missile silo. Hey, I know! I met up with one of them things when me and my old lady split. Mean suckers! Mean! *The Lawyer* will skin that *Alligator* and he'll leave that ring butt naked!"

A ruckus started up along the runway. In strutted a hefty man in black tails, a bow tie, and a tall stove-pipe hat, carrying a briefcase. Behind him trotted a harried secretary furiously jotting down notes.

Mullet Dosier, almost a duplicate of Mic Spalding, but bald and ten years younger, cleared his throat into the mike. "Ladies and gentlemen, boys and girls, for the first event of this action-packed evening, it is my pleasure to introduce to you New Jersey's finest counsel, *The Lawyer*! Here he comes. That man has a real killer instinct. He's so busy, he's so good at what he does— look at that, he's still working, right up to the ring."

"That poor secretary," Mic scowled. "Don't he ever let off? I see what you mean, Mullet...that's one...that's one vicious-looking dude if I ever saw one."

The crowd roared with a mix of boos and approvals. As the noise began to wane, Mic announced, "But I got tell you, I think he may just have met his match. Folks, give us a hearty welcome for the roughest, toughest, fightin'est reptile ever found in the Louisiana bayou! *Alligator*!"

The lawyer strutted around, prissily removing his bow tie and handing it to his secretary. She gently placed it just so-so into his briefcase. Then he removed his cuffs with their huge gold dollar-sign links and handed them to her. She placed them carefully into the lizard-skin case. Next, the harried secretary, who wore a banker's-blue business suit and half-glasses, helped

The Lawyer out of his jacket. She scurried from the ring with his case and jacket and waited dutifully at his ring post.

The Alligator swung into the ring. He followed The Lawyer around looking him up and down with exaggerated curiosity. He mimicked him and pretended like he was stripping off coattails and handing them to the secretary. The secretary sneered at him and kept pushing him away.

The Alligator suddenly ran to the ropes, looking up at the press box, and yelled, "What's this? I thought I was going to get me a piece of meat to chew on and I got this sissy in an opera coat?" Turning, pointing at The Lawyer, "What is that, anyway?"

Mic leaned into the mike, "Alligator, that is The Lawyer. That's your dinner tonight."

Alligator snorted and roared, swinging around to face all the audience, and bellowed, "Well, *Mister Lawyer*! I am the *Alli-gator* and you are the *Alli-ga-tee*!"

The Lawyer sniffed, raise his brow, looked down his nose. They squared off. With startling quickness, The Lawyer clamped his hooks into Alligator and flung him into the ropes.

* * * * *

Flashbacks— like living two lives simultaneously— electrical currents jumping from one contact to the other— one scene becoming confused with the other.

— Searching eyes scanned the scattering of vans and vehicles near the loading platform to the business end of the Sun Dome. Off to the side were the big cars: Lincolns, a Cadillac Limousine— probably Prince Albert's. The new Mercedes Kaminari Hitore drove. Car parked and locked, the eyes located every person in the area, and figured all of them to be undercover officers of one division or the other. Knowing it would be heavily guarded tonight only added fuel to the feverish desires that consumed. Through the walkways without a hitch.

The Wrestler Who Lost His Head

— *A dark corridor, tiptoeing softly. Echoes. Dim light outlining a partially closed door. Slanting shadows danced exotically. Noise!*

— *The roar jarred the fractured mind, bringing it back to the crowds. A parade of sweating bodies came into view— hands reaching out, the victorious slapping palms and shouting war cries and the screams of the fans leaning, reaching, grabbing!*

— *Sweat flew from the swinging, wet strands of mane and the spotlights lit the droplets, making them sparkle like diamonds. Massive shoulders oiled and straining.*

— *Yearning. He posed over the prostrate form, his masculinity staring at the ceiling, nodding approval. The loin cloth dragged along her writhing body slick with the heat of anticipation.*

The surprise. Immobility. The trophy.

— *Hiding in the dressing room an extra moment to get the eagerness under control.*

— She jumped from the seat and grabbed his arm. He shook free of her. Lips pulled back, teeth predatory, she yanked a hank of hair and planted a wet one right on his mouth. *Don't deny me, you son-of-a-bitch. The victor glared at her, but you saw recognition in his eyes.* He did protest too much. She followed him all the way to the locker room door and banged on it when he shut her out. He tells her to fuck off and she says, "Yeah..." *and he comes.*

— Don't take it off. I want to fight you, you sick bastard. I want to ride you like a bucking bull and make you eat and make you drink of me. You'll do my will...

...and you'll die for me. Another trophy for my wall.

Scarlet ribbons streaked her yellow hair.

— Prince Albert. I could tie that asshole up in a knot he'd never come untangled from. All the fanfare. And for what? For a few measly inches?

The evening wore on endlessly. Time seemed bogged in Karo. The stench of frenzy stained the air. *Scarlet ribbons...think of scarlet ribbons.*

CHAPTER XVIII

Mullet Dosier smirked, his voice smeared with sarcasm, "Ladies and gentlemen, from the Isles of Great Britain, from the center of European royalty...ladies and gentlemen, please, please let me have your attention. Protocol requires that we all stand and be silent while the...ahem...royal coach passes."

"I wish I had one of those long horns," Mic Spalding interrupted. "You know, those old whaddayacallits, French horns?"

"To welcome British royalty? French horns? You mean like they blew when Julius Caesar entered the hall in those Cecil B. DeMille movies?"

"Yeah, those."

Rising from his chair, Mic doing likewise, Mullet stood and placed his left hand over his heart. Into the mike he bellowed: "Announcing his royal hiney, *Prince Albert!*"

Rumbling up the entrance ramp came a wagon-like contraption being pulled by two recently defeated wrestlers. On the rolling platform stood an enormous can. An elaborate paper label scribed in curlicued, gold script listed the contents: *Prince Albert*, and below his name, an itemization of the ingredients. *One Gallant Lord, 230 pounds of muscle in one gigantic hulking hunk. Quality guaranteed.*

Ali, along with a number who'd never seen this act before, burst out laughing and clapped her hands with delight. Because he was a popular wrestler, one who's act had brought him local television fame, the crowd leapt to their feet, stomping, clapping and chanting "God help the Prince! God help the Prince! God help the Prince!"

Arriving ringside, at the best available camera angle, the slave crew laid down the enameled trace of the T-shaped frame and climbed upon the platform. It took both muscular men to pick up the five-foot silver-tone can opener and remove the lid.

The Wrestler Who Lost His Head

Out popped a smiling prince of a prince.

Naturally, during this elaborate process, Mic and Mullet used every cliché ever dreamed up regarding the releasing of canned royalty. The Prince stepped down from his make-shift coach. Regally entering the ring, Prince Albert unhooked his jeweled cape and handed it to one of his slaves. He then removed his jeweled crown and placed it upon a pillow offered by the second slave. After adjusting his glittering vest over his nickers, he turned toward the press box and stared coldly upwards at Mic and Mullet.

"Your most unkind words have gone not unnoticed." He raised his proud snoot in the air and glared down the long, slightly S-curved and battered remains of it, snorting with dignity, and, in a sing-song voice, cried: "Sticks and stones may break my bones but words can never hurt me!"

While Mic and Mullet ate him alive from their safe perch high above the roaring crowd, he strutted about the ring smiling prettily for the audience and flexing very impressive muscles, including those in his buttocks.

Then as suddenly as if an earthquake had shaken the Sun Dome, a hush fell over the thousands of fans. In the hot, bright circle, pooled by a spotlight beam that sliced through the darkened stadium, stood a shimmering silvery-white image.

Striding along the ramp like a true warrior, The Arabian Knight brought a wave of approval in his wake. Tonight, added to the elaborately sequined headdress and cape over his shimmering lycra bodysuit, he carried a beautiful, jeweled sword. Brandishing it as he marched toward the ring, he swung it high over his head in wide sweeps.

The man was breathtakingly handsome. He looked like an Arab sheik, though in reality, he was Anatole Spilotros, a Greek.

* * * * *

— Scarlet ribbons in the trophy box...

H. Churchill Mallison

* * * * *

The best seat she'd been able to wrangle was way in the back and about ten seats over from the wrestlers' entrance ramp that tunneled directly from the teams' locker rooms. She hated that because it made it virtually impossible for her to be seen and she hadn't wanted to have to stand around all night. It had taken a lot more than she'd wanted to give bribing a ring crew to call in sick and hand over his pass. Sixty fuckin' dollars plus the disgusting jerk wanted a blow job. But she got the pass. She sold her ticket, though, right before the gates opened, and got her money back and then some.

Beneath the work shirt and old jeans, she wore a lycra bodysuit— an iridescent turquoise that refracted emerald tones that flowed like restless waters as she moved in the light.

The ring crew foreman balked when she'd shown up, really annoyed, not only because Johnny had called in sick, but because he'd given his pass to a female instead of one of his usual crew standbys. She assured him she could outwork any of his men, then demonstrated her strength. He shut his trap fast, and in the end, he even told her he'd be happy to use her anytime as a backup crew. She and a handful of men were in charge of setting up the ring and tearing it down. She didn't mind. Usually it took the wrestlers about the same amount of time to leave after a match as it did for the crew to break down, and she thought it might give her an *in* with the men.

Meanwhile, during the fights, she didn't have to do a damned thing, so she'd slip into a personnel toilet room and take off the work clothes and stash them until later. She'd be more than visible when the wrestlers came back and forth from the ring, standing right at the ramp's mouth catching the edge of the spotlights.

* * * * *

The Wrestler Who Lost His Head

With binoculars, Jack watched the tunnel-like ramp all evening. From one bleacher section away, he studied every face he could pick up around the elevated seats that horseshoed around the entrance. There was a woman in a turquoise outfit standing on his side with her back to him who had bulky, dirty-blond hair tied back and bound with a jeweled turquoise net. He kept sending her mental messages to turn around, but the woman seemed fixated on the ramp or the ring and never so much as looked over her shoulder. Between the Alligator versus The Lawyer's match and the next event, he worked his way over to the other side. No seats were available, so he climbed to the Dome roof, found an inconspicuous space to stand, and trained the glasses on the opposite side of the tunnel. At first he cursed beneath his breath because the blond had vanished. However, she returned shortly and resumed her place at the edge of the activity. Just as he focused on her, The Arabian made his grand entrance and Jack saw nothing but leaping hordes of people in front of him entirely blocking the view of the tunnel. Then he caught sight of her reaching out to touch The Arab's arm as he passed. From the left, Bella Prunella ran towards him, dramatically reaching out to touch his hem, crawling on her knees. The crowd loved it— all but the blond, who snatched Bella Prunella up by the hair.

Bella, really angered by the intruder this time, grasped the stranger by the shoulders and said something to her. Jack, studying the scene through the binoculars, figured Bella was warning her that if she didn't knock it off she was going to get hurt.

The women swung each other around a bit and for the first time, Jack got a good look at the blond's face. Just as he thought: Gianconni. Even if he hadn't seen her face, he'd have known it was her by her next move. Bella, totally unexpecting a real fight, was suddenly flying through the air. She landed on her back and Gianconni pounced upon her, giving her an elbow drop to the throat.

H. Churchill Mallison

Meanwhile, except for those in the immediate vicinity, the crowd ignored them, focusing on the three-ring-circus in the bull pen where Prince Albert and The Arabian Knight were trying to out glamorize each other.

Jack quietly spoke into his walkie-talkie. "Landers, got 'er. Team ramp. At the moment she's got her own wrestling match with Bella Prunella and the two of them are rolling down the ramp towards the locker rooms. I'll hold this position if you can get somebody on the inside of that ramp in a hurry."

* * * * *

A maintenance man leaned on his broom and laughed at the two women, enjoying the lusty brawling while security men came running through the corridors. One of the officers literally skidded to a halt besides the tumbling women. The two uniforms each grabbed a squawking-mad hen and pried them apart.

"You both want to cool it downtown in a booking cell?" one of the men shouted to be heard over their screams and snarls.

Bella threw back her head hitting the officer on the chin with a solid whop with her skull. Realizing she might get arrested for assaulting him, she immediately stopped struggling and tried pleading instead.

"Look sir, this who-ever-the-hell-she-is broad keeps buttin' into my act! I don't know who the fuck she is or where the hell she comes from, but she ain't one of us!"

Gianconni, also realizing she was about to blow all her plans for the evening, suddenly backed off and became goopy-sweet to the officers, particularly the one hanging onto her.

"I apologize," Gianconni said. "I was under the impression that I was going to take over that role."

"Who told you that? Sure as hell wasn't me or my manager! You a wrestler? You a wrestler, what's your professional name?"

Gianconni held up both palms in surrender. "Okay, so okay. Yes, I am a wrestler, but I'm new locally. I don't have a manager yet."

"Where'd you get that badge?" Bella accused, "You steal that badge? She ain't one of us, officer!"

To Bella she said, "I'm on the ring crew, bitch." To the officer, "You can confirm that with Boss Perry. Works as ring crew leader. The foreman, you know."

The women, though both still mouthy, stood well apart and seemed relaxed enough. Bella's captor offered, "Listen, ladies. We don't want to have to take you two in. Why don't you both drop this crap and resolve it on your own time and somewhere else. Okay? Can we let you go and this shit isn't gonna happen again?" His raised brow, icy glare and grimace focused on each one individually. They both nodded in agreement. But on breaking up the squabble, Bella got in the last retort: "You can bet me and you are going to settle this one. And honey, if it ain't settled? I'm filing a formal complaint with the UCW and then you'll never work in this state again. Probably not in this country again. Got that?"

Gianconni's face didn't register anything, she just watched Bella disappear up the ramp and out of sight. She could care less who Prunella reported to, she was not and never intended to be a wrestler. Just like Bella Prunella had complained, Bella "is interfering with *my* act." Gianconni retreated to the personnel toilet and freshened herself up again so she could return to her position at the tunnel. *Damn it.* She'd missed most of the match and she'd better hurry or she'd miss him.

* * * * *

Defeated, The Arabian Knight stormed angrily from the ring barking noises that were supposed to be Arabian curses and charges of corruption intermingled with badly imitated broken English, shaking his fist at the referee. Gianconni waited for him at the foot of the ramp.

*   *   *   *   *

He pushed the broom and swept dirt and trash into a small pile, then leaned over and brushed it onto the dust pan.

Gianconni's pitch followed The Arabian all the way to the locker room door. He entered the door, slammed it shut in her face. A moment later, he opened it again. The maintenance man heard him say, "Tell you what. Maybe you got something there. We can talk about it. Just...well," his nodding head punctuated his thoughts, "...well, I'll meet you and we can talk about the possibilities."

Grinning, Gianconni resumed her position at the head of the ramp. Boss Perry came hurrying over, grabbed her by the arm, and dragged her down into the belly of the stadium.

His mouth opened, anger perched on his flexed tongue, all set to ream Gianconni out and fire her ass on the spot, he was caught from behind by two security guards who were asking him to come with them immediately. Utterly surprised, he let go with a staccato burst of "Uh— uh— uhs" and found himself being dragged off.

"Wait a minute fellas," he pled. "What's going on?"

A few minutes later, he came back to where Gianconni'd had the good sense to wait. Clearly angry, he came to within inches of her, pushing his face right into hers so that his nose almost touched hers. "Okay, Gianconni," nothing fake about this snarl. "I'm not firing you tonight. Yet. You make any kind of disturbance again and I'll see you don't work in this goddamned universe. Got that?"

"Yes, sir." Meekly.

"You stupid or something?" he shot at her and stormed off.

This time when she returned to the mouth of the tunnel to watch the rest of the show, she stayed back a little, out of the glow of the spots. Almost time for the main event. She spent the time waiting in deep thought.

The Wrestler Who Lost His Head

* * * * *

Kaminari Hitore stood almost a foot over six feet. A bull of a man whose arms were bulkier than most wrestler's legs. Who said Japanese were little people? His powerful neck muscles dwarfed his head. Slanted eyes gave him a particularly evil expression which he enhanced by wearing a jaw-clenching sneer. Championship contender of the first order is how Mullet announced him, his voice trembling with awe. Not an ounce of that three-hundred-twenty pounds was fat.

Mister Venus, once Mister America in the body-building circles, was a handsome auburn-haired man with skin like polished brass. He stretched his neck and spread his wings trying to look as massive as Hitore, but no matter what he did— all the jumping around in the world— nothing made him look anything but a good four inches shorter and just slightly smaller all over. But he was for-darn-sure prettier!

Hitore the monster. Mister Venus, the favored underdog. The Dome a cacophony of hoots, whistles, wails and jeers.

Hitore held Mister Venus above his head in an airplane spin. Around and around he spun, then slammed Mister Venus to the mat. Hitore ran to the ropes, climbed up at the ring post, bellowed an earsplitting *ki ai* and flew through the air. He landed on his victim with a power body slam. Mister Venus lay like a dead man. Hitore took a good look at him and gave him a couple of elbow drops to the throat for good measure. Then he stood and honked like a bull moose, strutting around in circles, thumping his chest.

Mister Venus stirred. The crowd screamed their encouragement. Shaking his head, he pawed the air, trying to find the strength to get up. Almost up, at least on all fours, it looked like he'd make it. Hitore casually walked over to him, looked down at him scornfully, grabbed him by the hair, and popped him a few good licks in his face.

Howling, Mister Venus begged for mercy. Then suddenly, as if God himself had intervened, renewed energy flowed into

H. Churchill Mallison

this American hero. He flew to his feet as if on angel wings. Samson's hair suddenly long and flowing again, this mighty warrior raged into the considerably larger Japanese *suigyu*, ducking his blows and landing a few of his own. A series of powerful punches to Hitore's chest and abdomen. Hitore bent double; Mister Venus caught him a good right hook to the chin. Hitore rose with the punch, caught a left to the chin, then another right. The tower of muscle staggered backwards a few steps, then fell like a downed redwood.

The dome rose a few inches off its moorings as the crowd came to its feet.

Mister Venus fell on Hitore's prostrate form. The referee threw himself on the floor beside them and pounded out three quick counts. Mister Venus jumped up, punched air with a balled fist, and leapt around the stage, glowing with victory, hysterically feeding off the audience's adoration.

* * * * *

Kaminari Hitore wiped the sweat from his face on a towel that was draped around his neck as he stood at the lockerroom door and looked the woman over.

A lopsided grin and lids at half-mast, Gianconni let her eyes leisurely roam over his massive form. "Can I touch?" Her voice drunk with admiration.

Hitore's slanted eyes, mere slits so that they appeared to be all black pupils and no irises at all, shot sparks as he let his gaze take in the muscular bitch before him. "Depends," he answered slowly, in perfect, unaccented American-English.

She reached a hand out, placing her flattened palm on the bulge of his pectoralis major. "Incredible pecs," the lopsided smile grew more so.

"You going to let me feel your pecs?" he asked.

"Depends," her delight spread the smile to the other side of her full lips.

"On what?" he asked, half expecting a price.

"On whether or not you'll wear your costume."

His brows raised, creasing his forehead and almost opening his eyes. "My costume?"

"Yeah," she drawled, apparently succumbing to an inner heat. "And you'll fight me."

"Fight?" he was confused.

"Wrestle. I'm stronger than I look." Her eyes closed as her hand traveled down his chest.

His thin lips spread across his face in a wide hot-doggy-daddy grin and he said softly, "So you want a *real* tumble?" She looked like she'd melt right there. His voice honeyed, "Okay. What's the plan?"

"Meet you out back. Follow me to my place. It's nice and private."

* * * * *

At the zero hour, that indefinable pause between midnight and morning when time slipped from January twelfth to the thirteenth, the moon, at ninety-eight percent on the wane, was barely visible. Even that faint reminiscent faltered behind thin vapors. Starlight, and a street lamp down the block that was half buried in the smothering arms of a water oak, colored the ground a lifeless gray; all else fell in deep shadow.

Sensing someone following her again, she'd passed Kaminari Hitore a note with explicit instructions and a hand-drawn map to her place. It said she'd be a few minutes late getting there because Boss Perry wanted her to help him unload the equipment back at a warehouse. Which he did, and she certainly wasn't going to refuse at this stage of the game. Being on his crew could be a big plus on her entertainment schedule. She'd followed Perry's van. When she left the warehouse, she started getting fancy with the driving, going around in circles, up and down streets, zigzagging in and out of traffic. No way could anyone be following her without it becoming evident! Though a

H. Churchill Mallison

little nervous about the hour, she decided to drive to the mall, park the junker, and pick up her Impala to take back home.

Confident no one lurked in the shadows, at last she drove to the duplex. Hitore waited. He said he'd only been there a few minutes. He'd stopped off and gotten a little juice and a couple of heavenly hits that ought to make the evening even more interesting.

His mass seemed to vanish in the gloom as he entered the front door. She told him not to turn on the lights. Blinded by total blackness, he simply stood still and waited for his eyes to adjust. Gianconni walked with arms stretched in front of her feeling around for the wall. The wall she ran into was pliable and radiated sensuous heat. They felt each other over. Her strong hands caressed his neck, his throat. A heavy kiss. Lots of preliminary exploring. Both seemed to think this evening would be even more exciting than anticipated. The lust contagious.

Stumbling around, they made it to the bedroom.

A small lamp flicked on. He made the room look too small. God, what a body. All the parts were in beautiful proportion.

* * * * *

"This is going to be too easy," he laughed.

"Come on. Come on." She held her hands like blades and stood ready to strike.

Hitore came at her playfully, planning to swing her off her feet, up into his arms, and then lay her out beneath him and ball the hell out of her. In a flash he caught a heel in the face which not only startled him, but hurt, too. Surprised, he stepped back, rubbing his chin, and stared at her. "Oh? So we know a little about martial arts?"

"A little," she teased.

He came in to her, planning to capture an arm and twist it up behind her, throw her down on the floor. There was no way she could hurt him, he was twice her size. Skillfully, she ducked his

The Wrestler Who Lost His Head

grab and caught him in the crotch with a knee, but not so hard as to curtail their fun.

"See?" she panted a little. "Better keep your guard up or you might lose the family jewels.

"You aren't gonna hurt me, baby." A slipery tongue licked his lips and his eyes narrowed to upside-down smiles. Hands extended, palms up, he flexed his fingers, motioning for her to come on to him.

While she warily danced around him, he hooked his thumbs into the elastic around the waist of his tights and started pushing them down around his hips.

"No, don't take it off."

"You're some kind of nut?"

"Hey, men like women in lacy garters. I like my men in sequins. Yeah, you can take that part off," she said as he unhooked a buckle and slipped off a sequined boot.

Hitore flexed his bared toes, adjusted his crotch, and stepped foreward. In a flash, he grabbed a hank of blond curls.

"God." Her eyes flamed. "Ouch, don't pull my fuckin' hair out," the grouse a pouty, purring complaint.

"You said you want it rough. You're getting it rough, bitch." One hand to her shoulder pressed her to her knees. "Okay, bitch. You want it, get it."

She looked up his massive torso from her humbled position with great eyes as her hungry hands felt their way up the insides of his thighs, over a bulge that made her gasp, to the waist of the tights. Clawing, she peeled the costume off.

"Open," he demanded.

"Not yet."

She did not have the strength to resist the guidance of his hands on her head.

"You're choking— "

He held her head and shuddered as she worked him over. Suddenly, he pushed her away and pulled her to her feet by her hair. With a sudden swing, he flipped her into the air and tossed her down on the matt on her back. A sudden swoop and he had her feet in his hands forcing her feet over her head. She took advantage of his leverage and rolled forcefully into a backward summersault, catching him by surprise, and she was free of him. She was on her feet and executing a flying scissor-chop before he realized what she was up to. A kick struck his chest. She landed with a graceful twist of torso so she'd be sideways to him and able to watch his movements. He caught her with an arm and swung her over his shoulder, holding her like a sack of potatoes. He dumped her on the mat onto her back, this time holding her down with a hand to her chest, forced her legs apart, and took her.

* * * * *

I heard the scream of maddening pleasure as if I were in a dream.

Trickling down. Rivers of it.

I'm lost in frenzied delusion— the violence a sensual, macabre dance— then panic. Get ready. I ache. With a struggle, I finally get my breathing under control. All is quiet.

Oh...Washed in the blood...the sucking, violent climax. You're mine. Mine. Another violent climax! Another trophy.

Surprise!

CHAPTER XIX

Hitore left around one a.m. The night lay heavy on the bush-shrouded lot, the moon gone. Feeling exhausted, he yearned for his own bed and deep sleep. The key slid into the car lock and the latch gave with a thump. He sat on the seat , car door open, with both feet on the ground for a moment before he hefted his bulk into the seat well and shoved the key into the ignition. Pulling on the seat belt, he fastened it and lowered the adjustable steering wheel in place. Instead of backing out, he pulled the car around in a tight circle and nosed onto the dimly-lit street. Between the wrestling match and the wrestling sex, he felt used up, though pleasantly so.

He wondered where she'd disappeared to? She'd gotten up to go to the john and never came back. So he put the missing parts of his costume back on since his street clothes were still in the car. He left without even a thank-you-ma'am. Kinky broad. But fun. He liked rough sex himself, though he'd never dream of treating his wife that way. What are whores for anyway but doing what you can't do at home.

Something cold.

A low voice, "Keep your hands on the wheel. Both of them. A three-fifty-seven makes one hell of a mess of your brain. — Ut! Do as I say Hitore, or die right here."

"You aren't going to shoot me while I'm driving."

"Don't bet on it. Most you're going to do is bump into the curb at this speed. You press the pedal to the metal and I'll blow you anyway. I got nothing to lose, so don't lose your head." A weird giggle.

"What do you want? I don't have much cash on me."

"Turn here left."

* * * * *

H. Churchill Mallison

The car pulled into the deep shadows. Hitore tried to see who it was behind him but couldn't even make out a silhouette, it was so dark. He grasped the steering wheel as he told. A sudden movement, so fast that it was done before it registered on Hitore's mind. The garrotte choked and twisted, cutting into his flesh. He tried to wedge his fingers behind the wire, but it cut so deeply he couldn't even feel it with his finger tips. He tried to reach behind him and grab the killing hands. Swelling with increased blood pressure, his eyes bulged grotesquely and his tongue popped out. A deeper darkness folded over his eyes. Blind panic; lungs desperately tried to suck air—

* * * * *

A chain fence ran along the edge of the shopping center's boundaries, skirting I-275 and Eisenhower Boulevard. A walk-in medical center was under construction in the middle of the vast parking lot behind Westshore society's favorite mall. The first day, although several people noticed the car parked way over by the fence next to the interstate and Eisenhower, nobody bothered worrying about it. The second morning buzzards and crows circled over it so the mall manager called a towing service to come haul the car off the property.

The tow truck driver sat on a stack of cement blocks tossing his breakfast all over the new walk-in clinic site. He'd moved his truck over there even before he radioed the police. Never in all his born days had he seen anything so sickening. I mean, yeah, car wrecks were horrible sometimes, but...well, they was accidents, not...not deliberate!

Cops of every variety swarmed like blue flies to a blow fish carcass. The tow truck driver just continued puking up his guts and wiped water from his eyes. Hell no, he won't cryin', but Jesus...

* * * * *

The Wrestler Who Lost His Head

Landers pulled his car into the lot of the new office building off Gandy Boulevard on the Pinellas side of the bridge. The Task Force occupied one floor of the mostly unoccupied building. A groan escaped. Far too many cars parked. If everyone working on the Task Force and all the employees of the three companies were here at the same time, there'd be maybe half as many vehicles. That only meant one thing. He spotted three vans, all painted with huge television channel logos and numbers, and that was but a drop in a thunderhead.

It had to happen sooner or later. The relative quiet— the lull in attention had been too good to hope for. He drove slowly through the lot, trying not to attract attention, heading for a side or back entrance to the building. Maybe, just maybe, he could get inside without being swept up in a tidal wave of media.

He'd just spent forty-five minutes getting his ass chewed out by Tallahassee, who'd had its gnawed on by the Mayor's office and the Sports Authority's director, Marvin Pickins. The mayor complaining that the city's efforts to attract major sports to the area was being ruined by these gruesome murders of athletes.

Forget the side entrance. In a matter of seconds, he discovered he could forget the back entrance and the other side entrance— all four were covered by media types carrying walkie-talkies so they could alert their teams if anyone tried to sneak past. Uh-oh, he was spotted. He looked like the Pied Piper driving around the building with this throng of reporters and crews gathering behind him.

Hell, if he was going to be mobbed anyway, he may as well go in the front entrance like a proper executive. When he pulled his Buick Regal into a space, he was swarmed like a sticky-bun sitting on the grass at a picnic. He grimaced at the pushing mob that literally held him trapped in the car. Finger to the electric window, he lowered it about two inches and yelled to be heard.

"You mind backing up enough to let me get out?"

Begrudgingly, a few pushed back a little, but surged again when those behind them tried to squeeze through and take their places. One tall cameraman turned his head and started shouting, "Make room so he can get out!"

Pushing with all his strength, he managed to force the door open against the stubborn resistance enough to squeeze through. Immediately a dozen microphones were shoved in his face. What sounded like a thousand voices started screaming questions at him. It was all he could do to keep from losing it and screaming at them. Instead, he raised his arms and yelled, "Let me get to the entrance and I'll make a statement!"

The aggressive herd pressed in on him harder screaming demands for information.

"If you don't let me through, damn it! I'm not going to tell you anything!"

Finally the crowd backed off just enough so he could swim upstream towards the building's entrance. Once there, he held up his arms, waved his hands about, and waited for them to quiet down enough to speak.

To a man who kept shoving a mike at his mouth, almost hitting him with it, he said, "You hit me with that mike..." His expression said the reporter would end up eating it, but he stopped himself short of verbally making the threat.

"Gentlemen! Ladies! Please! How do you expect to get any information with this chaos? Quiet down!" He waited a few minutes. At last the crowd got the message and settled down enough to be heard. "There's no news to report yet—" a wave of questions assailed him. He closed his eyes and started counting. The ebb retreated a bit. "We have a couple of leads—" another outburst. He turned as if to walk inside without telling them anything. That shut them up briefly. Turning around, he tried again. "Tell you what. Each morning you can pick up a press release here in the lobby."

The mob became angry and were now shouting demands and moving in on him again. Then he'd had it up to here. "Hold it!" he bellowed and the mob fell quiet. "Enough! Good grief! How about a little manners and some consideration! Back off! Now if you people want my cooperation, then you're just plain going to have to do a little cooperating, too! I will tell you what I can at any time during this investigation. Sometimes we cannot release information we have because if you print it, you can damage our chances of catching the perp.

"What I can tell you is that we have a few leads, but I cannot tell you anything else at this time. Now I know this is a high profile case, but I have to ask you to put the priority of solving these crimes ahead of selling newspapers. Like I said a minute ago, we will issue press releases daily and they will be on a table in the lobby of this building." All this time, Landers is having to shout over persistent questioning from the pushiest of the lot, but he continued. "That's all!" In answer to another wave of demands, he replied, "Hey, you don't let me go get the job done, how can I give you more information?" With a conciliatory smile that didn't reach his eyes, he turned about and struggled through the front entrance. Security guards held the crowd at bay while he entered the elevator. At least no one could get to the Task Force offices.

* * * * *

"You had her under surveillance. Two of you. Anybody see her leave with the victim."

"The victim had a name," grumbled Harry Francesco, "and it's John Ieyasu." He crumbled in the chair; wiped his face with his hands. Tears kept leaking.

Landers shot Francesco a glance, then softened. "I'm sorry. Sometimes we seem cold about these things." Francesco's head jerked in an indecisive nodding motion that said he knew that and it was okay but he was distraught and he'd like to fucking kill whomever had done this thing.

Jesse Hood slouched against the wall by the desk that Landers sat behind; Francesco crumbled beside it seated in a standard, uncomfortable green plastic upholstered chair. Jesse straightened up. When he did, Francesco took notice. The agent was a black man about six-four and built like a pro-football tackle. He had a face that could scare maggots, but a quiet intelligence and manner.

Jesse said, "I did. I followed her to a warehouse out on Adamo Drive and 42nd. From there, she zigzagged all over hell and back, but I followed her to Westshore Plaza. She drove into the covered parking, first level near the Robinson's entrance, and switched cars. Then I followed her home." Jesse looked up at Jack Robinson for support. They both felt awful. Jack stood shuffling his weight from one foot to the other, looking guilty. "Hitore's— Mister I-ee...how'd you pronounce that?— the victim, was there waiting for her in his car. I parked down the street, got out of the car, hid in the bushes for a while. Tried to peek in the windows, but the shades were drawn. Only one light came on after they entered: a dim light in the bedroom. Sounded like they were having a good time. I went back to my car and waited.

"He came outside at one-o-five a.m., got in his car, and left. He was alone. A few minutes later she came to the door and looked around, then went back inside and the bedroom light went out. I stayed around for another hour and a half. I'm telling you, she didn't leave that house. At least not until after two-thirty a.m."

Jack said, mostly to himself, "But she had a car stashed at the mall?"

"You didn't see anything else?" Landers asked.

Jesse squinted, then closed his eyes. "No."

"Nobody driving around?"

"No."

"No mysterious cars parked on the street that might not have belonged?"

"No cars on the street. People there either park in garages or in their driveways." Jesse slowly shook his head from side to side. "But, wait...there was an old van parked about a block away, but I didn't see anything going on there. Didn't seem unusual."

Jack spoke up. "I want to pick her up for questioning."

The Wrestler Who Lost His Head

"On what basis?" Landers asked.

"On what basis? She was seen with the other victims— "

"— We got no proof of that yet. And he was seen leaving her apartment alone."

"Bring her in and put her in a line up," Jack countered. He continued, "She had a car stashed at the mall where the body was found, for God sake, and we know the perp had to have stashed a vehicle to leave the crime scenes in all these killings. She's a body builder; she was in Los Angeles when Muncy was murdered; I don't know for sure yet, but I'm working on it and betting she was in Miami when Thornton was murdered. She is here and was seen at those matches with the victims at the Outlandish and Amherst. How much more do you need to pick her up for questioning?"

* * * * *

Jesse Hood and Joe O'Leary watched from Jesse's silver Buick LaSabre, which was parked curbside just south of Gianconni's Riverside address.

"There," Jesse's nod indicated an approaching Impala as it turned the corner ahead, drove slowly down the street, and turned into the driveway of the duplex. The driver, Gianconni, eyed the two men nervously as she passed.

Jesse started up the horses and pulled into the drive behind her. She stayed in her car and watched them in her rear view mirror, leaned forward as if ready to start up her engine and scram the hell out of there. Jesse already had his badge in his palm and held it up for her to see, guessing she might think they were there for some illicit purpose. O'Leary reached inside his jacket pocket for his badge as they walked over.

She seemed to relax a little when she saw the IDs and sat back in her seat, rolling big eyes up at them through a raised window.

"Miss Gianconni?" Jesse asked. She nodded affirmative. "Special Agent Hood, FDLE," he said, then indicated O'Leary,

"Detective O'Leary, Tampa Police Department. We'd like to have a word with you?"

She lowered the window a couple of inches. Jesse noticed that the car doors were all locked. "What about? I wasn't speeding."

"No ma'am, far as I can tell, you weren't. Would you get out of the car please?"

"How do I know you're police?"

Jesse and O'Leary glanced at each other, passing a look, then held their badges up against the glass of her windows. She took an inordinate amount of time studying them.

"Far as I know you're impersonators. How can I verify that you're who you say you are?"

"Feel free to call the FDLE." Jesse poked a calling card through the crack in the window.

"How? I don't have a car phone."

"Gimme a break, lady," Jesse's eyes rolled and his mouth pulled a frown.

Joe O'Leary spoke up. "Tell you what I'll do for you ma'am. I'll be pleased to pull the car up along side yours and you can listen to me call dispatch."

"Never mind," she snarled, having finally made up her mind to get out of the car. She unlocked the driver's-side door and swung her long legs out of the seat, then hefted herself up straight. "What can I do for you?" she asked in a bored voice.

"We'd like for you to come downtown with us for questioning, ma'am," O'Leary answered.

"What about?"

"About the demise of John Ieyasu."

"Who?" her whole face squinted expressing a combination of sarcasm and curiosity."

"John Eh-eeya-su," O'Leary over-enunciated. When her questioning expression didn't change, he added, "Kaminari Hitore, the wrestler."

It took a split second, but clearly long enough that she'd had to think about it, before recognition widened her eyes. She

The Wrestler Who Lost His Head

blinked, swallowed, and asked, "Demise? He have a wreck or something?"

"No ma'am, he was murdered last night."

Gianconni's eyes and mouth made an O and she tucked her chin in surprise. After a moment to collect her thoughts, she replied, "I don't know nothing about nothing. I ain't got nothing to say to you guys."

"Miss Gianconni," Jesse's manner quiet, "we just want to ask you a few questions. We'd like to talk to you at headquarters so you can look at some pictures for us and see if you can identify anyone. It could be mighty helpful to us if you would, but it's your option."

O'Leary shuffled his feet and gave her a fatherly expression.

"You arresting me?"

"No, ma'am, we just want to talk to you."

* * * * *

A group of women were herded through the doorway to the brightly-lit, enclosed stage that faced a wide, two-way mirror. They came in one at a time, mostly gazing at the floor, positioning their feet onto hand-painted footprints on the floor. All but one clasped hands behind their backs. Gianconni left her arms hanging at her sides and stared at her reflection. Defiantly, she jutted her chin a little, aggressively spread her feet, and squared her shoulders.

The woman, Addy Pierce, had arrived at The Tampa International Airport less than an hour ago, and was bleary-eyed from the trip. She studied each woman carefully, over and over again, without saying a word. Behind her stood Jack Robinson, Jesse Hood, and Ralph Landers. Landers gave an encouraging word every now and then. Tension mounted.

"Build-wise, number four fits, but something's wrong. None of the other women have the same kind of figure," she said at long last.

"Maybe the hair's different," Landers suggested.

"She does sort of look like— she's the type, you know? But, I'm sorry, I can't be sure."

"Take your time," Landers said.

Miss Pierce turned to meet his eye. Apologetically she murmured, "I'm sorry. But I can't say it is her if I'm not sure. It's been so long..."

After Pierce had been escorted from the room and before the next witness was ushered inside, Jack remarked, "Well, Miami wasn't as long ago, and the local witnesses are pretty fresh."

The Miami witness came inside: a young man about twenty-five. He was so tall he had to duck his head to enter the enclosure, but as narrow and lean as a blade of saw grass. Sitting down so he could see better, he let his eyes take in every detail of every woman in the lineup, particularly their breasts. Most of the women were hookers and dressed the part. Mister Roy Blasinger studied them like a gourmet diner at Bern's with a roomy credit card in his pocket. His eyes kept returning to number four. Smirking, he drawled, "It's number four."

"You certain?" Landers asked.

"Yeah. It's her. I tried to pick her up that night. Watched her dicking around with the wrestlers, but none of them was interested in her. So I thought I'd give it a try if she wasn't too expensive." He huffed an ironic laugh. "Turns out she'd not a pro— you know, prostitute— and she got all pissed off and got loud, making a scene. Like to the point I thought I was gonna get thrown out, you know? Bitch. Anyway, that's her."

"You saw her leave with someone?" Jack asked, seeking verification.

"Not just someone, she was putting the make on The Psychiatrist, and he was grinning like what she said sounded pretty good to him."

"The Psychiatrist?" Landers queried.

"You know, the wrestler. He went by The Psychiatrist. I don't know what his real name was."

"And she left with him then?" Jack asked.

"...Well, not...exactly. I mean, well, I knew they...I figured they came to an agreement."

"So you didn't see her leave with him?" Landers questioned.

Frustrated, Roy Blasinger blinked his eyes, his head vibrated irritably, and his lips pursed. He whined, "It was just *plain* that they'd meet after the fights. You don't have to be a wizard to spot a pickup."

"Had you ever had occasion to ask this woman out before this particular night?" O'Leary asked.

"No. Never saw her before."

"You sure?" O'Leary persisted.

"Yes, officer," voice sneering, "I'm sure that I never saw her before that night, and I've never seen her since, until right this very minute."

"You never saw her at any other wrestling matches in the Miami area?"

"Oh, my gawd, officer. How many times do I have to repeat myself. No, I never saw her before. I probably wouldn't even remember seeing her this time except that I tried to pick her up. There's anywhere from hundreds to thousands of people at these things. She just happened to be sitting near me and I saw her trying to pick up a couple of the wrestlers. Since they weren't interested, I thought I'd help out the little lady. That's all. But she wasn't interested and told me to, and I quote, 'Fuck off.' End of subject matter. Okay?"

CHAPTER XX

Jesse Hood and Joe O'Leary sat across from Belinda Gianconni. All three of them sat with hands palms down on the metal expanse of the industrial-weight, photo-walnut-grained plastic-surfaced work table in an interrogation room, and exchanged glances.

"Do you know a person by the name of John Ieyasu?" Jesse asked, resuming a heretofore meaningless exchange.

"No."

Jesse rolled large brown eyes. On anybody else, those yellow whites would mean a severe case of jaundice, but on Jesse, it was simply because he was about as black as an African-American could get. Even his fingernails were ebony. It had been previously decided that Jesse would be the good guy and O'Leary, who much preferred that role for himself, had to be the tough. But since she was a female Caucasian, to avoid any racial accusations, they let the Caucasian officer do the dirty work.

Since Jesse's size and a terrible case of uglies made him appear very threatening, and O'Leary's Irish rosy-cheeked cherub- like countenance made him look like Santa Claus, the effect confused Gianconni, thereby making her more suspicious, and hence, stubborn.

"Do you know a wrestler by the name of Kaminari Hitore?"

"You mean 'Did' don't you? You said he's dead. Yes, I *did* know Kaminari Hitore, but not very well. I just met him for the first time that night."

"For the sake of clarity, since we are taping this interview, would you state what night?"

"Saturday night, February twelfth at the Sun Dome UCW wrestling matches."

"Did you meet Mister Ieyasu at your apartment following the exhibition fights on the evening of— "

"No," she snapped.

"Let me finish the question, please Miss Gianconni, then answer." Jesse, a model of patience. "Did you meet— "

"No," she snapped again, her eyes bright with hostility. "I met Kaminari Hitore. I don't know who John Ieyasu is, except that you say he is Kaminari Hitore. But I did...have a date with Kaminari Hitore."

"...After the— "

"— Exhibition fight, as you call it," she interrupted.

"On the evening of— "

"Actually, since you want to get technical, it was probably February thirteenth, since it may have been a little after twelve by then. But I can't state for sure, since I wasn't timing him."

"When he arrived at your apartment?" Jesse asked. By now he'd begun to enjoy annoying her by being irritatingly calm and polite. She nodded an affirmative. "Please answer out loud, Miss Gianconni." A huge, meaty finger indicated the tape recorder.

"Yes, when...approximately, when he arrived at my apartment."

"What time did the deceased leave your house?"

"The deceased didn't leave my house," her sarcasm said dead men didn't go anywhere. A hint of a smile touched the corners of her mouth, but her eyes remained furious.

O'Leary turned his head toward Jesse and with a nod, he motioned Jesse outside. The two men left, closing the door behind them. In a moment, O'Leary returned.

Walking behind Gianconni, who still sat at the table with hands folded on top of it, trying to appear confident and calm, O'Leary barked, "Miss Gianconni, your attitude isn't helping you and it isn't helping us find the person who maliciously slaughtered a fine athlete." Suddenly, O'Leary swung around from behind her, banging both fists on the end of the table. She jumped. He leaned towards her, pushing his face very near hers, and enunciated: "What time did John Ieyasu leave your apartment?"

"Kaminari Hitore left...hell, I don't know. I'd say about an hour later. Probably around one a.m., give or take a few minutes." Offended by his startling actions, she pouted. "I want a lawyer."

"You want a lawyer?" O'Leary sneered as best he could. A sneer looked rather silly on Santa Clause. "You haven't been arrested for anything, so why would you want a lawyer? You feeling a mite guilty about something?"

* * * * *

Jack Robinson, Maddy Ulner, Jaime Cortez, and a FDLE Lab technician methodically searched Gianconni's apartment. The lab tech dusted for fingerprints and bagged a set of sheets found in the dirty clothes hamper that had semen stains. They would be tested for comparison with Ieyasu's.

Jack examined all of the shoes in the bedroom closet, which were thrown loosely about on the floor. None with blood stains. Next he examined each item of clothing or accessory hanging or shelved, again searching for some evidence that Gianconni had been in the bloody car. Maddy dumped each drawer one at a time on the bed, throwing each examined item back into its drawer when finished, then shoving the drawer back into its place.

Jack lifted several hat boxes down from the closet shelf. He set the boxes down on the foot of the bed and removed the lids. "Well-well-well. This explains a lot. Maybe." Maddy came over to see. "Wigs."

"Looks like a wig for each of those lycra outfits. I mean, I like to accessorize, too, but wigs for each costume?" She fanned the air with a hand and grinned. "Wonder if she ever wore wigs to the gyms? and that's why we never could get a lead on her?"

Jack pulled a face that said maybe.

Jaime Cortez hunched over a disorganized secretarial flipping through unpaid bills and miscellaneous papers. He found a calendar and started reading through it.

The Wrestler Who Lost His Head

* * * * *

"Did you have relations with the— Mister Ieyasu?"

"You mean sex?" she drawled, oozing boredom.

"Ahem, yes." Real tough guy, Santa.

"That is none of your business."

O'Leary thought that over for a moment, then replied, "Miss, we already know Mister Ieyasu had sex just previous to his death. We know he went to your apartment and met with you there for approximately one hour somewhere between eleven and one o'clock. You tell me he left you there around one o'clock in the marnin'." Joe O'Leary never had pronounced 'morning' any other way but 'marnin.' "Now, you tell me you did not have sex, then maybe he met up with somebody else? It would be far simpler all the way 'round if you'd just stop playin' games and answered the questions."

"I want a lawyer. You want anymore fucking information out of me, I want a lawyer here. I'm not saying one more fucking word. Got that Chubby?"

"Mister Ieyasu was murdered between the hours of twelve midnight and two a.m. in the marnin', and you are the last known person to be with him."

"Okay, okay. So, yes, I had sex with him. I may be good, Mister Detective, but he didn't drop dead from it. He hardly even breathed heavy. He left walking on his own two feet, got in his car, and drove off."

"Did you go with him?"

"What for?" Gianconni ve'ed her brow and glared at O'Leary like he was crazy. "Hell no. I went to bed."

* * * * *

Spiegel's Towing hooked up Gianconni's Chevy Impala that had been abandoned in the Westshore parking garage after the lab crew finished going over the scene. The towing company delivered the car to the crime lab for more finite testing. Then Spiegel's Towing picked up the '72 Galaxy jalopy, which a technician had already done a prelim on, and also took it in for the same careful examination.

* * * * *

Aubry Cox stood behind his client. "Don't answer that," he instructed when Jesse Hood asked Gianconni what Ieyasu was wearing when he left the apartment. "Listen, gentlemen, I haven't had time to discuss this matter with my client. She categorically refuses to answer anymore questions until we have had an opportunity to discuss this in privacy. And I want a copy of that taped interview. I want Miss Gianconni released immediately and I want twenty-four hours notice if you want to interrogate her again."

Jesse Hood and Joe O'Leary rolled their heads towards each other and pulled what-can-ya-do faces, raising their palms towards the ceiling. For good measure, Jesse told their backs as they walked out of the interrogation room: "Be sure your client does not leave town without first informing us."

Jesse watched the door close. To O'Leary he sighed, "If that broad farts I want it noted with the time and the date. I want a tail on her twenty-four hours a day."

"You can do that?"

"I'm going to see Landers right now and beg."

* * * * *

"Lab reports they found a few drops of dried blood in the back of Gianconni's Chevrolet Impala." Jack grinned. This could be the break they needed. "They're typing it now to see if it's a match." His eyes sparkled with excitement. "We got him placed at her apartment. That sample matches, we got 'er."

"Don't break out the champagne until that report comes in," Landers said.

The Wrestler Who Lost His Head

"What?— What?" Jesse barked, challenging the caution.
"I got a feeling, that's all," Landers replied.
"Yeah? Well, I got one, too," Jack's grin still plastered on his face. "And I'm telling you, this Gianconni's in this thing up to her neck. ...No pun intended."

* * * * *

Jack and Ali sat in the darkest corner of the Task Force's acre-size room corner staring at a video. He said, "Just see if you can spot her. She had to be at those matches somewhere."

"I thought you already had proof she was at the matches when those guys got killed, anyway. So what difference does it make if she was at the matches when nobody was killed?"

"Just look," was all he replied.

They both studied the films. Jack hadn't told her about the wigs. He wanted to see if she could spot Gianconni without that knowledge.

"Go back," Ali leaned forward in her chair as if that would help her see the large television screen better. "See that? I'll be darned! That could be her, couldn't it? The redhead — remember? At the Outlandish? Had on the crimson tights and cowboy boots? and kept trying to get Citrus Sam's attention? Oooooh..."

"Oh what?" Jack urged.

Ali looked confused, searched her mind. Gone. She shook her head negatively, "Something, but it's...I lost it. Something hit me, oh, damn. I hate it when that happens. Maybe it'll come back. Like at three a.m. when I'm sound asleep."

Jack reversed the tape again and stopped it on the close-up of the redhead when she'd pulled up on the ropes and was shouting at Citrus Sam. He noted the recorder's meter number and made a note to have the still blown up in a photograph.

Landers walked to the center of the room and announced in a loud voice that he had just received a phone call from the lab. Everyone dropped what they were doing and paid attention.

"Listen up! Got a call from the crime lab. First, the good news."

A groan rumbled through the room acknowledging the implication that all was not copesetic.

Landers continued: "The semen on the sheets matched." He paused, creating additional tension, "Now the bad news. The blood is Gianconni's type, which is 0 positive, according to her blood donor card. The victim is AB positive. So now we have positive proof that the victim was at Gianconni's apartment with her that night and did have sex with her. She is the last person known to be seen with him. But, although she did have a vehicle parked in the garage at the scene of the crime, we cannot place her there between the hours of twelve midnight and two a.m. *And* one of our own is witness to the victim's leaving and saw Gianconni at the house after the victim left.

"So where does this leave us?"

Someone weakly offered, "An accomplice? A jealous boyfriend?"

"However!" Landers grinned, pausing for effect. "Back to some good news. The California victim also had O positive blood." Breathless, hopeful silence. "I've requested a DNA on both Gianconni's sample and Muncy's, but that's going to take some time— minimum of five weeks— to get the results."

* * * * *

Jack stood at attention in the line of white-uniformed students. Gianconni explained the fine points of executing a *og oshi* hip throw. She selected one of the female students to demonstrate, letting the student throw her for a change. Gianconni lay sprawled on her back. She raised her head to look at her class, but did not rise. "Now, does anybody here remember what happened when Jack and I squared off that first day he joined our class? We did this same throw. Anybody?"

The Wrestler Who Lost His Head

If anybody, aside from Jack, remembered, they were too polite to bring up how she'd creamed him in less time than it takes to swat a pesky mosquito.

"Nobody remembers Jack's fatal mistake? You telling me, Jack, that you don't remember?" she challenged.

"I remember very well, but I thought someone else should answer."

Still silence.

"Okay. Jack, you tell me what you did wrong."

"I rolled over to get up."

"Right!"

Jack got an A on that one.

"So what happened then?" Gianconni asked.

"When I rolled over to get up, you pounced on my back, put a *hadaka jime* on me at the same time you wedged your heels under my hips for leverage, and knocked me out."

"So what's the point?" Her eyes scanned the lineup, seeking a response from another student.

"Don't roll over, just get back up onto your feet," someone volunteered, "Fast," he added.

In a flash, Gianconni rolled up to sitting position and then up onto her feet. "Who knows the definition of *hadaka jime*?"

"Naked strangle," a woman answered. "So all you got to do if someone tries to rape you is get him to roll over onto his stomach and jump him. Yeah, sure."

Gianconni, unflustered by the remark, grinned and took the opportunity to reiterate for the hundredth time: "Good point, Marcella. No matter how good a fighter you are, you're still probably going to be overpowered by a man if he wants to rape you and is bigger than you are. So, as we always stress, being alert is your best defense. Look the parking lot over for stragglers standing around before you walk to your car. You see someone standing around, go get a security officer to walk to your car with you.

"Okay. That's all for today. See you Monday." Gianconni *reyed* the class and they *reyed* in return.

H. Churchill Mallison

Jack stood in place while the others left for the locker rooms. "Mistress Gianconni," he bowed as he addressed her. "May I have a word with you."

Gianconni loved the formality in the *Do Jo*, and solemnly returned his *rey*. "Yes."

"I would like to invite the honorable *sensei* for a refreshing drink of nectar of fruit. And discuss a problem with her."

She considered, glanced at her watch, and said, "Okay. I have an hour."

Not often, but occasionally Jack invited her out for a glass of orange juice, and they'd developed a casual friendship. At least from her perspective; she didn't know he was an agent. From his perspective, he'd been careful not to be discovered during her interrogations, and his interest in her was a deception aimed at gaining her confidence. Same with Maddy Ulner.

They sat opposite each other at a booth in a Spanish sandwich shop. She drank orange juice; he sipped a Coke. He started the conversation.

"I think I'm ready to move to the next level."

"Almost."

"Why almost?"

"You've got the moves, Jack, but they still need perfecting. Get 'em down smoother. Your timing's off just a bit."

"Story of my life," he pulled a face that said he was a little disappointed. "Timing off, that is." He watched her eyes and softened his. "How come I never get past...you've got some kind of barrier up."

"Barrier?"

"Yeah. You got a steady boyfriend? You only like muscle men?"

"I like you fine, Jack. Just not interested in getting involved at the moment."

"No boyfriend?"

"Nope, and no headaches, either."

"I don't want to make your head ache," his voice ladened with innuendo.

The Wrestler Who Lost His Head

"Thanks, but no thanks."

"I know," he teased, "You're still carrying the torch for somebody."

"Hardly," her eyes paled with boredom.

"Someone's still carrying the torch for you?"

"Hardly."

"Then you're available?"

"Hardly."

"You're not a lesbian, you're not a nun, you're not celibate."

"Hardly."

"You're not cooperating," he started grinning.

"Hardly. This what you wanted to talk to me about?" she asked.

"Hardly," he mocked. "Nah. I really want to move up."

She grinned. Actually, when she relaxed and smiled, she was down right pretty. "Hardly," she said once more. "But, who knows. Maybe I'll change my mind."

"So you're saying I don't have any competition?" He waggled his eyebrows.

"But I do like muscle men," her expression implied he fell far short in the bulky-muscles department.

"So I'll take steroids?" he joked. "You date any fighters? You know, wrestlers or boxers? Body-builders?"

"Jackie, boy, stick to judo. My private life is none of your business." Her words were straight enough, but her eyes had finally softened and her pouty lips curled in a sexy, scolding way. She let her eyes roam over what she could see above the booth's table. "Actually, you aren't too bad. Tell you what. When you can beat me at *shia*, I'll take you on."

"Really?"

"Really."

CHAPTER XXI

I hate combination living/dining rooms. I like old fashioned dining rooms and real dining room furniture, too— not that formica dinette crap like I've got. I've got plans for this place.

Age yellowed shades cast a faint mustard light over the shadowy living room. Old lace sheers hung at the sides of the windows. It had been a plain rectangular space with the dinette at the kitchen end of the house, and the settee, rocker, and an ancient wingback with tattered, faded tapestry upholstery at the front.

The divider wall plans lay strewn over the formica of the four-seater dinette. Self designed, self built— building, that was. Actually, it would be a long time finishing it because of the problems encountered getting enough material— and money.

A faded photo, polaroid, actually, which never does retain its proper color, had turned brown in its tarnished, ornate silver frame. Mother, Father, sister Antoinette. I picked it up. *Mother always looked like she'd just bitten into a sour lemon. Father's eyes: dead. Tony now gone to fat and three screaming, spoiled brats.* Her husband was partner with some clown in a tree trimming operation. Ronnie. Always dirty. Dirt under his fingernails; dirt in his hair— ground into his skin permanently like some all-over tattoo that's turned him gray colored like a corpse.

Corpse. I smiled. The project was ready for the final stages.

The bathroom had a long hallway. One side held a combination linen closet and space for the overflow from the bedroom closet. Stored the work clothes in there. The other wall of the hallway is the back wall of the bedroom closet.

I always feel this surge of pride when I go inside my linen closet, push my clothes aside, and press ever so lightly at both edges of the wall board's panel. It pops out, you see, on spring hinges, so all I have to do is lift it off and set it aside to enter. I

The Wrestler Who Lost His Head

am so clever. Of course, if you paid attention to the dimensions of the outside of the building, you'd have to know there was a room missing on the inside. But who's ever around to notice?

It isn't a big room. About ten by eleven. Big enough. Inside it there's a work bench— two, really, considering I just use one to place things on I'll need later. And a long clothes rack like they have in laundries. More costumes, or at least articles from costumes— not mine, theirs. None really complete, but that's all right. Souvenirs to remember the glory of that sensuous evening— animal passions, almost like heated sex, and violence.

Put an exhaust fan in one of the boarded up windows. You know the kind they used back in the fifties and sixties in kitchens: set them in the windows and the fans blow towards the outside. I let ivy grow all over the outside on huge trellises to hide where I'd boarded up the windows. You could see them if you knew to look for them.

On my work bench sits the mold and the chemicals. But I'm not ready for that.

I take it from the freezer and wipe the gathering frost away. Placing it on the work bench, I gently, oh, ever so gently, brush off ice and water particles with a fine bristled brush. Brrrrr. Cold.

Actually, it probably would be better if I cast these immediately, but schedules just never work out that way.

Anyway, he's got to thaw a little before I can start painting him. I place a soft towel beneath him and dry his hair. Rich, black— actually, it isn't black. Why do people say Orientals have black hair? No. It's the richest of rich browns. Oh, to the indiscriminate it may be black, but not to the knowing eye. Deep, vibrant, blue-lighted umber. Straight as a fucking stick. The hair seems to have lost some of its luster. Hair conditioner should take care of that. I like Alberto VO-5, personally. I take up a bottle of it and rub some into my palms, then massage it into the thick, furry hair. With a brush I work it to a fine sheen.

H. Churchill Mallison

Feeling impatient— waiting for the skin to thaw enough to be pliable, I decide to leave the room for a while and busy myself with another project.

I know what you're thinking. Wrong. I'm a very clean person. Very particular. You can eat off my kitchen floor. Going over to the shade covering a square picture window, I slip a finger beneath an edge and peek outside. Nothing but oaks and pines. There's a slight breeze and the leaves of the oaks rock back and forth like an old man in a rocking chair.

Rocking chair. I sit in my old granny rocker, staring at where my planter will be. Actually, I have almost a third of the material already. I've stacked them in an arrangement. It's not a final arrangement, because I won't know exactly how I want to place everything until I have all of it together. But right now I have five— will have five— as soon as I finish this one, and five is enough to make a nice balance, so I can set something up temporarily.

I gaze into his eyes.

Scarlet ribbons.

The first one, Bulldog, looked just like a fucking bulldog. Ha!-Ha! Kept the collar. That was perfect with the collar. He'd been the first and I almost fucked it up. Sloppy cut. But the collar hid it.

Metal spikes like candy kisses. Fortunately, he hadn't put that back on. Picture that: trying to choke him out with a fucking leather collar on.

Growing dark. Like the dark. Have them dimly lit with a string of those tiny Christmas lights? The little white ones that blink off and on? Eerie effect. Love it.

Peek outside again. Slip out the front door. The property is heavily wooded, but still, who knows who might be snooping about. Some nosy kid. My dog howls. He's penned in the back. I let him out and he runs around the house a couple of times pissing on this bush and that, checking to make sure nobody's invaded our property. While he's running off excess energy, I go in to pour some Purina in a bowl and set it on the back stoop for him. Change the water in his bowl. I keep his dishes as clean as mine.

Dog's as black as the night. Like a ghost guard. You never see him and he don't always bark. He just comes up on you nice and quiet like, most times, then goes for the throat.

We got something in common.

Probably ready by now.

Back inside my studio. I sort through all the jars of makeup. Trying to find the closest color. Have to mix this one myself. A little of a dark tan, pour in a bit of pale beige to lighten it, but the color's too rosy. I pour a touch of black eye shadow powder into the liquid base and stir it around. Good. Almost good enough, but still too pink. Chinks aren't pink. Japanese chinks? I know Chinese are. Well, chink is good enough.

I experiment. Using my fingers, I apply the shades. So far, so good. I am a fucking artist with makeup. First I apply an even coat over all the skin. Neck, too. I got a lot of neck on this one. Getting better at this. Already evened up the ragged pieces, so I've got a nice, clean cut.

I want the eyes open, but he's so squinty-eyed, it's hard to tell if they're open or closed. I push back the fleshy part of the upper lid and deftly paint a heavy black line along the lash line using a water-based eyeliner that's applied with a brush. Blowing on the wet liner, I hold this until it's dry, then let go. Poking the flesh a little until the lid settles naturally, I study the results. Better. I line the bottom lid, touch it up with a Q-Tip. You still don't see much iris, but the eyeliner does an adequate job of accentuating the evil slant of his Oriental eyes.

Using gray, I contour the cheek bones and shadow the temples a touch to give his face added dimensions. A faint brush of rouge to the lips.

The first stage had been completed two days before. A spike is set in the bottom of the mold and the four sides are formed, but the block is hollow. The spike is placed about three inches to one side of the middle for easier installation of the head. The block is set aside on the other table. I carry it over now. I lift up the head and gaze at the severed end. Decision made, I position the head over the spike, then shove with a hard, clean movement. It sounds like skewering a chicken when the spike is driven through cartilage, ligaments, the brachial and esophagus tubes and bone.

I stoop down to look at the piece at eye level, make a few minor adjustments, then step back. No point in rushing things and making a mess of it. I take one step forward and rotate the block a little, then step back again. I do this until I've checked every angle. The hair's a little messed up, so I take the hairbrush and straighten that out.

The only real disappointment is I don't have an article to place in the block with him. All he'd worn was black Spandex bikini shorts and black laced sandals. Kept the sandals, but they'll be encased separately. A thought made me laugh out loud. What if I pulled his shorts down over his head? More I think about this the funnier it gets and my eyes are watering! I take his pants and pull them down over my head. Look in the mirror! Look in the mirror! I'm roaring— my eyes look like white holes peeking through the legs of his tights.

What's that?

Dog's barking.

Stop laughing. Stand dead still. Heart's pounding.

I slip outside my studio and snap the panel back in place. Damn it, I have to wash my hands before I touch my clothes. I decide not to make the noise by running water, so I grab a kitchen towel from the kitchen and wipe my hands on it, then return to the closet. Carefully, trying not to make any noise, I slide the clothes back over the secret entrance.

Dog's still barking. Barking like he does when somebody comes around. Fucking kids, why don't they drop dead?

I close the closet door. Back to the kitchen. A meat cleaver is in the drainage rack, so I take it for protection.

Slipping to the front window, I peek outside. I can't see anything, not even the dog, but I hear him growling and barking near the road. I decide to use the back door.

The Wrestler Who Lost His Head

Stepping onto the back stoop, I stop and listen. Dog's still out front. Keeping in the shadows, I work my way across the small clearing between my house and the thick shrubbery. I told you I keep a tidy place. I rake up the leaves every week, so I can sneak across the grass noiselessly.

My eyes adjusted. I saw him— Dog— crouched in a threatening stance pointing at a stand of bushes at the corner of my property. I stoop down and wait.

Maybe fifteen minutes go by. The dog and whatever's in the bushes are at an impasse. Nobody's moving, no body's talking, either, not even Dog. Moonlight glistens on the butcher knife, so I lower it into deep shadow, afraid I might give my position away. I'm about to decide nothing's out there and Dog's just spooked when there's a movement.

A tall, lean figure steps out from behind the bush. Actually, he could have been just off the road, but behind the bushes from my point of view. The figure cautiously moves along past my yard. Dog commences to barking again. The man is apparently worried about the dog and has decided to move on.

Then something strange happens. Dog runs up to the figure and then leans down and starts to eat something. I want to yell out Don't eat that you damn fool dog! He's probably poisoning you! The man— I'm guessing it's a man— there aren't any lumps on the silhouette to tell me otherwise, anyway, he starts easing into the yard. But Dog ain't no fool and he looks up and starts growling. The man stopped dead in his tracks.

Suddenly my dog starts whining, then before I know it, he's yelping and acting crazy, goes into fits. That bastard has fed my dog strychnine. He convulses about fifteen minutes before he falls into rigid quiet. All this time this shadowy person is crouched behind a tree watching my house. After Dog has laid quiet— dead, I figure— for another ten-fifteen minutes, the stranger starts creeping up to the house. I let him come. He goes up to my windows, but he can't see anything. Hides in the shadows by the front steps for a few minutes. I don't know what's going through his mind, my van's right there in the driveway, so he's got to assume I'm around somewhere. But this fellow acts like he thinks I'm off some place else. He finally steps up on my stoop and tries my door knob. Me, I'm just waiting for him to try the back.

I don't have to wait long. He turns and looks towards the street, then trots around the house towards the back. I see him trying to peek in every window, then he goes to the kitchen door. That is unlocked, so this damned fool slips inside.

Well, I don't need this.

I listen at my back door. After a while I hear a small noise that tells me he's fucking around in my living room, so I slowly crack the back door. Thing squeaks sometimes, but if you just open it a little, it's quiet. I get it open just enough to sidle inside.

I haven't made up my mind whether to attack or wait until he passes me in the shadows and simply grab him. I decide that as long as it doesn't sound like he's breaking anything up, I might just as well wait for him.

A long shadow precedes the stranger into my kitchen. I'm on the wall right beside that doorway, back in where the dust mop and broom are shoved between the fridge and the wall. My hand's already in position.

The shadow stops short of coming inside. Then he steps through.

Light catches on the meat cleaver as it swings down hard. Bone breaks as it severs the clavicle and lodges in the shoulder blade. The stranger gags and staggers to the left, falling against my range. I still got my hand on the cleaver, and I lunge from my hiding place. Blood is spurting everywhere! One of my hands grabs him by the throat, the other wrenches the meat cleaver free. His eyes lock onto mine in a brief moment of terror and comprehension, and then I bring the cleaver hard to the center of his forehead. It split like a coconut.

Fucking blood all over my kitchen, and I'd just cleaned it up real good last week. I shut the back door and turned on the light. A stupid kid. What I thought. Some nosey little jerk out for kicks. I grabbed a plastic garbage bag and yanked it down over

The Wrestler Who Lost His Head

his head to try to stop the blood from further spurting all over the goddamned room.

Like I needed this. Been so careful, so neat, and now this. Gore all over the place. I'd be the rest of the night cleaning this up.

Picked up his dripping body, stood it on its mushy head, and pulled another garbage bag over his legs. Too tall, the middle still exposed, blood continued to leak all over my floor. I gave up trying to contain it and picked him up bodily, carrying him out back. I dumped him at the edge of the woods, then went for Dog.

Spent the whole goddamned night cleaning up. Dug a hole first and dumped Dog and the boy in it. Had some lime— always keep that on hand for disposal purposes— anyway, dumped a bag of lime over the bodies, then shoveled in the dirt. Scattered leaves over the site, and by the time I finished, you couldn't much tell the area had been disturbed.

Now for the messy part. Cleaning up all that blood. Wash these clothes after I soak 'em in hydrogen peroxide first to break down the blood so it's more fully dissolved. And the rags. Wash the rags. Hose down the yard, the stoop. Damn, the stoop. Some of the blood had spilled all over the coarse cement. Have to do something about that.

Oh, shit. I've got to pour the block, too, before he thaws too much!

Dawn. Pouring slowly, really careful, trying not to disturb the hair much— it wants to float some— trying to get the air bubbles worked out of the head as the level creeps towards the top of the shell, I emptied the whole can of polycarbonate. My eyes burned from the fumes and from working straight through the night. But this trophy was worth far too much to risk screwing up. To date, this was my finest acquirement.

I'll call in sick and sleep later.

CHAPTER XXII

Jack Robinson sprawled in an office swivel chair pondering individual blow-ups of certain video tape frames. Something itched in his mind like a mosquito bite between the shoulders right where you can't scratch.

Everything pointed to her, but what if it isn't her? Could she be in cahoots with someone else doing this? Why? For the life of him, he couldn't figure out why. They have found her in every tape. In some she'd worn the coppery-auburn wig with the crimson tights, others she'd worn a long, black wig with an electric blue bodysuit. The night of the Dome fights she'd worn turquoise tights and no wig at all, but had the thick, matted blond mane contained in a turquoise crocheted net braided with sparkling beads.

But he's seen no indication that she wanted to be a wrestler, and even if she did, the men weren't her competition. Yeah, she liked wrestling the wrestlers for some wild sex, but that wasn't the kind of kink— at least Jack didn't think so— that indicated psychopathology, or even a deviation.

The tape from the Dome was already loaded into the video. He pressed the remote to start it running, stopping it every now and then to stare at the selected blow-ups.

Ali walked up beside his slumped form and laid a hand on his shoulder.

"Hi, baby," she purred.

He glanced up, startled to see her there, looked at his watch, it was six-thirty, then back up at her. He grinned. "Well, hi there, honey. This is a pleasant surprise. How'd you get in?"

"Landers let me in. He just left. On my way home and thought I'd pop in for a minute. You going to be late tonight?"

"Sorry. Probably. Actually, I'm kind of looking forward to most of the people going home so I can stare at these tapes and think. Frustrating, like something's on the tip of my tongue..."

She pulled up a nearby chair and sat next to him. "What are you looking for?"

"Some kind of motive, actually. I don't know. Whatever is happening, its here on these tapes, but we can't see it."

"Want me to go pick up something for you to eat? 'Tucky Fried or maybe a pizza?" she offered.

"Hey, you know... And why don't you get enough for two and you can watch these things with me. We haven't had a whole lot of time together. We can pretend like we're home watching movies."

* * * * *

I'd been wondering how the hell I was going to get the prize of all prizes— this year anyway— at the big fight in Indianapolis. That one will be so heavily guarded that it will be one hell of a miracle if I can pull it off. Not to mention that if I have to go to Indianapolis, how the hell am I going to get it back home? No point in taking that amount of risk, and I'm about to scrap the idea. After all, he'll be available again locally, though it will take a while. And now this.

A smile slowly stretched across the face much like a Doberman's anticipatory grin.

It's meant to be, that's all. When things work out this well, it's plain fucking meant to be. Like this is a dream come true. Like it could be years before such an opportunity strikes again. And the World Heavy-Weight Champion, too! Right in the center of the display. Right smack in the middle. God. This is wonderful.

I look in the mirror and study my image. I could be in that place. World Champion. Only I'm not even considered! And why? I've got personality, stage presence, I'm fucking beautiful, I have the best act in the business. I run my hands over my body. It's perfect. Not an ounce of waste. Solid, perfectly proportioned.

H. Churchill Mallison

Then the idea blooms— like watching rose pedals opening— I'm amazed at the sheer beauty, genius of it. How fantastic it would be to cast an entire form!

No, that would take up too much room.

Maybe create a mold and just pour the form. No body in it at all. Just, well, like a crystal statute. Of course, it'd just be polycarbonate, but the effect would be the same. I wonder if I could cast my own?

My smooth brow creases as I ponder my reflection in the mirror and the prospect of casting my own image. I shake my head. I don't see how. Takes too long to set the plaster, and besides, how could I get out of it without ruining the mold? Got to be a way.

Anyway, let's not get sidetracked.

At the UCW Championship fight in Indianapolis, he'll be fighting to keep the prize. For a brief moment I feel sagging disappointment, but quickly, I'm buoyed again thinking about the incredulous streak of luck. He's just been handed to me on a silver platter. You know what *they* say, *leave 'em wanting more. Quit while you're ahead.* Ha-ha-ha-ha-ha— quit while you're a_ head_! Die a champion!

"Laser Reygun." His name tastes sweet upon my lips. Six-nine, shoulders wide as a doorway. Trapezius muscles like nobody else in the business. When he flexed the deltoids, biceps, triceps and trapezius, the pectoralis majors— awesome— don't tell me that bastard never took steroids. No way. The definition of torso— flexed transversus clearly divided at the linea alba— a granite statute that rivaled any of the mythic Greek gods.

Maybe I should cast his body...even if I can't pour it for years, I could preserve that incredible form. I'd have to do it before I took the head. But how the hell could... Kill him there? At the apartment?

I don't know. If I stick to the tried and true, I don't have so many problems.

The Wrestler Who Lost His Head

* * * * *

"We *know* it's got something to do with her, but we don't know what it has to do with her. Her apartment was clean as a whistle. Same with the cars. Well, we did find a few drops of blood on the floor of the back seat of one of the cars, but it's her blood type. She said she cut her hand on one of those two-inch copper staples, lifting an awkward box out of the back seat of the car a few months ago. That's how come the blood. Sounds plausible. Reasonable. On the other hand, the blood type of the California victim is the same as hers. So we're running DNAs on 'em. We won't have those results for a while.

"Thought we had enough time before the Indianapolis fight to at least get the DNA reports back. Now this." Jack handed a photocopied memorandum to Ali.

The memo was from a local promoter and mailed to all the wrestlers and interested parties. Apparently an exhibition fight had been scheduled to benefit a special child who was in need of a liver transplant, and the parents were low-middle income class and didn't have medical insurance. Laser Reygun, the current World Heavy-Weight Champion, had agreed to a special performance to raise funds for the cause. Reygun, champion of the children, had three of his own, and was a soft touch when it came to children in distress. The match would be between Laser Reygun and Mister Venus on March 10th at the baseball stadium on Dale Mabry.

Silently Ali and Jack munched on fried chicken and stared at the television screen.

"Humph," Ali huffed and leaned toward the TV-video image. "Look at that guy. Looks like he's blind, doesn't he? Eyes like an albino or something."

"Where?"

"See Gianconni?" Ali pointed. "Well, now look two inches to the left kind of catty-cornered upwards. Black looking hair and...well, white eyes. You ever seen that actress on television?

The brunette with the almost white blue eyes? Looks weird. She plays a lot of psychotic roles because she looks spooky."

Jack studied the man for a moment, then went back to his own ruminating. He changed the tapes.

Ali wiped her fingers on a paper towel. "Think you'll be much longer?" she asked.

Jack checked his watch. Quarter past nine. "Where does the time go? Nah, let's wrap it up after a quick run-through of this tape. It's a short one."

"There she is again," Ali commented.

"Yeah. Once you realize she changes hair with every outfit, she's easy to spot. I can't believe it took us so long to discover that one. Hell, everybody knows you don't ID a woman by the color of her hair! Sometimes we get tripped up by the most obvious things. Don't see the trees..."

Ali watched the video. She turned her head and studied the blow-ups. "Hey, you know?" She fell silent.

Jack shot her a curious look.

She glanced at him, grinned, then said, "So we don't get home until midnight. Mind going back a little?" He rewound the tape, stopping every half second until she said stop. The tape began running again. "Stop!" she jumped a little. "Back just a couple of frames."

"What? What do you see?"

She squinted at the television screen, then turned back to the blow-ups. "There he is again."

"Who?"

"The blind man."

"Honey, what would a blind man be doing at a wrestling match?"

"Oh, I don't mean he's blind, I mean that guy with the albino eyes." She rose from the chair, walked to the screen, and pointed him out. "Can you have him blown up, too?"

"Got a reason?"

"Two different fights, and the same man sitting behind Gianconni. Maybe he's the ex boyfriend?"

"She said she didn't have an ex-anything."

"So maybe he's some guy who's got the hots for her and she isn't interested, so he kills off the competition."

"Is he the only one who shows up twice?"

"I don't know. Let's go back over the tapes again and see. Instead of looking for her, let's search the people in her immediate vicinity and look for repeats? You know, like him, the same person behind her at different fights."

"Let's finish this tape first," Jack suggested.

They watched in silence.

"Look, he's getting up. He's leaving," she said.

"Probably going for a beer or something."

The tape ran on, but the man didn't come back.

"Let's go over the previous tape," Ali said.

"That's the Dome fight, Ali, and that will take us all damned night. Let's go home. It's after ten and I'm bushed. Besides, we both have to get up in the morning." He rose and pulled into his suit jacket. "I'm glad you came by tonight. Not only because I've missed not spending more time with my bride, but because, my dear, you've been a big help. Tomorrow I'll continue this search."

* * * * *

The block set beautifully. Only a couple of air bubbles this time. Each one got better. If only I could get all the air out of the head. Don't want to soak it in water. Maybe alcohol. Formaldehyde stinks too much and I couldn't tolerate the smell. I don't want anything that would interact chemically with the polycarbonate, preventing it from setting properly.

I'm thinking this over while I carry Kaminari Hitore into the living room. Gently I place his block on top of a plain, solid one. I like the individuals to be surrounded by clear blocks, like framing each one with crystal. I have plenty of clear blocks. Now that I have five portraits, I can design a small wall of sorts.

H. Churchill Mallison

Five is a nice number— one in each corner and one in the middle— like the number five dice.

If I can figure out a way to keep all of Laser Reygun, I may just forget about repeating a matching wall on the other side of the dining room entrance, and use his statue instead. But to be frank, I'm not convinced I can preserve an entire body like that. Though, really, why not? I mean, it's air tight, isn't it?

Couldn't I cut the head off first, then place the body in the form, plug in the head, then remove the head later to insert into a block? Wait. Go back. Before that I have to remove the body, just smooth out any defects. While the mold seasons, start making the reverse side. Same steps. I could have the block ready before I even start to save time, so that once I have the front and back molds ready, I can just clean off the head, paint it, and place it straight into the block and pour. Minimum decaying time.

As for the rest of the body, I can just bury it out back with that stupid kid and my Dog.

* * * * *

Ali and Jack said good night to the guard as the guard let them out the front entrance. While Jack walked Ali to her car, he heard another car door open. He looked up in time to see a lanky frame hauling itself from the driver's side of a white Ford Fairlane. Jack recognized him immediately and pulled a face. He hurried back to his car and tried to make a quick get-a-way, but his pursuer knew he'd try that.

"Jack! Jack!" The man ran up to his car and knocked on the window. "Only need a minute."

Jack heaved his shoulders, sighed, and lowered the window. "Come on, give me a break."

"Just a minute? One lousy minute?"

"Don't you guys ever sleep?" Andy, a reporter from the Tribune.

"Guys? What guys? It's only me. One question. Just one question."

"Shoot quick, because I'm exhausted and want to get some sleep."

"Give me something. I already know there's going to be a fund raiser. What are you going to do about that?"

"Andy? What do you think we're going to do about that? We're all going fishing that night, Andy. Hear the reds are running off shore. Go home and get some sleep yourself. Christ. What are we going to do. What the hell..." Jack rolled up the window and started the engine. Andy made faces through the window and tried to get Jack to wait, but Jack didn't buy it.

* * * * *

"God, why do reporters do that?" Ali asked.

"It's called freedom of speech or something like that. They have a right to print whatever they can find out about anything, and damn the consequences. We have an obligation to run a case as quietly as possible so the news media doesn't spook our suspect. It's a royal pain in the ass, and I don't have a solution that doesn't infringe on somebody's constitutional rights. However, if it was up to me, I'd shoot the whole lot of 'em."

Ali slid over next to Jack on the couch and laid her head on his shoulder. He sighed and put an arm around her. In a minute, he started laughing quietly.

"What's funny?"

"I remember one time when I was a teenager. I'd just gotten my driver's license. Had this girl in the car that I'd been hot for since the seventh grade. She'd always ignored me until I got my driver's license and my own car. Fifty-six Chevy. Red and white."

"Thought it was supposed to be a fifty-seven Chevy?"

"Yeah, well, mine was a fifty-six. Anyway, I finally get this girl in my car and we're driving around. After spending all my cash on hot dogs and french fries and cokes, she finally slides

H. Churchill Mallison

over and snuggles. God, I was in heaven. I get so worked up— we're driving down Beach Drive in Clearwater— so I want to show how cool I am. So I turn and kiss her. Here I am trying to kiss her and see where I'm going at the same time. My mouth's like this," Jack screwed his mouth over to one side of his face, then started laughing. "Then what do you think? Here comes the fuzz! I get a ticket! Know what it says? 'Driving while encumbered!' Ha! 'Driving while encumbered!' Well, the judge threw it out saying there was no such offense that he'd ever heard of, but he reckoned I'd gotten the message. I did, all right. That girl told everybody in school."

CHAPTER XXIII

Monday morning hind-sight quarter-backing session of the Task Force. Landers opens the floor. "Anybody got any bright ideas?"

Doreen Jones raised her hand as if she were in a school class room. Being a minority's minority, an African-American female cop from St. Petersburg, one with a hefty dose of common sense, she tended to be politely aggressive as opposed to rabidly equal rights. Whatever worked. Landers' eye contact with her signaled for her to speak up.

Doreen stood up so she'd be heard better. She had one of those high-pitched, wee voices, a comical contrast to her striking good looks. Creamed-coffee skin, shoulder-length straightened hair of enviable quality, definitely African, beautiful features, and an all natural body to die for. She was used to firmly stating her position. "Since we're stuck with a dangerous situation, what with that extra fight being held here and three deaths to our credit already, what about we talk to the likeliest target and get his cooperation?"

Landers answered, "I've been thinking about that. My question is how do we choose the 'likeliest target,' and, suppose the murderer is a wrestler?— then we'd risk picking him and blowing it."

"Well," Doreen Jones added, "let's take a look at who was murdered and what role he'd played that evening. You know, was he always the baby-face or the heel? Did he always win? Was he heavy-weight or middle-weight? See how many common denominators we find."

"Good idea," Landers agreed. "Okay, so lets look at that. Detective Jones, why don't you compile that information for us and get right back to me with it."

* * * * *

H. Churchill Mallison

Doreen collected all the files on her desk and started sorting information.

Bulldog: Horace Muncy. Heavy-weight, mid-level fighter working his way up in the ranks. Bad guy, but underdog in the last fight. Lost.

The Psychiatrist: Emmanuel Thornton. Heavy-weight, mid- to- top level fighter. Sometimes a good guy, sometimes the heavy. This fight, the good guy. Last fight, won.

Long Kong Killer: Johnny Kon. Heavy-weight, lower level but moving up fast to mid-level fighter, and a potential major contender. Bad guy role. Last fight, won.

Billy Bob: Frank Van Allen. Middle-weight. Top of mid-level, but too small to be a heavy-weight contender. Sometimes baby-face, sometimes heavy. Last fight was heavy and lost.

Kaminari Hitore: John Ieyasu. Heavy-weight, major contender for heavy-weight championship. Bad guy. Never an underdog. Last fight, lost.

FUND RAISER MATCH: Main event, Laser Reygun versus Mister Venus.

Laser Reygun: Larry Reagan. Current Heavy-Weight Champion of the World. Baby-face. Always the good guy. Last fight, won.

Mister Venus: Warren Stephens. Mid-level Heavy-weight, on the small end of Heavy-weight status; baby-face, underdog. Won last fight against victim, Hitore.

Doreen studied the list. Okay, so who else was on the card the nights of each of the deceaseds' last fight? Any common denominators there? Back to Bulldog.

* * * * *

Tuesday morning Ralph Landers called another early morning meeting. This time Harry Francesco and Paul Spiegel were invited to attend.

Landers stood at his charts and looked out over the room filled with agents and detectives from all over the Tampa Bay area, and then nodded an acknowledgment to their guests.

They'd tried to smuggle Francesco and Spiegel inside, but the press caught sight of them and had started shooting questions. Landers took a moment to comment that since Mister Francesco and Mister Spiegel were involved with promoting the sport of wrestling, it was natural that they'd seek information from them, and no, there had not been any new breakthroughs. He stressed that any second-guessing by the stations or newspapers could damage chances of apprehending the perpetrator. He preferred that Francesco's or Spiegel's presence at this meeting not be mentioned, and hoped that cooperation from the media would continue.

Harry Francesco, the major international promotor of the sport in the state of Florida, was a former heavy-weight champion himself. The only other man in the room of comparable physical size was Special Agent Jesse Hood. Francesco pushed back on the hind legs of his chair and laced his fingers across his stomach. Probably because he was so tall and so long-legged that sitting on a metal office chair on all fours was just plain awkward. Jesse Hood tended to do the same thing.

"Mister Harry Francesco, here," Landers spoke, "is the promotor for both Laser Reygun and Mister Venus, the main event for the Willis child's fund raiser. What we want to discuss here is whether or not to ask one or both of those two wrestlers to let us use him as a set-up.

* * * * *

Francesco cooperated with Spiegel in planning the card. Spiegel promoted on the lower level, which consisted of beginners. They decided to use his most talented, home-grown newcomers for the warm-up, which would be a good break for a beginner; a good middle-weight match for the lead-in, and then

H. Churchill Mallison

have the main event. Spiegel wanted to include one female match, but Francesco nixed that idea, saying he wanted to use that time for promoting the cause. He agreed that maybe they could use a couple of women wrestlers for that promotion, though. Get a couple who were mothers themselves.

After some negotiating and discussion amongst themselves and a number of wrestlers, it was decided that the card would read: A tag-team match with Da Brain and Mama's Boy versus Alligator and The Lawyer; a high-level middle-weight match with Nippon Ji-Shin versus Spanish Fly; Bella Prunella and Peachy Keene to pitch the campaign for the Willis child along with special guest announcer Mullet Dosier out of Atlanta; and then the main event, Laser Reygun versus Mister Venus. Of course, there'd be short pitches for contributions between each fight, and they could pull up any visiting wrestlers who came to the match to watch and wanted a free plug and a chance to pitch with Muller Dosier.

A local television station, maybe two, would broadcast the fights a week later, but that broadcast wouldn't be announced until after the fight. They need to draw a maximum crowd, then use the footage for a second pitch to the public for funds for the child.

* * * * *

Landers and Francesco met again, this time in Francesco's office at his gym. "How well do you know the people you've set up for these fights?"

"Personally? I only know Larry and Warren...what you'd call *well*. These other players, ah, with the exception of Nippon Ji-Shin, whose real name is...let me think...Oh, yeah, Won Fu, and Spanish Fly, whose real name is Al Gardino. Both Fu and Gardino have done lead-ins for nationwide televised events for us a number of times. I know them, but I don't promote them."

"Can you trust them?"

"Who? Fu and Gardino or Larry and Warren?"

The Wrestler Who Lost His Head

"I'm sorry, I mean...is it Larry and Warren who are the main event? I'm confused," Landers shook his head as if that would shake everything around and it'd settle right side up.

Francesco laughed and scratched a cauliflower ear mindlessly. "Larry and Warren. Laser Reygun and Mister Venus."

"Yeah. Right."

"Do I trust them. Yes, I think I can say uncategorically that I trust them. Both of them are nice men. Larry's married and has three kids, and Warren, who is presently between marriages, is foot-loose, but he's a very decent guy, too. I'd almost stake my life on those two."

"You said 'almost.' What does that mean?"

Francesco gave him a cynical smirk, then his face softened, "As much as anybody can tell about anybody else. I guess the only person who knows his dark side is himself, and maybe half the time, he don't even know."

"So...I'll call them by their stage names because that's the only way I can keep 'em straight in my mind...Laser is married. Mr. Venus, Warren, is single. Way I figure it, Warren is our likely man. Right? The one most likely to be propositioned."

Francesco reared back on his chair and pulled a face. "Oh, not necessarily. Those arena rats go for anybody they can. Care less if they're married or not, so long as the old lady isn't around. Fight like this? Larry's wife might come, might not."

"And if not, then he's game? He usually...screw around?"

"Nah. But that don't stop somebody from trying."

"I really don't want to use a married man. I mean, you know, we'll be right there and nothing is going to happen to the man, but you never know...something could go wrong." Landers' head shook in short, curt no's. "Nah. Rather go with the single guy."

"Suppose she don't go for Warren? I mean, yeah, he's a good looking guy. Former Mister America. But Laser Reygun is far and away the most popular wrestler alive today. Just as good looking, bigger, better... You got an arena rat on the prowl, she'd going for the finest cheese first."

"You think we can talk to both men?"

"Frankly, that's what I'd do. Then whomever she goes for, he's prepared. Knows what to do, what to expect. I don't think you have to worry about either one of them giving away the show. But what makes you think she won't go for one of the other fighters?"

"So far she's been picking someone from the main event, though not necessarily the winner. Naturally, we're keeping our eyes and ears open, watching all of them, but concentrating on the odds. Even if it isn't the woman who's doing the killing, somehow she seems to be connected. Killer could be one of the fighters or...well, anybody."

* * * * *

"That's a whole lot of assumption," Larry Reagan's eyes said these jokers must think he's stupid or something. "You tell me you don't know if she's in cahoots with somebody, or even if she's knowingly connected, and then again, she might be the actual killer."

Jack Robinson couldn't help but smile a little. It did sound absurd on one hand, and perfectly obvious on the other. He assured, "We'll have you covered all the way. From the time you leave your house to go to the stadium. Someone will be in the locker room at all times. We'll also have Warren covered one hundred percent. All we are asking is that if she comes on to you, take her up on it. Let us know you took her up on it, of course. Even if she goes after Warren instead of you, we'll have someone with you throughout the entire evening. And we've got her covered for the entire day and evening of the matches. Someone will be on her tail every breath she takes." He watched Larry for some positive sign.

Larry's cheeks bunched with a grimace and his eyes crinkled into worried triangles. "I've got a wife and kids to think about."

The Wrestler Who Lost His Head

He let out a sad sigh and let his massive shoulders sag as much as they could, which wasn't much. "Hell, I'll go along. But I gotta tell you, I don't like this one damned bit. I'm going along because...what choice do I have? I had a lot of respect for John Ieyasu. You know there was a good chance he'd fight me for the championship? Like it hurts, man, that talent like that is senselessly lost."

"How about you?" Landers addressed this question to Warren Stephens, whose face was riddled with doubt.

Warren straightened up in his chair. "Ahem," he cleared his throat, then his face flickered as numerous false starts raced through his mind. "I guess...like Larry says, what choice do we have? I sure as hell don't plan on quitting the game because some nut's on the loose. You say you think they're being strangled with a garrote by someone hiding in the back seats of their cars? I've got an alarm on my car. Somebody breaks into that, it's going off."

"Do us a favor. Don't engage it that night."

"Some favor. Talk about sticking my neck out." He had to smile at that.

CHAPTER XXIV

Belinda Gianconni stood at her closet staring at the row of costumes, undecided what image she wanted for the evening. She had to be really spectacular. After all, *Laser Reygun*, and if she couldn't get to him, well, Mr. Venus was A-O-kay, too.

She'd tried her damnedest to get on the ring crew for set-up and tear-down so she could get in free and hang out in the dugout. But, despite Boss Perry's promise to use her again, he'd never returned her phone calls. When she approached the crewman she'd bribed before, he told her in no uncertain terms exactly in which warm dark place she could deposit the dough because she'd almost cost him his job.

Gianconni released a sad sigh. This fucking state was too much. In L.A. people didn't act like she was some weirdo from Planet Zork. She fit right in. She loved it out there until someone started following her around, watching her all the time. Finally, the paranoia grew so intense, she had to leave. Hated New York, so that was out of the question. So she decided to try Miami. Same feelings there. Shadows. Like they'd followed her from L.A. The thought occurred to her: she liked sitting with her back to a wall and she liked living on the edges of the country— no way could she stand living in the Plains States.

Now Tampa, too. Shadows. Why didn't people just mind their own business. And unfriendly. Well, she'd known she'd have to figure out how things were done here. Some places were harder to operate in than others. But let me tell you, out in L.A., the crowd loved it when she went after the wrestlers acting love struck. The wrestlers liked it too. This Tampa Bay area ...too...conservative?— is that the word? Some kind of red-neck mentality. Southerners. Who needs 'em. It never occurred to her that Florida's population was about as eclectic as California's.

The Wrestler Who Lost His Head

She swelled with determination and pride. They're just jealous, the women— hell, even some of the men. Well, she was something to envy, so let 'em eat their guts out. She pulled out three suits and looked them over. Needed some new outfits. Wore the red, the blue, the turquoise already. Tonight, the Silver Star routine? Yeah. She hadn't done that one here. Besides, that would go great with either Laser Reygun or Mr. Venus. She'd look like part of the act, like one of the men's managers. Yeah. Demilo, Mister Venus' manager. Hmmm. She liked that. Or René Reygun?— no, René...Star?...Mars?...Destiny? Destiny. René Destiny. Hmmm.

The silvery-white bee-hive wig hid her thick, blond mane, which she'd pinned and then netted for extra hold. Her hair was so heavy it would pull out with just ordinary hairpins. Imitation ruby, diamond and sapphire stars twinkled from a swirl that started at one temple and wound its way to the top of the foot-high hairdo. A matching streak of stars spiraled up one leg, around her torso, and ended in a twin set of bursts over her bosom. The bodysuit had a whitish sheen with silvery highlights, creating a hot glare effect rather than a pewter-silver color. For shoes, she wore clear plastic pumps with sparkling chrome spikes. This was her dress outfit. Special occasions only.

Gianconni pulled the drape aside and peeked out the front window. She could see a small square of street at the end of her driveway, though most of the view was blocked by the overgrown shrubs. She liked the privacy those bushy, fifteen-foot-tall viburnum provided, but at times like this, they hid too much. From where she stood, at least that little bit of street was clear. The only thing visible was a garage door with its wide, opaque fan window of the house across the street.

She opened the front door, looked around, and then locked it behind her. The '79 Impala was parked near the steps. Since the police had torn it apart and put it back together again when they couldn't find anything, she'd taken it to a shop and had it repainted, reupholstered, and detailed to the nth degree. All naugahyde this time, no damned cloth to soak up stains. It had cost a bundle, but still, it was a lot less than buying a newer used car in as good a shape as this one. She'd had it since she'd bought it new and had always taken good care of it. A chill passed over her just thinking about those fucking cops tearing her car up like that. The junker, she didn't care. She kept it for hauling equipment or trash or whatever dirty work she had that she didn't want to use the good car for.

Unlocking the car's door, Gianconni slid inside. She checked the rear view mirror, then started up the engine. Still nothing in the rear view mirror. She shoved the stick shift into reverse and swung the car around in an arc, then pushed into first gear. Slowly she edged to the street, nosing out carefully from the hedge row, and stopped. Looking both ways, she noted there were no cars at all on the street. She sighed relief and pulled onto Riverside.

Gianconni knew they wouldn't let her in through the service dock, so she'd bought a ticket and entered the proper gate. She didn't care what seat she'd gotten because she didn't intend using it. The passageways were mobbed as hordes of people hunted for the gateways to their seats. Finding a snack bar, she stopped long enough to buy two cokes and a box of popcorn. She wove her way through the crowds, heading for the dugout nearest the service gate, figuring that most likely would be the stage entrance for the matches. Some of the wrestling fans did double-takes when she passed by and they bumped into others who were also watching her instead of where they were going.

A guard stood near the dugout turning folks away and directing them to their proper gates. Gianconni approached, avoiding eye contact, having decided the best approach was to simply walk right in as if she belonged. It worked. He took one look at her outfit and the tray of drinks and food and paid her no attention.

She slipped into a maintenance closet and placed the drinks and popcorn on a clear shelf. Taking one of the soft drinks in hand, she left the closet and made her way up the ramp.

The Wrestler Who Lost His Head

The stadium filled rapidly. She watched as the crowd amassed. An occasional stadium cop would notice her, give her a curious, admiring glance, then go on his way. Nobody said anything to her aside from an occasional "Evenin' ma'am."

Though she stayed topside most of the time, she didn't miss much of what was going on below. She saw the wrestlers and their managers, promoters, make-up men going to and from the locker room. This night both the babies and the heels used the same locker room and ramp. Here came some competition— arena rats. Next to her they looked like a pack of mangy rodents, at that. Gianconni knew all about arena rats, but she didn't consider herself one. She considered herself a professional martial arts *sensei*, and thought she'd make an excellent addition to some hunk's act as a manager. She had no earthly intention of ever rolling on a mat with another woman. But one way or another, she was getting in on the big time money scene via somebody's back.

For the opening, world famous announcer— at least in the wrestling and body-building world— Mullet Dosier, entered the ring with his microphone. A number of wrestlers who weren't on the card for the evening came in full dress anyway. Mullet Dosier kept apprised of who had arrived and wanted to make announcements to help promote the cause. He would call them up one at a time, spreading them across the entire evening's program. As each wrestler came up into the ring with Mullet, the wrestler would slip him a card with his data so Mullet would know what to say or do.

"And you are..." Mullet made a big deal out of holding up the card and studying it, as if astonished to see what was written there "...*Dirty* Girty?" He stepped back a little and looked her up one side and down the next. Pulling a face that said he didn't want the likes of her close to him, he remarked, "What on earth are *you* doing up here? This is going to be an evening for kids, Dirty Girty."

"Yes!" she shouted like a Baptist preacher in the throws of ecstacy, "Yes! And I am up here to tell all those folks out there that they ought to thank their lucky stars that they have their health! That their children haven't had to suffer serious defects or debilitating disease. I'm a mother, you know."

A dramatic pause as Mullet continued to size her up, "That's what I hear." His voice implied a mother of quite a different variety.

"Now don't you get too smart with me Mullet Dosier. I know you're supposed to be some kind of big shot up there in Het-lanta, but down here in gator land, you ain't nothing but another *re*-tired wrestler who can't do nothing but run his mouth."

Mullet blew up as if inflated with helium, looked mighty insulted, and said, "Lady, and I use the term loosely, I think you'd better get out of the ring and let somebody— "

"— Now hold on there a minute." She dug in. "I ain't moving until I tell you— tell *all a you*" she waved her arms and spun around, indicating the entire stadium, "what I got to say. Now I know you got that prissy Bella Prunella and that sissy Peachy Keene to come up with you tonight to talk to them folks out there about little Timmy Willis. But you got me all wrong! I'm all heart for that little Timmy Willis. And I'm tellin' *all you folks* that for my next fight, I'm donating all my earnings to the Timothy Willis Fund!— 'Cause I'm not all bad and *I know I can put my money where my mouth is."*

Mullet fell back like he was startled by this sudden revelation that Dirty Girty could do something down right decent. He said, as if in awe, "Why Dirty Girty? That's plumb...that's plumb-tee mighty nice of you! I am impressed. Are you turning over a new leaf?"

"You want something turned over? I tell you what I'll turn over. You get that sissified Peachy Keene up in the ring with me, and I'll turn something over for you. Her leaf! Ha!-Ha!"

A disturbance broke up this interchange as a dazzling white image came striding up the ramp towards the ring. The Arabian Knight. Mullet Dozier turned his back on Dirty Girty and watched the majestic approach of one of the best looking

The Wrestler Who Lost His Head

wrestlers in the business, even if he wouldn't ever make it to the top. Still, the Arab was a crowd pleaser and he'd been booking more and more major network shows as lead-in acts for the main events. Beside him trotted a woman dressed in virtually the same tights, but accessorized differently. He was sequined and draped with a robe; she was bejeweled and capeless, showing off a perfect form.

* * * * *

Gianconni trotted along side The Arabian Knight.

"I thought you said we were going to have a conversation," she said. "Just you look at me. I can help you."

"You help me as it is," he smiled. "And I don't have to pay you."

"I could be your manager. We could put together a killer act."

He stopped and smiled down at her. The audience loved it— was this the beginning of a new ring romance? A smile that would melt granite. Words spoken softly so nobody else but Gianconni could hear it, he said, "I work alone. Feel free to adore me, even kiss the hem of my robe. I'll let you follow me to the ring. But I'm not putting you on my payroll. You can weep and kiss my ring and follow me back to the dressing room. You can kiss my ass, darling, but I will still work alone."

"Okay, that's the way it is," she said, surprisingly agreeable. "What the hay, maybe I can get somebody else's interest when they see me working with you. I want in somewhere and you're a start."

"Just don't get in my way," he kissed her hand while she stared into his hypnotic eyes. She felt her heart leap; he turned his back on her. There was something terrifically threatening about him and it turned her on. She followed him to ringside, holding onto the hem of his beautiful cape, kissing it— well, pretending to. She didn't dare risk getting lipstick on it.

H. Churchill Mallison

* * * * *

Jack Robinson worked his way along the third row. He sat down about four places from the end, by the ramp the wrestlers' would use for their grand entrances. He became immediately engrossed in a hot-dog he held with both hands. With a finger, he poked some escaping pickle relish back into the folds of the bun. Mouth watering, he raised the mustard coated dog to lips, all set to sink his teeth into it. "Excuse me." He looked up and three people filed by. He leaned back into somebody's knees behind him, protecting his hot-dog. He'd commenced another attack on the sandwich when he saw the glittering damsel walking up the ramp sipping from a large paper cup.

At first he didn't recognize her, and if he hadn't been looking for her, figuring she'd be dressed up in some kind of costume, he wouldn't have. Gianconni looked better tonight than he'd ever seen her. The white wig didn't make her look older, it turned her into someone glamorous. That is, if you liked your glamour dolls with muscles. Although, he had to admit, if she wasn't flexing, you didn't necessarily realize just how muscular she was.

* * * * *

While The Arabian Knight kibitzed with Mullet and smiled beautifully for the packed stadium, rotating slowly so everyone could get a good look at him, holding his arms taut at all times to streamline his muscles, Gianconni strutted around the outside of the ring. Occasionally she'd shout instructions to him as if she managed his act. This time she was ringside before Bella Prunella had a chance to show. She saw her coming along the opposite side of the ring. Bella began hissing at her and making clawing motions at her. Gianconni put her palms on her rump, elbows swung back so that her breasts poked out like eyeball-headlights on a sports model racing machine, and took long strides in Bella's direction. Bella hissed louder, baring her long

The Wrestler Who Lost His Head

teeth and longer fingernails, backing up and occasionally giving the audience nervous looks, as if she was scared of Gianconni, but too proud not to put up a hissy.

Both women kept their ears open for cues in the conversation between the Arabian and Mullet Dosier. In order to get away with the sideshow, they had to respect that there were times to knock it off and be quiet. Times such as fighters advertising their upcoming bouts or when Timmy Willis' plight was the topic. Gianconni picked up on a cue and fell quiet and still, leaning against a corner post, listening to what was being said. Bella did the same, though she kept her eye more on Gianconni than she did on the spotlighted business at hand.

Mullet was talking about The Arabian Knight's record. "I gotta tell ya, A-rab, I really felt a lot of disappointment that you let a cream puff like Prince Albert get the best of you in February! Wha— what happened? I mean, boy, he canned you that time!"

"Meester Mullet," the Arabian Knight enunciated with his fake accent, "I am not a man to whimper, but ees a crookeed mash. Thees refereee, ees— how you say?— on ze tek. A com-pew-teir cannot count zes fast!" He gestured to the audience how badly he'd been insulted. "I know zee pipple 'eer, like honest fight! Yes?" He waved, palms upwards, to encourage audience response. They roared a mix of approval and some jeers. A small group of adolescent boys sat in a cluster ringside booing and cajoling. The Arabian walked over to the ropes in front of them, flexed his entire body, and then looked down at his nose at them. "Look at you! All of you healthy boys! I'm glad you come tonight to help out this leetle boy who is not so fortunate! You mek geeft of your lunch money all week?" He turned his back on them and returned to Mullet. "Meester Mullet, I sink we should talk about leetle Timmy Willees and not about how a crookeed referee count me down." He spun and looked around as if searching the crowds for Timothy Willis, "Leetle Timothy Willees, for you! My next match I ween for you and I geef you all ze money I mek from that fight!" Then,

H. Churchill Mallison

snarling just enough to look tough, but not to spoil his handsome features, he said to a middle distance, "And as for you, Prince Albert, I geet you in an honest fight, you leave in your can weeth your feet sticking out ze top!"

A referee came ringside and slid beneath the ropes. He held a quick conference with Mullet, then politely returned to the ropes. Mullet quickly wrapped up his conversation with The Arabian Knight, and then held up his hands for the audience to pay attention. While he announced the first match on the card, the Arabian quietly exited the ring.

Bella Prunella came around the ring as if she intended following the Arab off stage. She feigned great distress when Gianconni glared her down, backed off, and sulkily slunk back to the opposite side of the ring. Gianconni turned and trotted off to catch up with the retreating white knight.

She caught up with him about ten feet from the locker room. "Mister Spilotros," she called in hushed tones. He turned and stared at her as she approached. "Wait just a moment."

"Do not use my real name," he warned.

"I'm sorry. I just wanted to impress you that I do my homework. Can I give you my card?" She slipped a calling card out of her bra, grinning, held out her hand toward him.

"You're stubborn," he said factually.

"I'm a martial arts expert. Black belt. California Women's Champion. I'm not interested in wrestling myself, but I am interested in the managerial end of it. Entertainment— you know, the typical cornball stuff. It's fun. I want to do it. I mean, like tonight? Bella Prunella's finally catching on that we can play off each other and really get the audience going."

"Who's your agent?" he asked.

"Don't have one. Don't know anybody locally. I mean, well, yes, I've picked up a name here and there, but haven't found my way through the doors yet. Maybe you can direct me to somebody? Give me a recommendation?"

"Not interested."

The Wrestler Who Lost His Head

"Oh, come on. You had to start some place, didn't you?" She pushed her brows together and pouted prettily. "Oh, I don't necessarily mean I have to hook onto you. You want to remain a lone wolf, fine. But if you can direct me, maybe I can get in on the ground floor with someone."

"I'll give you a name then you'll go away?" he asked.

"I promise."

"Call Paul Spiegel and maybe he can put you onto somebody."

"How do I find him?"

"If you can read, why don't you try the telephone book?"

She thrust out a hip and planted a fist on it. "What's the matter? You don't like women or something?"

"What I like I get. I don't like solicitors of any sort. I like my privacy." He spun about and disappeared into the locker room.

CHAPTER XXV

Gianconni sighed as she stared at the closed door. Maybe she should try a different tact. She knocked on the door. Nobody answered. She pounded with her fist. A skinny man who looked like an aging Paul McCartney of the '60s Beatles wearing shirt-sleeves and an apron tied about his waist opened the door and stuck an irritable face through the crack. "Yeah? Waddaya want?"

"Tell Mister Spilotros that his...manager from Miami wants a word with him."

The door slammed in her face. She counted. The Arabian opened on the count of seventeen.

Squinting meanly, Spilotros asked her, "So what is it now?"

"I thought I recognized you, but I wasn't sure. The Arabian Knight my ass. In Miami you were Anu the Mesopotamian. Why the change?"

"Look. What do you want from me? I am not taking you on, so what do you want?"

"An introduction."

"To whom?"

"Laser Reygun."

His mouth dropped. "You...I don't *know* Laser Reygun."

"But you are in there with him and you can meet him and you can tell him I'm a professional martial arts instructor and would like to meet him."

"And if I don't."

She shook her head from side to side, knitting her brow as if in deep thought. "You know? The more I think about it, seems like I know you from somewhere else, too."

"Look, Belinda— "

"— Belinda! How the hell do you know my name?" She stepped back, heart thumping a ragtime beat.

He stepped outside the door and closed it behind him. "You just gave me your card. Remember? ...Besides, I already know who you are. I'm an admirer of yours. I remember you from Miami, too." He snared her unwilling eyes with his strangely pale ones and reeled her in. He leaned against the door, his hands behind him, still clutching the door handle. Full lips smiled sweetly, but the expression didn't touch his eyes— eyes like pale, blue diamonds. "I've watched you with the wrestlers. You don't need my help."

"Aw, come on. Is he in there?"

"Look, I'll see. No promises, but I'll see."

* * * * *

Gianconni hung around the tunnel so long she began to wonder if there was an exit from the locker room she didn't know about. Most of the crowd was gone. About the only people left were the ring crew, maintenance personnel, security guards, and a few autograph hounds that, like her, wouldn't give up. Then the door to the locker room opened wide and a noisy group exited. The Arabian Knight left with a cluster of make-up men and local-yokel promoters, businessmen, and the likes. Two seconds later another bunch left with three other fighters and a couple of hounds.

Mister Venus opened the door and immediately, as if from the pores of the cement block walls, four arena rats and a gaggle of fans emerged and descended upon him. He took a moment to sign autographs, then disappeared around the corner with the rats in tow. Gianconni listened to their chatter echoing as they clomped off towards the service exit. Mister Venus, Warren Stephens, cut a fine figure. He could be a doctor or a lawyer dressed in a suit and nobody'd ever guess he wrestled but for his exceptional build. His caramel sun-streaked hair grew thick and he combed it to the side, John Kennedy style. She smirked, feeling disgusted that he'd let those ragged rats cling on him like that.

The tunnel grew so quiet she decided she'd been stood up. The hounds even fell silent.

The locker room door opened once more. Several men stepped out with Laser Reygun. They grouped for one more huddle, then dispersed. The hounds descended upon him like buzzards to road kill. He cheerfully signed autographs and joked a little with his admirers, then told them it was time to go. Like all good folks, he needed his rest, too. Laser Reygun watched them vanish around the corner, then he turned to the lone woman. A broad, handsome grin spread across his face.

"Hope I didn't keep you waiting too long."

A lopsided smile, drooped eyelids, a purr, "I was beginning to think you'd beamed up and took off."

"Wanted everybody out of here. Thought they'd never leave. I'm married, you know, and all those folks know my wife. See?"

"You don't need to explain."

"Been thinking about your offer. Gotta tell you, it's ...interesting."

"You got your costume with you?"

"Yes, I sure do. I like your get-up, too. You look like a bolt of lightening."

"Heat lightening, sugarman. Mister Laser Rey *Gun*." Eyes smoldering. She was already so aroused she could have eaten him alive right there in the tunnel. Would have, too, if he'd said the word. She let her gaze fall to his crotch, then travel slowly upwards again until her eyes locked on his deep marine aquas. She walked up to him and pressed her body full length against his. She felt his response as she rubbed him with her belly. He was so tall he made Gianconni feel delicate.

She tilted her face up and stared deeply into his eyes which grew hazy with lust. Laser grasped the nape of her neck with one hand and pulled her tightly to him. His lips crushed hers. The canvas flight bag thumped to the floor at his feet.

She undulated against his muscular thigh and felt the straining bulge pressing against the softness of her belly. He grabbed her ass and hiked her higher on his leg. She swung her leg over his and climbed him like a tree.

The Wrestler Who Lost His Head

She bucked; he buried his face in her bared cleavage. She nuzzled his neck and bit him, but not hard enough to leave a mark. Then he took both hands, grasping her at the waist, and slid her up his torso until he had her almost over his head. She wrapped both legs around his neck and he puffed hot air into the waiting divide, then raked his teeth across the meeting of the four seams. Lifting her again, he let her slide down his body. Then he stepped back from her.

Panting, flushed with heat, he managed a chuckle. "This is hardly the place. I follow you?"

"Yes."

Gianconni spun on her heels and began swinging those hips as she sallied down the tunnel to the service exit. Like an eager puppy, he followed.

* * * * *

She leaned against her front door jamb, one arm stretched along the frame above her head, the other at rest along the slow curve of her body. A hand splayed suggestively on the inside of her thigh. While she watched him get out of his car and retrieve the flight bag with his costume, she stroked her thigh and ran her hand up her body and to her breasts. He came to her at the doorway, crushing against her. His mouth sought hers, then trailed down her neck. Both hands squeezed and tugged at her breasts while he licked them. Her tights were too tight for him to free them, but that didn't stop him from trying.

She gave a mighty shove and pushed him away.

"No. Get your costume on. You want it, you fight for it."

He tried to nuzzle up to her again, but she slapped him hard against the face. He adjusted his pants, thought for a second, then backhanded her. She stumbled into the house. He shut the door behind him.

Gianconni felt her way to the bedroom door and flipped the switch to a small lamp inside the room. He'd stayed behind at

the entrance, unable to see where to go in the darkness. She made a silhouette in the lighted framework of the bedroom door.
"Change there," she instructed.
"Here?" he asked, surprised.
"There. Then come into my room. I'll be waiting for you."
"You don't have a bathroom where I can change?"
"Just do it there. You can use the bathroom later."
"Okay, if you say so."

* * * * *

Jack had looked at every single face of every single person in the sections surrounding the dugout, looking for the white-eyed man who inevitably popped up in close proximity to Gianconni at these wrestling matches. No one fitting that description sat in this area. He spent the entire evening searching. People constantly walked up and down the aisles going to the rest rooms or a snack bar, some left, late ones arrived. He watched the vendors as they slowly worked each row of benches; he noted the face of every security person or maintenance man. No white-eyed man.

Special Agent Allen Tolliver contacted Jack by radio as soon as he and his troop of people left the locker room and he'd gotten back to his car. Tolliver, a body-builder himself, had remained inside the locker room for the duration of the fights, and then left with Mister Venus, Warren Stephens.

"All clear here. I'm going home with Mister Stephens and put him safely to bed. I'll contact you when I'm through there."

"Ten-four. By the way, you didn't happen to see a man with funny looking eyes, you know, kinda albino-looking? Real, real pale eyes? Gives him a bit of a strange look? Dark hair, though," Jack asked. "Anybody like that in the dressing room maybe?"

"Nah." Silence. Then Tolliver spoke up again. "Hey, you know? Except for...ever take a good look at The Arabian Knight? Good looking guy— well, I think the women find him

The Wrestler Who Lost His Head

good looking. Anyway, he has black hair and real pale eyes. Like *real* pale eyes. Looks strange as hell."

"The Arabian Knight?" a hushed tone to Jack's voice; he felt jolted. "Jeez...anybody tailing him?"

"Uh...no. We just covered the men who were on the card to wrestle. The Arabian was just a show. You know how they come all decked out in case they can get some publicity."

"Shit."

"Why? You think he's got something to do with this?"

"I don't know, but I damned sure want to find out. It feels right."

"So what do you want me to do?" Tolliver asked.

"Nothing. Just go on as planned. I'll get ahold of Landers and pass the info on to him. See if he can check him out." Jack clicked off, then placed a call for Landers.

* * * * *

Paul Spiegel said, "No way. You gotta be kidding. Anatole Spilotros? He's one of the nicest...he's a gentleman, for God's sake. I never heard him say a bad word about anybody. Jealous? Of who? True, he isn't big enough to make it to the top, but he's as good as they come in the middle-weights. Gets plenty of television coverage. Makes decent money now. Good enough money so's he don't have to hold down a full time job anymore."

"Who does he hang with?" Landers asked.

"Nobody I know of. Isn't married. Don't know of any girlfriends in particular. Guarantee you, though, that boy ain't gay."

"Well, for now, just give me his address. We'll worry about his character or sexual orientation later when we've got time for philosophical discussion. Know what he drives?"

"Okay. Okay. Let me see."

Landers waited restlessly, knowing that Spiegel was flipping through records at his end of the telephone line to find the address.

"Okay, here it is. Anatole Spilotros, Route twelve, Box one-nineteen-twenty-three, Zephyrhills."

"Where the hell is Route twelve? You don't have a street or road name?"

"'Fraid not."

"What does he drive?"

"Drive?"

Silence. Landers could almost smell Spiegel thinking.

"Sometimes he drives a beat-up van, but I don't know what make it is. White, I think. And he drives a VW Rabbit. I don't know what year."

"Thanks." Landers hung up without waiting for a response.

Landers sat at his desk for a moment thinking. He'd recently met a Postal Inspector at a friend's house. The inspectors knew who the Postmasters were and had the authority to roust 'em out of bed any time they wanted. He telephoned his friend, who didn't sound too friendly since he'd already gone to bed.

Landers placed a phone call to Hank Dorey. The CID Postal Inspector took a little convincing, but finally he agreed to look up the Zephyrhills Postmaster and get him down to the Post Office. Forty minutes later Dorey rang Landers. "We're here. Got the address registration card in my hand," he said. "Got a pencil? You want to take these detailed directions down exactly, or you'll never find this place."

* * * * *

"Off Morris Bridge Road. Now read 'em back to me so I know you got it right," Landers spoke to a Pasco County Sheriff Deputy. He listened as the young man read back the directions. "Right. Get on it. Stay in radio contact."

* * * * *

A Pasco County sheriff's car drove slowly along Morris Bridge Road, nearing the Pasco-Hillsborough county line and the back door to the University of South Florida. Solid ground gave way to mostly swampy savanna in an area that became a confusion of feeder streams. The deputy almost missed the gravel turn off, and then later, the postal box, a rusted black standard issue that was nearly invisible in a stand of weeds.

A dirt drive led to a small house set back from the road about a hundred feet or so. A scraggly forest of water oaks and scrub pine, thick with thistles and the usual underbrush, surrounded the property. At one a.m., it was mighty dark and he wasn't too happy with the prospects of investigating that spooky looking little bit of a place.

He slowly pulled the squad car into the drive, stopping as soon as his headlights fell squarely on the house. Pulling out a search light, he ran its beam over the grounds. The deputy picked up the mike, speaking quietly. "This is Alpha-Lima-Tango two-eight. My ten-twenty is Morris Bridge Road near Blackwater Creek and the Hillsborough River in the middle of snake country. Ten sixty-five?"

"Copy," the dispatcher's voice seemed as friendly as a mother's when a kid wakes up in the middle of the night with monsters hiding in the closet.

"So far nada. No vehicles in sight. I'm going around to the back. Ten twenty-three."

"I'm here," the dispatcher responded. Wasn't much action around Zephyrhills evenings; he wasn't exactly under a strain trying to keep up communications.

The deputy put the car in gear and let it drift along on its hyped idle position, which kept it moving about three miles an hour, unless he had a little upgrade every now and then. No way was he getting out and walking around if he could circle the house in the car. He kept the spotlight trained on the ground ahead of the car to make sure he didn't run over something that might blow a tire or damage the underside.

H. Churchill Mallison

Coming along side the house, he braked and ran the light over the walls. One window towards the front, none from about half way back all the way to a kitchen door. Then a kitchen window. The pool of light slid down the back door, across the small threshold, then along a worn path that crossed the back stretch of ground all the way to the encroaching forest beyond. The light pool skirted the path until it highlighted a wire burning barrel where the owner disposed of his trash.

The ground was clear enough for easy driving, so he continued around. He noticed by the worn turf and weeds that the owner also parked his vehicles in the back sometimes. But none were in sight. He continued his circuitous examination of the grounds and the house's exterior.

"Come in," he spoke into the mike with more confidence.

"Ten-four."

"Ten-five FDLE Clearwater Field Super Landers that there's no vehicles at the site. No sign anybody's home. Somebody does live here, though. Request further instructions. Ten-four.

"Ten-four."

Now that he'd driven around the house and found it deserted, his courage bolstered. He drove to the kitchen entrance again, parked with the lights trained on the door, and got out of the car with a flashlight.

What was that stain trailing down the steps towards the path? Looked like spilt blood or something. Whatever, someone had tried to clean it up and hadn't done a very thorough job.

* * * * *

Landers put out a call to all men. "All units, keep a look out for man with black hair, light blue eyes, very strong and possibly armed. Driving a white 1970 Ford van, license plate HCG six-one-eight or a blue VW Rabbit, ah, 1978, tag HLM four-nine-two. Name Anatole Spilotros, a.k.a. The Arabian Knight. Pick up for questioning. Use restraint if possible."

The Wrestler Who Lost His Head

* * * * *

The deputy tried the back door. Locked. He'd expected that, but one never knew. Stooping down, he took a closer look at the rust-colored stains absorbed into the raw cement steps. His eyes followed a worn path.

Then he heard something rustling at the edge of the woods. He looked from the forest's edge to his car and back to the trees again. Heart thumping wildly, he opted for the car and jumped inside. He grasped the spotlight and turned it in the direction of the sound.

At first nothing. Then that strange ultra-red glow from animal eyes shown like hovering fireflies with a broken light switch. Two sets. No, three. Coons? Eating from an illegal garbage dump, probably. Still. He radioed for backup. "Something's back there in the woods and coons are eating it. I don't like this. Looks like a trail of blood from the kitchen, too."

"Now don't tell me you're afraid of a raccoon!"

"You so brave, you git your ass out here and go back into that black woods by yourself with something slurping and slobbering back there. Not me, buddy. Not on your life."

CHAPTER XXVI

Ed Tolliver rode with Jack Robinson along Riverside. They passed Gianconni's and kept on going.

Maddy Ulner sat on the hood of her car, which she'd backed into the Newton's garage. Mister Newton kindly removed his Oldsmobile around to his back yard to make room. The Newtons had been more than willing to cooperate with the police. The police almost had to drag them off to a hotel for the night, they were so excited by the unfolding mystery they'd wanted to hang around and see what was going to happen.

Maddy was in position an hour before Gianconni had left for the matches. She finished a spy thriller; ate a large pizza and drank a quart bottle of cola over the course of four hours. Fortunately, the Newtons had been considerate enough to leave the door from the garage to the kitchen open so she could use the microwave and the bathroom.

* * * * *

She's gone already. I drove by Belinda's. I passed her house nervously thumping my chin with my fist. Knowing I'd made a stupid decision, I still felt determined to take him home this time and not leave him somewhere to be found. Anybody but Laser Reygun or Mister Venus. Either one of those bodies...I began working on the details again of how I could cast the entire thing and also use the head for one of the blocks.

Before I hadn't really had a *blood* problem because it was all left in his car or around it, and I didn't track any home with me. This way, I'd absolutely ruin my van. That meant I'd have to dispose of it. Drive it off somewhere in a swamp and burn the thing. No, better yet, ditch it into one of those bottomless phosphate pit lakes. It would never be found. Shit, and I'd have to ride a bicycle all the way back, so it would have to be only

The Wrestler Who Lost His Head

twenty or thirty miles away. God, creativity could get complicated.

There. I see a place to stash the van. Back of a dead strip shopping center on Armenia. It had a ten foot cement sound barricade separating it from its neighbors to the rear that would muffle any sounds and hide my actions. I parked it and locked it, then began walking up the street. Found a Winn Dixie; bought a week's supply of groceries. Called a taxi to take me home.

Took my time getting ready for the fund raiser. Had to be at my best tonight. Every time I put on the white tights I feel a surge of power.

I use a lot of black eyeliner so that my unusual eyes stand out. Look at my eyes? Aren't they really great? It's the eyes that set me off from everybody else, don't you think? They're like...like water. No, not blue! Oh, there's a hint of blue, like the blue sky diluted by sheer white clouds. They do look like an albino's eyes, but I'm not an albino. And they may look weak to you, but I've got keen eyesight. My mother had one blue eye and one brown one. My father had pale eyes like mine. Not quite as pale as mine, but almost.

You might say I'm vain. Well, yes. I am. When I enter the ring, people adore me. Women lust after me. Do I like women? No, not really. But I don't...frankly, I don't give a damn about women one way or another. Gay? Don't be ridiculous. No, I wouldn't say I'm sexually attracted to men, but...well, when I do these things. Maybe it's just the adrenaline, the excitement.

I mean, if I was sexually attracted to men, wouldn't I get some kind of turn-on from the body contact when wrestling? No, what turns me on is beating them on the mat— showing 'em who's boss— over-powering 'em.

I watch Gianconni when she throws these muscular, tremendously strong men down on the mats flat on their backs. Sometimes I get inside; sometimes she doesn't close the shades. She gets 'em by surprise. And they let her get away with a lot.

*   *   *   *   *

She stood in the middle of the bedroom. Laser gaped. The entire room was one gigantic bed. Mats from wall to wall. This nutty broad slept on the floor mats? Three doors. The one he stood in, a closet door, and one to the bathroom.

"What's this?" he asked, though he knew.

"My play pen," she didn't smile. She bowed a *rey* to him, then let out a shriek and flew at him so fast she caught him completely off guard. He caught a foot on his chin and stumbled back, stunned.

"Whoa!" he blurted.

"I told you I want a fight," she warned.

With a sheepish grin, he half raised his arms as if in defense. She began prancing around him.

"Look," he said, dropping his arms.

As soon as his arms dropped, she flew at him. This time he responded, catching her wrists. He made the mistake of looking her in the eye and she kicked him a good one on the shin. With exasperation, he whipped her around and scooped her up, holding her like a sack of potatoes over his hip. She thrashed around a bit, then he threw her to the floor and pounced on top of her. He sat square in the middle of her torso and planted her arms to the ground with his hands.

"I'm trying to talk to you. Think you can relax here a minute?" he asked reasonably.

"Yeah? About what?" she challenged, eyes alight with excitement.

"I...I can't go through with this."

Her body went flat with shock and she stared up at him. After a second to absorb what he'd said, she grunted, "Huh?"

"I can't go through with this. I'm sorry. I shouldn't have come."

"Oh, give me a fucking break," she snarled, sounding angry instead of disappointed.

The Wrestler Who Lost His Head

"Hey, I mean, this sounds great, but I'm...I'm about as married as a man can get. I can't go through with this."

She rolled her eyes, sucked her teeth, then tried reasoning with him. "I'm HIV negative, sweetums, and I have a current card to prove it. And I don't have any designs on you outside of tonight. Come on. One for old time's sake."

"What old time's sake? You know what the problem is? You're coming at me with all this karate shit and I see my ten-year-old kid when he wants to play rough. We wrestle like this. Me and my ten-year-old!"

Gianconni sank into the mat. She wished she'd sunk through the mat and vanished. Falling utterly limp, she droned, "Well I fucking well can't compete with a ten-year-old, can I." It wasn't a question. "So get the hell up and get the hell out."

Laser glanced at his watch. He hadn't stayed long enough; the cops wanted him to kill at least half an hour. "Say, you think we could have a cup of coffee or something?"

"Do what?"

"A glass of water? I...I really didn't mean to hurt your feelings, Belinda."

A smile touched her eyes for just a second, then they went cold again. "Don't sweat my feelings, Laser Reygun. Hey, I got more out of the famous man than those autograph hounds. You kiss as good as you look like you do. And that over the head thing?— remember in the fucking tunnel at the fucking stadium? You forget that already? You sure you want to go home?"

He swung free of her flattened body and rose to his feet, extending a hand to help her up. His eyes told her all she needed to know: no go, babe-o.

Eyes to the ceiling said to him that she thought he was naive and stupid, but hey, so okay. "Tell you what you can do for me though." A thought brightened her smile. A faint rise of his brow asked what. She responded: "I need in. I want to get in on an act. Not to wrestle. That's not my goal. I want to manage a fighter. You know, come on like Shelly Sheela and Cheetah-Man."

H. Churchill Mallison

Grinning like he didn't really mean what he was about to say, he asked, "This like blackmail or something?"

"No, no," her face drew in like she smelled something terrible, then she said, "I'm not into that, Laser. I'm asking you for a favor. You don't want to oblige me, then fine. Go home. Without a fucking cup of coffee. But you help me," impishly, "I'll make you the best cup of instant caffeine you ever drank."

* * * * *

I see— hear actually— that things are progressing nicely and right on schedule.

I slip around the overgrown hedges quietly. Looking over his car from the deep shadows, I wonder if he has one of those car alarms. Everyone now-a-days hooks those awful things up and you can't even get close to the damned cars without the alarm going off.

I take the lock jock out of my back pocket, ready to slide it down between the window and the door and open it. I try the handle, set to run like a son-of-a-bitch if the alarms went off, but it doesn't. The driver's door isn't even locked, which is nice. But on the flip side, the car's a T-frame two-door.

I quietly open the door and pull the seat forward. Buick Riviera T-frame coupes don't have a lot of leg room in the back and he has the seat pushed back as far as it will go. I groan. Hoping he won't notice, I ease the seat up a notch or two, then wedge myself in the back. Thank God it's dark as Satan's hell outside.

* * * * *

Maddy Ulner watched the house. Then it hit with all the urgency of a digested A-bomb! *Oh, shit*! she thought as her head frantically turned from the garage window and the kitchen door and back again. The urge struck again, and this time it was answer the call of nature or have a very embarrassing disaster.

The Wrestler Who Lost His Head

She bolted for the kitchen door, flung herself down a short hall to the guest bathroom and barely got her pants off in time.

Whew! That was close!

As rapidly as possible, Maddy returned to her post. Guilt assaulted her. She should have known better than to finish off that entire pizza! But these watches were *so* boring. Ha. Well, at least she wouldn't have to double up on her gym time next week to work it off!

Studying the little square view of the house across the street, she didn't see anything different. Larry Reagan's Riviera, appearing undisturbed, still waited in front of Gianconni's.

* * * * *

The front door opened.

Maddy saw Gianconni and Larry Reagan standing in the frame, back-lit by a dim glow. They stood there talking for a few minutes. Then Larry descended the steps and walked over to his car. With his hand on the door handle, he turned back and was still talking to Gianconni.

Maddy reached inside her car and pulled the mike through the opened window so she could talk on the radio and still keep an eye out the garage's fan window.

"He's getting in the car," she said.

Tolliver responded to the call while Jack drove. Jack immediately swung over to the side of the road, let a car pass, then made a U-turn and headed back, speeding up as he drove.

"See anybody get in the car before him?"

"No."

"No? Could you possibly have missed it?"

Silence.

"Ten sixty-five?" Tolliver asked.

"I copy you. I had to go to the toilet a few minutes ago."

"Oh, for chrissake!" Tolliver shouted into the mike.

Maddy withered inside a little, knowing he was fully justified at being miffed. "Sorry, but it wasn't a choice."

"How long were you gone?" he barked.

She paled and spoke to the ceiling somewhere above her in fathomless darkness, "Maybe five minutes."

"What's happening right now?"

"He's standing at the car door talking to her. She's in the doorway of the house. Uh, he just opened the door. Oh shit. Where are you?"

"Close but not near close enough. You stay there and watch Gianconni. She leaves, you tail her. Tell me which way he turns."

"Gianconni just went back inside."

* * * * *

Larry opened the Riviera's door. It was immediately obvious to him that the seat had been moved and his heart started pounding painfully against his ribs.

Oh, God, please protect me. Just in case we screw this up, please forgive me for all the stuff I've done wrong and watch over my family.

He tried to swallow but his throat was so dry it ticked. He ran his tongue around the inside of his mouth, trying to stir up a little saliva, but he was dry as a mummy's kiss.

He tried to see in the back without really looking, and he'd swear he saw a black hump. But how much could you really see in the all-black interior in an all-black night.

He leaned down and tried the electric seat control to see if the seat would go back any further. The least he could do was make the son-of-a-bitch uncomfortable. Assuming, of course, there was somebody in the back. It didn't budge. He snorted a nervous laugh and thought of all those horror movies he'd seen as a kid. Chain-saw Massacre— stuff like that. Trying very hard to act normally, he quickly shot a glance at the surrounding tree-like bushes, wondering where in God's name all the cops were who were supposed to be charging in here right about now to rescue him and catch the murderer.

The Wrestler Who Lost His Head

Stall.

He turned his back to the door and leaned his rear end inside just enough to sit on the edge of the driver's seat, then he bent forward to tie his shoe. He tried to peek through his underarm to see if he saw something in the back, but again, just solid black. Too fucking-solid black. His hands began to tremble.

Where the hell are they?

Then he heard the garage door open across the street. He knew they'd positioned someone inside there to watch— at least that's what they'd said. Feeling better immediately, Larry sat up straight. He took a deep breath and swung his legs inside the car. A pause. Nothing. He started up the engine and punched on the headlights. Nothing. He put the car in reverse and swung in an arc, then headed toward the street. He stopped at the edge of the drive and stared straight into the open garage door ahead of him. He could see a Pontiac's front end in his headlights, but he didn't see any cops. If the officer was inside the car, Larry couldn't tell it.

Larry couldn't help it, he felt so frightened he thought for sure he'd pee his pants. He kept one hand flat across his neck, hoping that if someone suddenly garroted him, they'd catch his knuckles instead of his throat.

He felt a bump against the back of his seat, but before he could respond, a cold voice instructed.

"Don't get cute. I've got a three-fifty-seven magnum aimed right at the base of your skull. Don't reach back with your hands. Put both hands on the steering wheel and keep right on driving like you are."

Larry's eyes flashed to the rear view mirror. All he saw was a large silhouette. And no headlights— no fucking lights at all— following him.

CHAPTER XXVII

Maddy spoke into the mike. "Larry Reagan turned south on Riverside and turned west at the first corner. I didn't see anyone inside with him."

Tolliver responded: "All cars be on the lookout for an eighty-three Buick Riviera, silver, license plate Lima Alpha Sierra Echo Romeo. The driver may have an armed and extremely dangerous kidnapper with him. Car last seen driving west on Peru off Riverside heading towards Armenia.

"Take all precautions not to harm the driver, Larry Reagan. Identification of suspect kidnapper unknown at this time, but may be a professional wrestler. Stay in radio contact."

Jack whipped the little blue Skylark around the corner onto Peru and gunned it.

A static burst on the radio, then O'Leary's voice came through. "Got him. Man in the back seat of the car. Can't see what he's up to, but he's directly behind the driver. Turning south on Armenia."

Tolliver spoke, "Go straight on through the intersection if someone else can pick him up."

"I see him." Doreen Jones' voice cut in.

"Don't get too close," Tolliver warned her. Jack pulled onto Armenia and tried to close up the distance. "Follow him until I tell you to turn off, then run parallel to us when I've got him. When we close in, I want you there in seconds.

"He's slowing down," she said. "Pulled over on the side of the street. I'm passing him. Can't see what he's up to without being obvious. Anybody got him?"

"I see him." Tolliver said as they caught up to within a block and a half of him. Jack pulled to the curb and doused his lights. Tolliver got out of the car and took a walk to one of the darkened buildings. He stood in the shadows watching Jack while Jack watched the car up ahead.

The Wrestler Who Lost His Head

Jack shouted, "Get in! He's moving again." This time Jack left his headlights off for a few minutes, driving up the parallel parking lane, hoping to attract less attention. He turned them on after he let the car get a half block's distance further ahead since there was no traffic on the street at this hour and he wanted the killer as relaxed as possible.

The Riviera's tail lights flashed. Larry Reagan hit the break three times, then turned into and drove behind a deserted strip shopping center.

"Hit it!" Tolliver shouted into the mike. Everybody, surround the Armenia Short-Stop Athletic Mall. Pronto!"

"No siren yet, let's get there fast and quiet."

Jack gunned it.

* * * * *

"Pull over by the curb," the man said.

Larry saw the man's eyes in the rear view mirror. Those eyes locked onto his in the reflection.

"I know you..." Larry said.

"Tough for you," the man replied.

Larry started to turn around, but the man swatted the back of his head with the barrel of the pistol.

"One more move like that and I'll kill you right here."

"You're The Arabian Knight! What the fuck— you crazy man?"

"Just do what you're told and never mind the essays." Anatole Spilotros slid from directly behind Larry enough so he could look out the back window and still keep an eye out if Larry made any sudden movements. He watched for a few minutes. "Okay, go on."

"Where?"

"Just keep going until I tell you to turn. You're going to turn right, so stay in the right-hand lane. Keep it slow."

Larry drove on. He felt stunned that the killer was The Arabian Knight, a wrestler who had everything going for him!

His mind was torn from fear of dying and shock that this man in the back seat was one of his fellow athletes.

"Mister Spilotros..."

"I said no essays, so shut up. Start slowing up." Spilotros looked out the rear window again, then said, "Turn in here. Go around back."

Larry began sweating profusely.

"Pull up next to the van."

He pulled his Riviera along side the van.

"Turn off the engine and douse the lights."

Spilotros kicked the passenger's seat back forward with a foot, then leaned on it and opened the passenger's door, all the while facing Larry and aiming the gun at his face. "Both hands on the wheel. You flicker a fucking eyelash and I'll blow your jaw out, then I'll blow your nose off, then I'll take out one fucking eye at a time. Got that?"

Cops? Cops? Larry's eyes locked onto those weird white eyes and felt himself go a little insane with terror. He recognized a soul of ice in those glacial white eyes, not a hint of humanness. Trapped by a demon from hell. He saw no remorse; he saw no sympathy. He saw lust.

Spilotros managed to extradite himself from the back of the car while never taking his eyes or the point of the pistol off his victim. He pushed the seat's back to its upright position.

"Slide over here nice and slow-like and get out on this side."

Spilotros backed up in direct proportion to Larry's movement towards him, keeping at a safe distance. Once Larry swung his feet to the ground and pulled himself upright using the car's door for assistance and balance, Spilotros backed up to his van. Using his left hand, Spilotros felt around on the van's back double-swinging doors and slid its bar latch free of its hasp. "Get in and sit down with your back to this door."

"You nuts? I'm not getting in that van."

"Oh, you're getting in it. One way or the other. You cooperate and maybe you'll live to tell about it," he lied. *Give 'em just enough hope to make this easier.* "Give me any crap and you're dead Mister Laser Rey*gun*. Don't make me no nevermind."

Explosion— Screaming sirens, whopping tires against the curbs, screeching rubber— seven cars careened into the shopping mall's vacant parking lot from both ends, sliding around the corner to the back, blocking the van and the two startled men.

* * * * *

Time all but stopped! Laser Reygun's head rotated to the north, then south when the cops burst upon the scene. In that flash reaction, he'd lost his advantage letting the cops distract him. He felt his torso retract, expecting an explosion from the .357 magnum.

With a roar that came all the way from the soles of his feet, Laser Reygun went ballistic before he'd even had time to correct the turn of his head and focus on his enemy. His peripheral vision saw The Arabian Knight's reflex action was a hair slower than his.

His mass knocked The Arabian off balance and the two crashed to the pavement. The Arabian hit the ground rolling in a tumbled tangle of limbs, with Laser ending up on top, astride him. Laser struggled to grab the wrist of the hand with the gun, but The Arabian Knight held him back. His left arm ram-rod straight against Laser's chest, he held him at bay long enough to shove the steel barrel up Laser's nose.

"Move, fucker," The Arabian warned, dead eyes burning into Laser's. "You go with me, hero, so don't get excited." He cut his eyes to the side, making contact with a set of equally cold grays.

Jack Robinson fixed on those white eyes. He stood, feet spread, not three feet away with his .9 millimeter aimed right between Spilotros' eyes. Neither one of them blinked.

"You got about twenty eager guns aimed right at your head, Spilotros."

H. Churchill Mallison

"You breathe and I blow this fucker to smithereens," The Arabian sneered.

* * * * *

Laser's mind snapped back from it's shock. Time sequence normalized. He stared wide-eyed down the length of the .357 which pushed his nose up as far as it would go without driving it into his cringing brain. Spilotros' eyes had fixed on a cop to his right, but his head hadn't budged an inch. Astride The Arabian's chest, he felt his opponent's knees pulled tightly against his back. Wedged between those powerful legs and that cold barrel, Laser was off balance and couldn't hold this position forever. The slightest movement and Spilotros would blow his brains all over hell and back. He knew he was dead if the cop shot— Spilotros would pull the trigger in reflex. He knew he was dead if he so much as trembled. He knew he'd just run out of options.

A surge of power and his arm sliced across Spilotros' chest, caught Spilotros at the elbow, jackknifing his arm. The gun exploded.

Laser's eyes and mouth O'ed with surprise and he reared up, grabbed his bosom, and toppled over.

Before the stunned officers could react, The Arabian threw the man aside, rolled him onto his stomach, and flung himself astride his back. He grabbed Laser by the hair and pulled his head back, jamming the pistol against the base of his skull, holding, as if waiting for a count of three.

The circle of cops closed in. By now, six more cars had crammed into the narrow space between the mall's back wall and the sound barrier, adding to the barricade of vehicles and drawn weapons.

Spilotros' unblinking stare still held Jack's as he dismounted his victim and tried to drag him to his feet by his hair. But Larry Reagan laid limp as a dead mackerel. Spilotros put his first two fingers of his left hand at the pulse point on Larry's neck and realized he was still alive if not conscious. He worked his arm underneath the inert body to get a grip on it.

"Tell 'em to hold their fire, hero," he said to Jack, "or this guy will be dead. All-a-you! Back off!"

Nobody moved.

"Back off or I shoot. What I got to lose?"

The cops understood that and the circle retreated a couple of steps, but nobody put their weapons away. That is, everybody but Jack.

"You," he said to Jack, "get his feet. *Get his fucking feet!*" Spilotros had raised Larry's limp body waist high, but his dead weight, and him having to lift with one arm, proved too much. "Help me get him in the van."

Keeping the gun at Larry's head, Spilotros and Jack half carried, half dragged the body to the rear of the truck. Spilotros propped Larry's upper body against the van's floor, then aimed his pistol at Jack while he hiked himself into the van. Now keeping a bead on Jack, he instructed. "Roll him inside."

Jack struggled with the limp body, but couldn't manage it alone. "Need some help."

Spilotros glanced around at the cops right behind Jack who still held their weapons on him. "You," he pointed his pistol at O'Leary, "throw down your weapon and help this guy get Reygun in the van."

O'Leary and Jack lifted Larry's body onto the lip of the van's floor and rolled him inside.

Spilotros waved the pistol at O'Leary and ordered, "Get back. You tell your buddies to clear a path for me and let me drive out of here, or this guy and your cop-friend here are dead right along with me."

To Jack, he said, "Get in. No, clown, after you throw your pistol away. You think I'm stupid?"

Jack climbed into the back of the van. Spilotros ordered, "Face against the wall. Spread 'em!" Holding his gun on Jack, Spilotros ran a hand down one side of his body and then the other, looking for hidden weapons. He found a small pistol strapped to his ankle, pulled it and threw it out. Holding Jack by the collar, he backed away an arm's length, let go, then edged backwards towards the front of the van. "Okay, hero, pull Reygun into the van, shut the doors, and latch 'em from the inside. Don't get cute."

Jack put his hands under Larry's arm pits and struggled, dragging him deeper into the van so that he lay lengthwise to the floor. He walked to the opening, bent almost double due to the low ceiling, and looked out at O'Leary and the circle of expressionless faces that hid a palpable aura of fear.

O'Leary locked his eyes on Jack's. Maddy Ulner shouted the order: "Clear a path. Let'em through and hold your fire."

"Tell 'em if one fucker follows me, you're dead even if you're driving a hundred fucking miles an hour. Then get your ass up here in the driver's seat."

Jack reached out for one of the two hinged doors. Looking at O'Leary, Jack emoted in a voice far stronger than he'd expected: "Do not follow us. You do, he shoots me regardless of how fast I'm driving. I repeat, do not follow." He swung the door closed and reached out for the other one. To O'Leary, he said, "Seriously, Joe. Don't."

The second door slammed home and Jack dropped the latch into its hasp.

The Wrestler Who Lost His Head

CHAPTER XXVIII

Jack crawled forward and climbed into the driver's seat. He expected Spilotros to take the passenger's seat, but he didn't. Instead, he knelt behind Jack and gripped him by the nape of his neck in a hand as strong as a steel vise. The other hand crammed the .357 painfully into the base of his skull.

"Easy, now. Put'er in gear and let's slowly roll through all your buddies. No by-by waves. Both hands on the steering wheel at all times where I can see 'em."

Jack had to lean forward slightly to reach the floor gear stick and pull it to drive. The van began rolling and the sea of stricken officers divided like the Saint Andreas fault on a bad day: a ragged rending of order by violent force. Jack saw only those faces in front of the van as they parted.

Spilotros put a choke hold on him while Jack drove through the officers. Though he held firmly, he didn't strangle. Instead he stuck the pistol in Jack's ear. He whispered, "Like lovers. Cheek to cheek. Get to I-75 and head north." Spilotros grinned at the remaining few officers within their field of vision, then they were back on Armenia. Jack started to turn north. "Not that direction, hero. Go south to Howard, then double back and get on the Interstate."

Once on the street, Spilotros let go of Jack. "Show's over," he sat down cleanly out of reach in case hero got any stupid ideas. "Nice and comfy now," he said in a voice that implied this whole thing was a game. "I really didn't want to blow off Laser's head, but I got no compunction about spattering your brains and ruining that boring mug of yours. I got other plans for Laser Reygun. Gonna immortalize 'im. You? You can keep my Dog company."

* * * * *

O'Leary barked into the radio, "Get a helicopter up there. Tell the pilot to contact me immediately. I don't want the suspect to know the 'chopper's got 'im if we can find 'im, but I want to know what roads he takes. He's armed and extremely dangerous. Two hostages, one already injured and possibly dead. Van last seen heading south on Howard."

* * * * *

Spilotros liked having a captive audience. He told Jack all about himself. How the kid made him kill him because he'd killed Dog and then went inside his house and saw his collection.

"Only thing that pisses me off, now I gotta pull up stakes and move on. Had a good thing going here and you got to start nosing around. Hey, clown, keep within the speed limit, but don't under-do it. Don't want no more problems tonight, don't need to attract any more flies. Keep your hands off the rear view mirror. You take a hand off that fucking steering wheel one more time and that's all she wrote. You can see to drive, but you don't need to look me in the eye while we converse. I don't mind. Don't mind a-tall. Okay, fuzz-boy, hang a U-ey and let's get rolling to 75.

Then he started talking about his special collection, leaving out few vivid details. Spilotros kept up the chatter. Jack zoomed onto I-75. Two a.m., not much traffic. A few semi-tractor trucks hauling through while Tampa traffic was as at its ebb. An occasional automobile.

"Get off on Busch. Go east." Then, "South on 30th."

They spent the next forty-five minutes zigzagging all over northeast Tampa making sure nobody followed behind. Jack drove north along 56th street, intersected with Fletcher, turned north on 30th Street again, which became State Road 584, along Trout Creek.

At State Road 54, Spilotros told him to turn east. They passed through the small intersection of Wesley Chapel and drove beneath I-75. Before they reached Zephyrhills, he told

The Wrestler Who Lost His Head

Jack to slow down. They turned south on Morris Bridge Road. After a while, Jack saw a road sign that pointed west to Hillsborough River State Park.

Spilotros said, "Slow up. Gonna make a left up here in a minute." Jack slowed. "Stop!" Spilotros shouted in his ear. "Back up ten feet and pull off on that gravel road. Drive down it nice and easy."

About a mile later, "There, on the left at the mail box. Don't turn in, just slow up and drive on by." Jack did as he was told.

Spilotros studied his house as they passed. Nothing. No cars, no nothing. "Okay, back up and pull in. I want you to drive all the way around the house to make sure nobody's back there to surprise us."

Jack pulled in, following a tire-track drive to a door on the side and to the rear of a small frame house. Except for a kitchen door and window, the entire west wall was covered with jasmine and ivy vines overtaken by wild grape that had crept in from the encroaching scrub forest.

An eerie, breathless void enfolded the place like a long dead underground mine. No light anywhere except for the two shining holes the van bore through the vapors, which pooled on the woods behind the property.

It wasn't until they'd come full circle that it occurred to Jack that the Task Force hadn't found this place after all, or had entirely misjudged Spilotros, thinking he wouldn't dare return home. He was alone and unarmed with a maniac and a corpse.

The van lurched to a halt by the kitchen stoop. Instantly, Spilotros was on his feet, scrambling for the van doors. Knowing Jack had no weapons, he didn't feel immediate concern about him. No way could Jack prevail if he were stupid enough to try to physically attack him. He threw the latch free and flung open the doors. Then he turned around to see what Jack was up to.

He'd expected Jack to fling himself out the door, that's what he'd have done if he'd been in his shoes. But he hadn't. He'd turned around, an arm over the back of the seat, and was struggling to climb into the back, but his hip was caught by the steering wheel. Spilotros took quick aim and fired; Jack ducked as soon as he saw Spilotros' right hand move and the shot missed. But now Jack was wedged, still tangled up with the steering wheel and now caught between the console, which separated front seats, and the dash. Frantically, he began scrambling backwards, finally getting his legs free of the steering column and seat bracket, and had one knee on the floor frame. Another shot hit the console between the seats, missing Jack's head by a fraction.

Spilotros, still near the rear of the van, took a step closer inside and took careful aim. "By-by, buddy-boy."

Fast as a rattlesnake, two massive legs coiled and rammed straight like an exploding piston! A shot rang out, hit the ceiling and punctured the metal with a scream.

Spilotros slammed against the frame and the left hinged door fell open. Inertia swung it partially closed. Off balance, he stumbled against the loose door and it crashed wide open, spilling him to the ground.

The forest exploded. Guns fired from every direction. Jack ducked as low to the floor as he could get, reacting to the furious, shattering noise.

Dead silence.

Jack raised his head cautiously and looked over the seat toward the rear. No Spilotros. He heard a noise and ducked. A voice spoke from the floor behind the driver's seat.

"Reckon that took care of The Arabian Knight."

Jack whispered, "That you, Larry?"

"Who the hell do you think it is?" Puffing.

"Holy Christ, man, I thought you were dead."

"Takes more than a .357 to kill the Laser, man." Silence again. "But it sure did make a hole in my shoulder. I could use some help."

Jack crawled in the back with him and the two of them edged towards the rear of the van. Peering over the floor's horizon, they saw The Arabian Knight sprawled on the ground looking like so much ground steak.

Then shadows emerged from the trees. It looked like the Calvary, there were so many of them.

Joe O'Leary walked up to the body and kicked it with a foot to see if it moved. His raised his head and looked at Jack, "What took you so goddamned long? We been sitting out here swatting mosquitoes— bet there ain't a fucking quart of blood left in the whole damned bunch of us put together!"

Maddy Ulner pulled her walkie-talkie from her hip and radioed, "Get the ambulance up here pronto. No, get two. One on standby's for a wounded soldier. Don't rush the backup, the other guy ain't going nowhere but hell."

CHAPTER XXIX

Daylight.

The crime lab groaned the minute they ventured into the living room.

"That's not all," Jack said. "You've got a grave site out back with a boy and a dog in it that's relatively fresh. Probably ripe as hell. Looks like the coons got at 'em, too. At least these poor stiffs in here're encased and don't stink."

The few who'd been allowed inside stood in a group and stared, clearly horrified. Five men's heads were cast in clear polycarbonate cubes. Their eyes stared back lifelessly, all expression gone from their once lively faces, though they'd been carefully made up to look more alive.

There were other cubes containing articles of costumes, carefully placed below the owner of each item. These had been stacked to form a divider wall between the dining area and the living room. There were enough clear cubes to fill in the blank spaces, but it was obvious that Spilotros needed quite a few more trophies to finish the job.

"Guy's a regular freakin' artist," one of the crew picked up one of the heads and stared at it. "Know who's who?"

"Not yet, but will soon as we match 'em up with their photographs. Except Hitore, I recognize him. Saw his last match," Jack sounded tired. Sick and tired. "Just when you think you've seen it all..."

"You believe he used Christmas lights to make the fucking blocks glow?" somebody groaned.

One of the lab men, a guy called Chubby, because he was, turned around and eyed Jack curiously. "So where'd he do it? He didn't make these things in here. Got a shack out back or something? This had to be messy."

The Wrestler Who Lost His Head

"Has a lean-to, but it's full of junk. Scraps, some yard tools, stuff like that. No work bench." O'Leary offered.

Jack said, "While he was spilling his guts in the van, he mentioned a secret shop."

Chubby walked the inside of the house, being careful not to disturb anything, then asked Jack to walk the outside with him. After they'd circled the house and returned to its center, which was basically to the west side of the living room, Chubby commented. "Don't fit."

"You mean the house seems bigger on the outside than it is on the inside?"

"Like a room's missing."

"Guess his secret shop's in here? He's handy enough with his hands to wall up a door and cut him a new one," Jack added.

"Bathroom's got a mighty big linen closet for a house this little."

"Let's see," Jack said.

They opened the louvered folding doors. After a quick glance at the setup inside, they both began tearing clothes off the rack and throwing them onto the floor. They stood staring at the back wall.

"Got a sledge hammer or an ax?" Jack asked.

"Is the Pope a Catholic?" Chubby answered. He hollered over his shoulder at one of his helpers, "Dwight! Go get me the fireman's ax and bring it here."

Dwight ran out and was back again in less than two minutes. He held out the long-handled ax toward Chubby. Chubby looked at him like he was crazy or something.

"So bust in the wall, Dwight. You think I'm gonna do it? That's what I pay you for. Me boss, you peon."

Chubby and Jack stood clear. Dwight, a little put out at having to do such a menial job, stepped just outside the closet. He couldn't get a good hearty swing going because the hallway was too narrow, but if he raised the ax over his head and swung down at an angle, he could get better leverage.

H. Churchill Mallison

He took a deep breath, raised the ax, and brought it down with all his might. The ax crashed through the wallboard, rebounded, took the panel with it, and the entire spring-loaded wall came crashing down on Dwight. Jack and Chubby moved fast and caught it, so he didn't get hit with its full force.

A stench poured forth like lava from a volcano— thick, oozing, hot— a strange combination of toxic chemicals, dead flesh and the unmistakable copper odor of blood. The bare bulb in the linen closet let enough light through the hole in the wall for a man to step inside and find a light switch.

Nobody rushed in. Instead, they busied themselves helping Dwight get freed from the wallboard. He could take the honors.

Grumbling, Dwight ran his hands over the wall on either side of the opening until his hand found a switch. Four forty-inch florescents lit the room like a noon-day sun.

The men stood in stunned silence as they eyed Spilotros' workshop.

Finally, a weak voice: "What the hell are those? Looks like caskets without lids?" Dwight spoke through a handkerchief.

"A mold, I think," Jack said. "One's the top, the other the bottom. He mentioned making some kind of cast of Laser's entire body as a monument to his supreme talent. I didn't understand what he was talking about, but now that I see it... Spilotros blabbed the whole time he had me driving all over Pasco and Hillsborough. He told me all about having a unique collection that he'd let me see before he blew me off."

"Wonder how he made 'em?" O'Leary asked.

"Easy. He was gonna pour polyurethane or what ever that stuff is into the form, let it set up a little, then put Laser in it and do one side of him. That second form would be for the other side. What I can't figure, and I damned sure wasn't going to ask, was how he planned on getting him loose from the form once it set."

"Easy," said Chubby. "You wax the hell out of the form with paraffin before you put it in. Once the polycarbonate sets, you heat it up enough to melt the wax, then lift the body out."

"Christ," Jack complained. "I haven't thrown up in years, but damned if I don't think— " he bolted from the room.

* * * * *

Jack and Ali walked down the beach hand-in-hand. Jack talked quietly and endlessly. She just listened. Once in a while she'd ask a question.

"So who was the boy?" she asked.

"Some kid who lived in Zephyrhills. He had a record for breaking and entering, a burglary or two. TVs, radios, stuff like that. Fourteen years old. Parents both drunks."

"His dog?"

"No. Dog must have been Spilotros'. Autopsy showed it had been poisoned with strychnine. Apparently the dog was the one living thing Spilotros had respect for. Fed him well; found Vet bills, gave him heartworm medicine, the whole works. Kid must have fed him a piece of meat with the poison on it to get him out of the way. The boy was murdered in the kitchen."

"Stabbed?"

"I don't want to talk about it. I'm sorry, but..."

"No, I'm sorry. I must sound like a morbid bystander," she squeezed his hand.

"Just, what a horrible way for a kid to go. For anybody, for that matter."

Jack finally fell silent and they walked the last mile home listening to the waves lapping the shore.

They crossed the small dunes that ran in a narrow strip separating the homes from the beach strand. At the foot of the deck steps, Ali stopped and looked up at Jack.

"So, what about Gianconni? What was her role in all this?"

"Apparently, she didn't realize she was being followed. Not by Spilotros, anyway. She got spooked when the police started following her. ...Tell you the truth," he said, eyes staring at a middle distance, "The way she was pushing her luck with him at the matches, I think she was beginning to suspect him.

H. Churchill Mallison

"Every time she picked somebody up, he wound up dead. Get's a little too much to call it coincidence after a while. First time in L.A., well, she'd pass that one off. Then again in Miami. Maybe you could pass that off. But three guys in one city, and every single person you date... Can't prove it, but I think she was contemplating blackmail. But, no, I don't think she was part of the set-up. Without Spilotros' testimony, we'll never know for sure."

"You buy that she was innocent?"

"Haven't found anything to say different, though I'm not sure I'd exactly call her innocent." He chuckled.

"Why was Spilotros following *her*?"

"Maybe he liked her taste in men."

"Well, what next? Think maybe we'll get a breather?"

"God only knows. Oh! By the way, speaking of breathers... Chief Charlie and Maddy Ulner and a date are coming over tomorrow night for a cookout. Know somebody we can fix Charlie up with?"

Ali's face fell. She rolled eyes up at him that would chill a iceberg. "Maddy?"

Jack laughed. "Sugarbabe? Don't sweat it. Wait until you see her date. Know who she's going with? Huh? You aren't going to believe this."

"Who?"

"Citrus Sam!"

"You're kidding!" Ali's eyes lit up. Well, that was another story. Excitement growing in her voice, she asked, "Do you know his real name? I'd feel kinda stupid calling him Citrus."

"Cahill. Bill Cahill. What are you so excited about? He's with her, sweetie-pie, so don't get goose bumps." Jack swatted her on the fanny.

"Ha! Who's jealous now? Huh? Huh?"

"Come on, now," he said, changing the subject. "Who can we fix Charlie up with?"

* * * * *

The Wrestler Who Lost His Head

"Life can be good. ...Ever thought about quitting."

"Daily. But I won't."

"Why not?"

He thought about that for a few minutes while they climbed the stairs. "I guess because I know at least I'm doing something that matters. Even if we never manage to stamp out crime all together, there's got to be some folks out there that try. Why don't you quit counselling those hopeless, abused women?"

"Not all of them are hopeless," she answered. Then she, too, thought about what he'd asked. "I guess, like you, at least I feel useful."

"Know what I'd like?" his face suddenly relaxed, releasing the pent-up tensions at long last. "I'd like a good, stiff drink and a sandwich later on and I'd like to sit on our deck and do nothing for a while."

"You got it."

* * * * *

Ali brought out a tray ladened with two stiff drinks and a plate piled high with sandwiches, potato chips on the side. She set the tray on the low table between the two lounges and then stretched out next to him.

An hour later, he said, "Time for us to plan our honeymoon trip. How about a cruise to Jamaica and Mexico? Think about it. Meanwhile, I think I'd like to haul my bride off to the sack. Ummm...wanna wrestle?"

The End

ABOUT THE AUTHOR

Churchill Mallison, an observer of human nature, attended a seminar put on by the FBI in or around 1990 on the psychological make-up of serial murderers in an effort to discover why one sociopath lives out a relatively normal life while another becomes a serial killer. Because of her curiosity about what makes a murderer tick, she has written several thrillers, and other mysteries. Jack Robinson appears in several of her thrillers as a detective, advancing to Special Investigator for the Florida Department of Law Enforcement.

A Tampa Bay area resident since 1970, she is also an active artist and owner of a small bed and breakfast. She wrote several books while living in Tampa, Florida, but since moving to Bradenton, Florida, has been involved in developing her bed and breakfast, assisting with the repairs of a lovely 1913 home in downtown Bradenton's historic district, and fine art painting to the extent that she temporarily ceased to market her writings. Now being settled, and having narrowed her focus considerably, she is concentrating on polishing and publishing her novels, working on digital arts instead of oils, and creating and teaching web design.

"I find that painting definitely affects my writing, and vice versa. More than once I've had gallery visitors say they "read my pictures." Conversely, I write so you can *see* my stories."

You can view her artworks and short stories by visiting her web site on-line gallery at www.tizart.com.

Printed in the United States
3462